Thirteen Guests

Thirteen Guests

J. Jefferson Farjeon

With an Introduction
by Martin Edwards

Poisoned Pen Press

Originally published in London in 1936 by Collins
Copyright © 2015 Estate of J. Jefferson Farjeon
Introduction copyright © 2015 Martin Edwards

Published by Poisoned Pen Press in association with the
British Library

First Edition 2015 First US Trade Paperback Edition

10 9 8 7 6 5 4 3 2 1

Library of Congress Catalog Card Number: 2015938525

ISBN: 9781464204890   Trade Paperback

Poisoned Pen Press
6962 E. First Ave., Ste. 103
Scottsdale, AZ 85251
www.poisonedpenpress.com
info@poisonedpenpress.com

Printed in the United States of America

Contents

Introduction

Thirteen Guests is a country house mystery story, firmly in the tradition of the Golden Age of Murder between the two world wars. For decades, detective fiction written during that period has been associated with a handful of "Crime Queens"—Agatha Christie, Dorothy L. Sayers, Ngaio Marsh, and Margery Allingham—and the worthy achievements of several of their male contemporaries have tended to be overlooked. One of Sayers' own favourite crime writers was, in fact, J. Jefferson Farjeon; she much admired his "creepy skill". He published this book in 1936, the year before *A Mystery in White*, which has been enjoyed afresh by thousands of twenty-first-century readers following its reissue in the British Library's series of Crime Classics.

The story begins at the "gravelly" railway station of Flensham, where an accident introduces John Foss to a lovely widow called Nadine Leveridge. Nadine takes it upon herself to invite Foss, a young man who has reached a crisis point in his life, along to Bragley Court to recuperate. This is the home of Lord Aveling, an ambitious Conservative politician, who is about to host a week-end social gathering. Assorted fellow guests include a county cricketer, a novelist, a society painter, a gossip columnist, a Liberal MP, and a retired "sausage king". Aveling had planned on a party of a dozen people; Foss is the thirteenth guest.

Foss is not superstitious, and in any event, as the cricketer tells him: "The bad luck would come…to the thirteenth guest who passes in through that door." Last to arrive at Bragley Court are an enigmatic couple called the Chaters, and it is the husband who proves to be the thirteenth guest. Farjeon soon ratchets up the tension with a sequence of strange incidents in which the violence escalates. A painting is damaged; a dog is killed; a stranger's body is found in a quarry; finally, one of the thirteen guests meets an untimely end.

Country house murder mysteries were a staple of Golden Age detective fiction. E.C. Bentley's *Trent's Last Case* set the pattern, and was followed by Lord Gorell's now forgotten *In the Night,* and Agatha Christie's unforgettable *The Mysterious Affair at Styles*. *The Red House Mystery*, by A.A. Milne (yes, the man who later created Winnie-the-Pooh) poked fun at the form, while the iconoclastic Anthony Berkeley played an ironic game with it in *The Layton Court Mystery*. Yet country house murder mysteries not only survived, but flourished, continuing to be written and published in almost industrial quantities. The reading public of the 1920s and 30s loved them, and it is easy to understand why.

The "closed circle" of murder suspects to be found at a country house party provides readers of a whodunit with a chance to pit their wits against the author. The portrayal of conflict and tensions in a small community has a powerful and enduring appeal, and over the past three-quarters of a century crime novelists have shown much ingenuity in creating "closed circle" mysteries. Think of relatively recent books as different as P.D. James' final novel about Adam Dalgliesh, *The Private Patient*, a book firmly within the genre's traditions, and Stieg Larsson's *The Girl with the Dragon Tattoo*.

James and Larsson shared a strong interest in human behaviour and motivation. Characters in Golden Age mystery were, if conventional wisdom is to be believed, invariably "made of cardboard", but this criticism is itself both clichéd and misleading. Whilst plenty of Golden Age novelists focused solely on the puzzle element of their stories, others showed a genuine interest in exploring character. J. Jefferson Farjeon belonged to the latter group; he depicts the suspects with a zest that remains appealing to this day.

Joseph Jefferson Farjeon (1883–1955) came from a literary family. His father Benjamin, his sister Eleanor, and his brother Herbert were accomplished writers, while his grandfather was a noted American actor, and Thomas Jefferson an ancestor. *The Master Criminal*, Farjeon's first novel, appeared in 1924, and he proceeded to publish dozens of books, mostly under his own name, but occasionally using the pseudonym of Anthony Swift. *No. 17*, a play as well as a novel, was filmed twice, the second time by Alfred Hitchcock. *Mountain Mystery*, published in 1935, and *Death of a World*, written in the aftermath of World War II, saw Farjeon venturing into speculative fiction, and even in more down-to-earth thrillers, like *Thirteen Guests*, he seized every opportunity to indulge his romantic streak. Shortly before he died, a story he had written in the Thirties for radio broadcast, "Murder over Draughts", was adapted for TV, prompting *The Times* to gaze into its crystal ball: "how eminently natural it seems to turn to the television for a story. Perhaps these experiments will tempt some modern authors to write stories directly for television."

Farjeon's work, then, enjoyed sustained commercial success during his lifetime, and made a contribution to the popular culture of the day. He honed his skills as a writer, so that although he never lost a taste for melodrama, he learned how to marry it with engaging characterisation and deft plotting. Perhaps, like many popular novelists, he wrote too much, but his detective fiction certainly does not deserve the neglect into which it had fallen before the success of *Mystery in White*. *Thirteen Guests* earns its place in the British Library's Crime Classics series as another novel that displays Farjeon's "creepy skill" and provides lively entertainment as well as a teasingly constructed mystery.

Martin Edwards

www.martinedwardsbooks.com

Chapter I

Completion of the Number

Every station has its special voice. Some are of grit. Some are of sand. Some are of milk cans. Some are of rock muffled by tunnel smoke. Whatever the voice, it speaks to those who know it, sounding a name without pronouncing it; but those who do not know it drowse on, for to them it brings no message, and is merely a noise unilluminated by personal tradition.

The voice of Flensham station is gravelly. The queer softness of it is accentuated by the tunnel and the curve that precede it. The tunnel throbs blackly and the curve grinds metallically, but Flensham follows with a gravelly whisper that is as arresting as a shout. With eyes still closed the familiar traveller sees the neat little platform gliding closer and closer. He sees the lines of equally neat bushes that assist a wooden partition to separate the platform from the road. A notice, warning passengers not to cross the track when a train is standing in the station. A signal, arm slanting downwards. A station-master, large and depressed, fighting the tragedy of Cosmos with a time-table.

Of the two passengers who alighted at Flensham from the 3.28 one Friday afternoon in autumn, only one had an advance vision of these things. She was a lady of about thirty, and Puritans and Victorians would have called her too attractive. Her hair was tinged with bronze. Her nose delighted your thoughts and defied your theories. Her complexion was too perfect. Her frankly ridiculous lips annoyed you because by all the rules of sanity they should have disgusted you, yet they did not.

She had been described by her husband, now lying peacefully in his grave, as one of life's most glorious risks, and he had consciously taken the risk when he had married her. "Let her tear me to pieces," he said on his wedding-day. She had done so. She had jolted him from heaven to hell. And he had never reproached her. He had loved her without her make-up, and three hours before he died, during one of her rare moments of repentance—even the worst of us are softened as we watch the sands run out—he had waved her regrets aside. "How can you alter what God made?" he had said. "Some one has to suffer."

The other passenger was a young man. To him the gravelly music of Flensham station told no story, and for this reason he almost ignored it. The lady was already on the platform, interviewing a liveried chauffeur, before the man realised that the train had stopped.

"Hallo—Flensham!" he exclaimed suddenly.

The train began to move on again. The young man jumped to his feet. On the rack above him was a suitcase. He seized it with one hand, while the other groped for the door-handle. A moment later the suitcase shot out on to the platform. The sight amused the lady, to whom every sensation was meat, but it insulted the large and depressed station-master, to whom every sensation was a menace to routine.

Worse followed. The owner of the suitcase shot out after his belonging, and as he shot out his foot caught in the framework of the door. Now the lady's amusement changed swiftly to anxiety, and the station-master's indignation to alarm.

"Quick! Help him!" cried the lady.

The station-master, the chauffeur, and a porter ran forward. The train chugged on. Its late passenger sat on the ground, holding his foot. He had been pale before; he was considerably paler now.

"Hurt, sir?" asked the station-master.

"Of course I'm hurt!" he retorted unreasonably. "Why the hell don't you show the name of your station in larger letters?" Then he noticed Nadine, and apologised.

"Quite unnecessary," Nadine answered graciously. This young man was immensely good-looking. He had a smooth, boyish face, and his eyes, though drawn with pain at the moment, held possibilities. "Swear as much as is good for you—and that's probably a lot."

He forgot his twinges for a moment. Nadine had the beauty that drugs. Her commanding ease, also, was a consolation, dissolving the oppressions of an unimaginative station-master, a staring porter, and a rather too superior chauffeur.

"Thanks—I'm all right," he said, and fainted.

"Coo, 'e's gorn off!" reported the porter.

"Looks like a case for a doctor," muttered the station-master.

"Definitely," nodded Nadine.

The chauffeur glanced at her, and read his own thought in her eyes. There was a faint green light in them. It generally came when she was intensely interested. Her husband had called it, anomalously, the red signal.

"Could you get him into the car, Arthur?" she asked.

"Easy," replied the chauffeur.

"Then, if you don't mind, I think we'll stop at a doctor's on the way."

"Dr. Pudrow, madam—the same as attends Mrs. Morris. He's the one." He turned to the porter. "Give us a hand, Bill. And remember he's not a trunk."

The station-master interposed. He himself had been the first to suggest a doctor—he was glad of that—but a certain procedure had to be observed. This was his platform.

"You'd better wait till he comes to," he said.

"Of course," agreed Nadine. "We're not going to abduct him."

In a few seconds the young man opened his eyes. He now fought humiliation as well as pain.

"Did I go off?" he gasped, momentarily red.

"We all do silly ass things when we can't help it," smiled Nadine. "Don't worry. But I think you ought to see a doctor."

"*She* thinks," reflected the station-master. "Taking it all to herself!"

"Believe you're right," murmured the young man. "Something or other seems to have gone wrong with my foot. Could you—send one along?"

"I'm glad you're keeping your sense of humour."

"Eh?"

"Why send one along when I can take you along?"

"That's really frightfully decent of you."

"Say when you're ready."

"Well, if it's not too much trouble—sooner the better."

She made a sign to the chauffeur, then turned back to him.

"Grit on to yourself. It mayn't be nice when they lift you. I know what it's like—I hunt."

He closed his eyes, and kept them closed for two very unpleasant minutes. Then he found himself gliding through a land of gentle undulations and russet October hues. Above him the sky was crisp and clear. The tang of autumn was in his nostrils. The sounds of autumn came to him, too. Dogs bayed in the distance. He recognised the quality, and pictured red coats among them. From an opposite direction cracked the report of a gun. Now he pictured a pheasant flashing downwards from the blue dome, to end its short uneasy life in fulfilment of its destiny. Closer at hand were branches as gold as the pheasant's breast. Closer still was a bronze curl....His eyes, as they opened, focused on the bronze curl.

But pain intruded. Stags and pheasants were not suffering alone.

"How are you feeling?"

"Not too bad."

"I expect I'd say the same." Nadine's voice was appreciative and sympathetic. "We'll soon be at the doctor's."

It occurred to him that he ought to thank her, but when he began the bronze curl moved a little nearer to him and she placed her hand over his mouth. He rebelled against the pleasure of that momentary contact with her fingers. They were cool, while they warmed. He rebelled because he knew that she was conscious of his pleasure, that she had deliberately produced it. But he did not know that she was conscious, also, of his rebellion. She took her hand away. She had the sporting instinct. She did not fight a man who was down.

"But stags and foxes, eh?" her husband had once taxed her, when she had been forced to point out this virtue to him.

"They're different," she had retorted.

"Of course they are," he agreed. "They don't start fifty-fifty—and they can never get up again and smack you."

The conversation had preceded one of their biggest rows.

The Rolls glided on. A small vine-covered house peeped over one of the brown hedges on their left. The sun, nearing the end of its shortened day, sent a low arrow of light into the vines and picked out a brilliant little plate-inscribed: "Dr. L. G. Pudrow, M.D." The house was less pretentious than the plate, and therefore needed the plate to dignify it. But for the useful illness of a rich old lady and the daily visits this illness imposed, the house might have been even less pretentious. No doctor, however, could visit Bragley Court every morning, and sometimes every afternoon as well, without comfort to his bank-balance, and Dr. Pudrow had found Mrs. Morris a godsend. That was not why he had devoted so much earnest thought and care to the business of keeping the suffering old lady alive.

When the Rolls stopped outside the house, Dr. Pudrow was actually engaged in that rather unchristian occupation. A maid informed the chauffeur that her master was out.

"He's at your place," she said. "If you hurries you'll catch him."

"Is he coming straight back?" inquired Arthur, with the practical sense of one who has to deal with grit in carburettors.

"No, he's not," answered the maid, and added pertly, "he's got a baby coming at six."

Arthur considered. It was now eleven minutes to four. He pointed out that the baby was not due for over two hours, but the maid retorted that you never knew, and that the doctor was going right on anyway. "This'll be No. 8—it's that Mrs. Trump again," the maid observed. "*I* call it disgusting!" She believed in good looks and Marie Stopes.

The chauffeur returned to the car and reported. Nadine looked at the young man. The green glint in her eyes was dancing once more.

"There's only one way to catch the doctor," she said. "And there's only one doctor to catch. He's attending a patient at Bragley Court—where I happen to be going myself. Shall I take you on there?"

"Why not deposit me here till he returns?" asked the young man. "I mustn't go on being your responsibility like this."

Nadine explained the situation. The doctor might be hours before he got back. Some babies were optimistic, and hurried; others showed less anxiety to enter a troubled world.

"Then—would you take me—?" began the young man, and paused.

"Yes? Where?" inquired Nadine.

Obviously, even a man who fell out of a train had some destination beyond the platform. For the sake of the adventure she had delayed referring to it.

"Not sure," said the young man, and the reply pleased Nadine. The autumn sun was in a very generous mood, and she had no wish to end the adventure. "Isn't there an inn somewhere?"

Nadine turned to the chauffeur, who was still awaiting instructions.

"Bragley Court, Arthur," she said, "and don't worry about speed limits."

There was always something vaguely personal in her use of the word "Arthur." It implied no social unbending on her part, and permitted no familiarity on his, but it recognised his existence; almost, his male existence. Now it added two miles to the speedometer.

"Bragley Court doesn't sound like an inn," commented the young man wearily. He found he couldn't fight.

"It certainly isn't an inn," answered Nadine. "The only two inns within reasonable distance—as far as I know—are the Black Stag and the Cricketers' Arms. The Black Stag is by the station. No stag has ever been known there, although I think there *is* a rumour that years ago one hid behind the bar, but there's plenty of blackness. It comes from the tunnel. I believe the inn puts up one traveller a year, and never the same traveller. The Cricketers' Arms is *much* more lively.

That's why it is even less desirable. All sorts of company. And I'm told the bed, like Venice, is built round seven lumps. I really think, if you went to the Cricketers' Arms, you might die of it."

He did his best to smile. Watching him closely, she assured him the smile was not necessary.

"You're quite understanding," he said suddenly.

"I know you're in pain," she replied. She had to restrain an impish desire to give him a more personal answer. "I was thrown once, and couldn't listen to a funny story for a week. Does my prattle worry you?"

"No, please go on."

"I don't know if there's anything to go on about. Oh, yes—Bragley Court. We are racing there to catch the doctor before he leaves one patient to go on to another, that's all." She laughed. "You are to be sandwiched between old age and youth—an old lady of over seventy, and a baby minus two hours."

It was true her prattling did not worry him. It helped him wonderfully, for there was a vital quality behind its levity that forced some part of his attention, diverting it from his pain. But he did not quite know how to handle it.

"I hope the old lady is not very ill?" he said rather conventionally.

"She is very ill," returned Nadine. "She does jig-saws, and is a lesson to everybody. That is, if anybody ever *is* a lesson to anybody else, which I doubt. I've only known two people in my life who could make me feel a pig. She's one of them."

"I know what it is," thought the young man. "She's so confoundedly *natural*!" Aloud he asked, "Your mother?"

"It would have been politer to have asked if she were my grandmother! I forgive you. She's neither. She is our—my hostess's mother. Bragley Court is the place of the Avelings, you know. Or don't you know?"

"What! Lord Aveling?" She nodded. "I say—do you think you'd better take me there?"

"Why not? Are you Labour?"

He did not reply at once. He was frowning. In the distance the dogs were barking again. A bird, too fat to emigrate, sent a note of shrill sweetness from a bough. "I have just eaten a worm," sang the bird. It was happy. The snow was a long way off.

"I don't know whether you realise what *I'm* realising," said the young man seriously, "but I may have to stay a bit where you set me down."

"That's exactly why—since you've given me no other address—I'm taking you to Bragley Court. I've already implied that if I took you to either of the local inns here I might be had up for murder."

"But—"

"Do you think, if you tried terribly hard, you could stop worrying? If we catch the doctor, let him decide."

"And if we don't?"

"Then Lord Aveling can decide. And I know *his* decision in advance, or I wouldn't risk inviting it."

"I'm not too sure of that," said the young man. "You do take risks."

"Do I?"

"You've risked—*me*!"

"So I have!"

"What makes you think Lord Aveling won't kick against having a stranger lumped upon him, even temporarily?"

"Three things, my dear man. Is that too familiar? One, Lord Aveling. Conservatives with ambition are splendid hosts. Two, myself. I've an instinct—and Lord Aveling likes me, and knows I'd never let him down. Three—isn't that an old school tie?"

This time he laughed.

"Satisfied?" she laughed back.

"Sounds pretty good," he admitted.

"Thank God for that," sighed Nadine. "Because here we are, and there's no turning back now. By the way, what's your name?"

Chapter II

Inventory

Half an hour later John Foss, bandaged and stretched out on a rose-coloured settee, reviewed his position.

He had been received at Bragley Court with the utmost ease and courtesy. Indeed, when he realised the vastness of the space in which Lord and Lady Aveling moved, he became a little less anxious over the dislocation he would cause. His advent at the Black Stag or the Cricketers' Arms might have created a flutter, but Bragley Court gave no outward sign of vulgar emotion. The indoor and outdoor staff numbered twenty-six, and each member had been trained to meet any situation or emergency with smoothness and efficiency. Emotionally there was no difference between passing a toast-rack and conveying a stranger with a crocked ankle from a car to a couch.

Nevertheless, he was conscious that something more important than efficient service had dealt with his arrival and had sanctioned it. He might have been treated courteously as a necessary evil—his sensitive mind would quickly have fathomed that—but instead Lord Aveling had appeared in person while the doctor did unpleasant things to his leg, and had even half-humorously held the end of a bandage for the doctor, thereby proving (as Nadine pointed out later) that he, also, could be influenced by an old school tie.

Then, when the doctor had concluded his task, and had impressed on an elderly woman hovering in the background the necessity of frequent applications of surgical spirit, Lord Aveling had insisted that it would be wise for him to remain on the settee a while longer.

"You won't be in the way here," he said. "We can move you to your room later."

"He will have to be moved very carefully," commented the doctor.

"Why move him at all?" suggested Nadine. "Why not move the couch? When I missed my fence two years ago, I was rolled for the night into the ante-room."

"Excellent idea," agreed Lord Aveling. "Some time after tea."

"Yes, when the poor man gets tired of being looked at," smiled Nadine.

Lord Aveling had departed amiably. "The right sort," ran his thoughts. "Good family, obviously. Interesting. Not many youngsters this week-end. Bultin coming down by next train. Make good paragraph. Yes, Bultin will use it. Another example of Aveling hospitality. Followed by list of guests. Wonder if this was the right week-end for Zena Wilding? And the Chaters? Still, of course, I had to have the Chaters....Pity this young chap makes the thirteenth...."

But welcome alone did not reign in the spacious lounge-hall that glowed in the late afternoon sunshine and flickered in the light of an enormous log-fire. Something brooded as well. The shadows seemed to contain uneasy secrets, and none of the people John had so far met reflected complete mental ease. Lady Aveling, when she had momentarily deserted a card-table in the drawing-room for a kindly peep at the casualty, had appeared nervously anxious to get back again. Two guests—a thin, angular, cynical man in a black velvet coat and large artist's tie, and a short, stout, grey-haired man of the retired-pork-butcher-and-made-a-damn-lot-out-of-it type (he had made a cool hundred thousand out of it, which alone explained his presence here)—struck a vaguely jarring note when they passed through the hall together. The elderly woman deputed to apply surgical spirit at intervals had been grim. A pretty maid on her way up the carved staircase with a tray had been flushed. A butler had followed her to the stairs, and then turned round and vanished.

"Something's wrong," reflected John. "What is it?"

He wondered whether the two new people who were just entering the hall would continue the impression.

They were a man and a girl in riding kit, and they bore the dust and atmosphere of hard going. The girl's cheeks were tingling from her ride, and she instinctively brushed her hand across her forehead as she entered, as though to sweep away the sudden fuggy warmth of the blazing logs. She was beautiful, in a slim boyish way, and although she looked well in her dark green riding habit, a stranger longed instinctively to see her in more definitely feminine attire. It was odd that a certain hardness around her mouth, a hardness held there by the set of her lips, did not detract from her beauty. Possibly because one could not quite believe it.

The man, large and well-built, reminded you pleasantly of cricket, which in fact he played.

"Half-past four," said the girl, glancing at a clock on her way to the wide staircase.

"Does that mean tea in your room?" inquired the man, pausing to light a cigarette.

"No, I'll be down," she replied. "But the bath comes first. These things are sticking to me."

The settee on which John lay was fitted into a shadowed angle of the wall. The sun was slipping down behind a distant wood, preluding quick gloaming, and a servant entered the lounge-hall and switched on lights. The girl at the foot of the staircase turned her head and saw the patient.

John endured an awkward moment. It occurred to him that perhaps, after all, the routine of Bragley Court had its little flaws. It should have protected him against the necessity of explaining himself. Yet it was unreasonable to expect some one to be in perpetual attendance on him, and even Lord Aveling's generously-planned staff did not run to a Cook's guide. So, after enduring the girl's curious scrutiny for a moment or two, he remarked bluntly:

"I've had an accident, and Lord Aveling's been good enough to give me temporary shelter."

"Bad luck," said the man. "Not riding, was it?"

"No—a prosaic train. I jumped out while it was moving, and it tried to take my foot on to the next station."

The man smiled, and held out his case.

"Have one?" he invited. "We smoke anywhere. Reassure him, Anne."

The girl advanced with a little nod.

"Of course—quite in order," she said. "I am Lord Aveling's daughter. And this is Mr. Harold Taverley."

"Thanks awfully," answered John. The momentary awkwardness created by these two had vanished very quickly. "It does help knowing! Mine's John Foss. And my whole object in life just now is not to be a confounded nuisance. Please don't delay that bath."

Anne laughed. Her mouth lost its hardness. She turned and ran upstairs. But her companion lingered.

"Don't *you* feel sticky?" asked John.

"Oh, I've got a few minutes," replied Taverley. He had a clear, full voice, but rarely raised it. The retired Pork King could only make his carry when he shouted. "I suppose there's nothing I can do?"

"Well—yes, there is," said John impulsively. This was the kind of fellow you could talk to. "I'd like to know something about the people here. One feels such a fool, you know. Rather like a monkey in a zoo."

"I know," smiled Taverley. "That is, if monkeys really do feel like that." He squatted on a stool. "I suppose you'll be staying a bit?"

"There's been some talk of rolling me into an ante-room for the night. Everybody's frightfully decent."

"The ante-room? That's where—" He paused. "Well, let's run over the inventory. Who've you seen so far?"

"Lord Aveling."

"He's easy. Fifth baron. Hopes to be first marquis or earl. Conservative. I hope politics don't make you feel suicidal?"

"One has to bear them; but I'm not particularly interested."

"Just as well. You'll be able to keep out of arguments. Have you seen Lady Aveling?" John nodded. "She needn't worry you. She follows her husband's lead. The daughter you've just met. The Honourable Anne. Keen on horses. Hunting people here, you know. And golfing. Private course. Anne can drive two hundred."

"I like her," said John.

"She's O.K." Taverley paused for an instant, then added: "She liked you."

"You made up your mind quickly!"

"So did she about that. So did you. Well, let's finish the family. There's only one more."

"The son?"

"No. That's the disappointment. Lady Aveling's mother. Mrs. Morris. You're not the only invalid in the house. But you won't see Mrs. Morris—she sticks to her room!"

At that moment Mrs. Morris was lying two floors above, propped up on pillows, in an ecstasy of joy. She was almost free from grinding pain. The world was very good....

"Fine old lady," said Taverley. "Example to the lot of us. Right. Now for the guests. Who have you seen of those?"

"A lady brought me here."

"Rather large and stout? Impressive glasses?"

"My God, no!"

"Would 'distracting' be the adjective?"

"I can't think of a better," agreed John, fighting an annoying moment of self-consciousness.

"That sounds like Nadine Leveridge. I heard she was coming on the 3.28. Was that your train? The one that tried to pull you to bits?"

"Yes. And Leveridge was the name."

"Our attractive widow. Susceptible people need to keep out of her way. She can break hearts while she passes."

"That almost sounds like advice," said John.

"Well, if it is, it's good advice," parried Taverley unrepentantly. "That kind of woman can put a man through hell. Make pulp of his will-power. And—what's the use?"

"I see you don't like her."

"You're wrong, Foss. I like her immensely. What's a woman to do with her beauty? Scrap it? One sticks to oneself. I like her, and I liked her husband. He and I played cricket together. He used to tell me that the only moment he could forget Nadine was when he brought off a leg-glide. There's something about a leg-glide. Then only he got perfect peace. After he'd passed through a particularly difficult time you could always bowl Leveridge l.b.w.—he *would* try for that leg-glide. Even with the ball on the off-stump."

"Did they quarrel, then?" asked John.

"Like hell," answered Taverley. "And loved like hell. The

person who next marries Nadine will know all there is to know. Well, that's Number One of the guests. Seen any more?"

"Yourself."

"Sussex. Batting average, 41.66. We won't talk about the bowling average. Lord Aveling loves a show, and I'm part of it." He laughed, then frowned at himself. "Don't get a wrong impression of our host. He's all right."

"It seems to me you think everybody's all right."

"So they are, if we dig down far enough. But you'll need to hold on to your faith this week-end—you'll bump into some odd people."

"Here come the only others I've bumped into," said John, as the front door opened abruptly and the velvet-coated man and the retired merchant came in. A draught of keen air came in with them.

"Brrh!" exclaimed the retired merchant, rubbing his hands together. "Shut the door, quick!"

"Mistake to admit you're cold in company," commented the velvet-coated man. "It stamps you with a hot water-bottle."

"Well, I love my hot water-bottle, and I don't care a damn who knows it!"

"You'll lose respect. Life, being itself hot, only sympathises with a poor circulation."

"Oh, does it? Well, blood ain't the only thing that circulates!" The retired merchant tapped his pocket and laughed. "Life respects *that*! Besides, where's your company, anyhow?" Then he became conscious of it. "Ah, Taverley! We've just been across to the studio. It's going to be a masterpiece. How's the patient? How's it go?"

"First rate, thanks," answered John. "I shan't be on your hands long."

"Glad to hear it. I mean, glad you're feeling better. Nasty things, these twisted ankles. I bunged mine up once playing draughts. Ha, ha! Well, come along, Pratt, or we'll have no tea."

He strode to the stairs and disappeared, but Pratt paused for a moment before following.

"Described *us* yet?" he inquired.

"No. You're next on the list," smiled Taverley. "So you'd better hurry!"

Pratt smiled back and left them, with just enough speed to indicate that he could respond to a jest without losing his dignity. John grinned.

"*Leicester* Pratt?" he asked. Taverley nodded. "Rather the rage just now, isn't he?"

"Very much so. That's why he's here. Women flock to him to be painted, and Pratt ruthlessly reveals their poor little souls. Queer, isn't it, how some people will strip themselves for notoriety—and not know they're doing it?"

"I saw one of Pratt's pictures last May. I thought it was clever, but—well—"

"Horrible?"

"Struck me that way. What's this latest masterpiece? Is he painting anybody here?"

"The Honourable Anne," answered Taverley. Both men were silent for a few seconds. Then Taverley continued: "The other was Mr. Rowe. You won't have heard of him, but you may have breakfasted with him. Pratt—who has a cynical name for everybody—calls him the Man Behind the Sausage. When he paints Mr. Rowe, as he's bound to do one day—Rowe is rolling in it—he'll elongate his head just enough to let everybody know but Mr. Rowe. That's his devilish art. He finds your weakness, and paints round it."

"I don't think I'm going to like Mr. Pratt," mused John.

"Take my advice and try to," responded Taverley. "Well, that's four of us. Five—the large lady with impressive glasses. Have you read *Horse-flesh*?" John shook his head. "You're luckier than about eighty thousand others. Our large lady wrote it. Edyth Fermoy-Jones. Accent, please, on the Fermoy.

She'll die happy if she goes down in history as the female Edgar Wallace. Only with a touch more literary distinction. Quite a nice person if you can smash through her rather pathetic ambition."

"I'll do my best," promised John.

"Six, Mrs. Rowe. Seven, Ruth Rowe—daughter. There isn't really much to say about them, except that Ruth will be much happier when—if ever—she escapes from the sausage influence. Let's see—yes, that's the lot of who are here. But Number Eight is coming by car—Sir James Earnshaw, Liberal, wondering whether to turn Right or Left—and there will be four more on the next train. Zena Wilding—"

"The actress?"

"Yes. And Lionel Bultin. Bultin will write us all up in his gossip column. His method in print is rather like Pratt's on canvas. He says what he likes and what others don't. Who are the last two? Oh, the Chaters. Mr. and Mrs. I don't know anything about them. Well—that's the dozen."

"And I make the thirteenth," remarked John as Taverley rose.

"I hope that doesn't worry you?"

"Not superstitious."

"That's fortunate, although, even if you were, you'd be clear. The bad luck would come, wouldn't it, to the thirteenth guest who passes in through that door?…Well, I must be moving. See you later."

Before going up, Taverley waited while the pretty maid with the flushed cheeks—they were still a little flushed—came down. John turned his head to watch the Sussex cricketer depart. A sudden gasp from the maid brought his head round again.

She had vanished, but he was just in time to glimpse a form flashing by the window.

Chapter III

At the Black Stag

The brilliant amber of the day had gone. The sun had changed into a dull red disc and had dropped below the fringe of Greyshot Heath. Already the nip in the air had lost its pleasantness, and the sly old fox at Mile Bottom was opening its eyes in its earthy den to ponder on pheasants and mice and rabbits. One day the sly old fox would itself be hunted, and only for this reason had it escaped sharing the excommunication of the pole-cat. It was too good a runner to waste its agility in the north.

In a little wood half a mile from Bragley Court a cock pheasant fluttered heavily to his roosting place. He had no fear. Death, that odd, incomprehensible thing, came to others; but *he* had survived a dozen shoots, and he knew how to evade its shadow. If a stoat or a cat prowled too close, an old bird could easily raise the alarm and find some other retreat. Like all living things, the cock pheasant was immortal to himself, because he had not yet endured the experience of extinction. When extinction came, he would not know it.

The doctor's brass plate had ceased to glow. It was now merely a cold flatness surrounded by vines. The sentinel dog outside the Cricketers' Arms had risen, shaken itself, and gone inside. A lamp had appeared in the uncurtained window of the Black Stag overlooking Flensham station, and the gravelly railway station itself was a length of grey shadows broken by the occasional dim lights of platform lamps and of an inadequate waiting-room. Somewhere to the south loomed a large black hole that was a tunnel. You were conscious of the hole, but you could no longer see it, for its blackness had merged into the blackness of the hill through which it bored and of the sky above the hill.

A man sat at the uncurtained window of the Black Stag, staring with moody eyes at the deserted smudge of platform. He had arrived that morning on the 12.10. He had partaken of an unpalatable lunch, and had spent the early afternoon strolling about in a purposeless way, smoking incessantly, and almost as incessantly consulting his watch. He had returned to the inn at three o'clock, and had sat at the window till the 3.28 had drawn in. He had watched the two passengers alight, and had witnessed the accident. It had not interested him particularly, because his interest was centred in one thing, and one thing only; every event outside that one thing, every circumstance that bore no direct relation to it, was as unreal and shadowy as the platform at which he now stared. Had the man who had tumbled been seriously hurt? It did not matter. What was the lady doing? It did not matter. The scene was being enacted within a short distance of him, but for all the effect it produced upon his emotions it might have occurred in Siam. When it was over, and the train had gone, and the platform had become once more deserted, he had taken another purposeless stroll, again smoking incessantly, again incessantly consulting his watch. And now he was back again, and a large, heavily-breathing woman had brought in a lamp.

"You'll be wanting tea?" asked the woman.

He was a rum one, this one was, but even rum ones took tea.

"The next train's 5.56, isn't it?" replied the man.

She told him that it was. She had told him the same thing three times already. Then she repeated her question about tea.

"Eh? Yes, I'll have some tea," he replied, without interest.

"What would you like with it? Just bread and butter? Or we've got some nice seed cake."

"Anything. Yes. Whatever you've got."

The woman evaporated, and appeared ten minutes later with a tray. She placed the tray on a sideboard, covered a stained table with a scarcely less stained cloth, and moved the tray to the table. The seed cake presided with dejected majesty on a tall, glass-pedestaled dish. Its mission appeared to be to make thick slices of bread and butter look appetising by comparison.

"Excuse me, sir," said the woman, lingering. "But will you be staying the night?"

"What?" replied the man.

"Will you be staying the night?" repeated the woman. "If so, I could have your bag taken up—"

"Don't touch my bag!" cried the man, interested at last. ("You'd have thought some one had trod on his toe," the woman recounted later.) Then the man added: "I'm not sure. Yes, perhaps. I'll let you know presently."

The bag, a black one, was on a chair. When the woman had gone, the man went to it, opened it, looked inside, closed it, locked it, and moved it, for no reason that he could have explained, to another chair. Then he returned to the table and began his tea.

From the bar across the passage came suddenly the sound of raucous music. Some one had put a penny in a grotesque piece of machinery, and was receiving his money's worth. The man plugged his ears with his fingers and glared at his teacup while the music ground on. After a minute he removed his fingers, then hastily shoved them back again. His forehead throbbed. His head seemed on the point of bursting. A poor man's pleasure was filling his heart with hate.

"God above!" he shouted.

But nobody heard him. The music across the passage was even louder.

When at last the music ended, he found himself laughing. He did not remember beginning to laugh. He stopped abruptly.

"This won't do," he muttered. "This won't do."

He finished his tea quietly and returned to the window.

Chapter IV

Over the Yellow Cups

The teacups at the Black Stag were thick and white. At Bragley Court they were thin and yellow, and they began their clinking in the drawing-room, a long, lofty room of pink and cream, and then followed the guests to their various locations. If you disliked pink and cream and a preponderance of elderly feminine society, you stayed away from the official headquarters, confident that the yellow cups would find out where you were and come to you. Mohammed, at Bragley Court, would not have been put to the trouble of going to his mountain.

John's cup came to him at exactly five o'clock, on a brightly-polished mahogany tray. It was brought and deposited on a small, low table by the pretty maid, and John watched her with interest to discover whether she still bore any traces of her recent agitation. Outwardly, she was now quite calm again, and because of her pleasant friendly quality he hoped that her appearance reflected the truth.

"Is your foot better, sir?" she asked.

"I am sure this interest is unconstitutional," thought John, "but it's nice." So he did not discourage it. He told her that his foot was very much better. The lie did not impress itself on him at the moment.

A cushion had fallen to the ground. The maid picked it up and fixed it behind his head with a bright smile. Then she put another log on the crackling fire and departed.

It was a small, trivial incident, but later on, among a collection of incidents less trivial, John remembered it.

He was staring at the fire, watching the flames crackle upwards towards the chimney, when a voice said:

"Well, how are you getting along? Do you want some one to pour out your tea?"

He did not have to turn his head. Even if he had not recognised Nadine's voice he would have sensed her personality in the faint silky rustle of her approach and the less faint aroma of expensive perfume. She disturbed the air as she drew near, breaking it up into little emotional ripples.

"Hallo," he answered. "I'm all right. And thank you."

"I could have my tea here with you," she suggested, having already made up her mind not to have it anywhere else. "Shall I?"

"I'd love it," replied John. "Only I feel I'm upsetting things terribly. You ought to be with the other guests, oughtn't you?"

"Why? There are no oughts here. We do as we like. Haven't you noticed it?"

"I've noticed they don't worry you much."

"Of course you have. The house is run on lines of the most highly-organised freedom. You may flirt desperately or read the *Encyclopædia Britannica*. Just follow your mood. No one will interfere with you, or display any vulgar curiosity. Even a man with a bad foot isn't pestered with attention. But you can be quite sure the name of Foss has been looked up in Debrett." He laughed. "Is it to be found there?"

"I've an uncle who fills a dozen dry lines."

"Lord Aveling won't find the lines dry!" smiled Nadine,

sitting on the low stool lately occupied by Harold Taverley. For the first time he took in her rather daring tea-gown, with its provocative glimpses. It was a compliment that she should waste all this wealth of subtle femininity on him. Or was she wasting it? "Debrett and the old school tie will chain you here for the week-end, however your foot progresses! Lord Aveling can't run a country—though he wishes he could—but he can run a country house, and he lives for these house-parties, you know. The little thrill of them—the little notoriety of them—the little excitement of them—and the little things that happen in them. And, sometimes, quite big things."

A desire swept through John to ask, "And what do *you* live for?" But he quelled the impulse, and asked instead:

"Are any big things going to happen this week-end?"

She regarded him quizzically for a few moments, then replied, "I shouldn't wonder."

She turned and nodded to the pretty maid, who had reappeared with another highly-polished little tray gleaming with yellow china. The second tray was deposited beside the first tray. As the maid departed, Nadine's eyes followed her.

"Pretty, isn't she?" said Nadine.

"Very," answered John.

Two people came down the staircase. Harold Taverley and Anne. The signs of the road were no longer upon them, and both had changed to indoor clothes, but John noticed that Anne still favoured green. She was wearing a rather severe, close-cut frock that indicated without exploiting her slim boyish figure. Her dark hair was neat and smooth, and slightly waved. John gained an odd impression as she ran forward to greet Nadine that, while conceding to the moment, her real spirit was elsewhere.

"Nice to see you again, Nadine," she exclaimed. "Wasn't the last time Cannes?"

"Yes—drinking coffee at the Galerie Fleuries," answered Nadine. "Did you have a good run?"

"Wonderful! You must try my new mare. She goes over everything."

"I'd love to. But you'll want her to-morrow?"

"Please! You can have Jill, though. We've still got her, and you always liked her, didn't you?" She turned to John. "Do you ride? How's your foot? Or are you sick of being asked? I'd be!"

"It's the penalty of being a pampered invalid," replied John; "and I don't mind it at all. My foot's fine, thank you. But I'm afraid it wouldn't be well enough to join you to-morrow."

"Beastly shame," said Anne. "Never mind, we'll fix you up with jig-saw puzzles. Let me know if I can do anything, won't you? See you later, Nadine. Come along, Harold."

Taverley smiled at John.

"We'd stay, but you're being looked after," he remarked. "Be good to him, Nadine."

When they were alone again, Nadine frowned.

"Beastly man, that Mr. Taverley," she observed. "He's so hatefully nice!"

"I like him, too," replied John. "Is niceness a vice?"

"Yes—like water. You must have something with it."

"I imagine he's got a lot with it."

"Rather. All the virtues, and a perfect off-drive. And he hates *me*!"

"Oh, no, he doesn't!"

"How do you know that?"

John coloured at the quick question, and at his clumsiness. He decided not to retreat.

"We talked of you," he said. "Do you mind?"

She glanced in his cup, noted it was empty, and filled it.

"Of course I don't mind," she answered. "What else do people talk about but other people? But don't tell me what

Mr. Taverley said about me. Whatever it was, I am quite sure he forgave me, and so I'd have to forgive him, the beast!"

An interruption occurred. A uniformed nurse—Bragley Court could even materialise that—appeared abruptly and insisted on an application of surgical spirit. Surgical spirit during tea! But the nurse explained apologetically that she had a few minutes now, and might not have later.

"Does she look after Mrs. Morris?" queried John, when the nurse had soaked his foot and gone.

"Yes," answered Nadine. "Poor old lady. She ought to be dead."

"You mean—the release?"

"Of course! What's the use? You shoot a horse or a dog when it's incurable, but God wants humans to go on suffering!" She shuddered, and for once in her life misinterpreted the expression of a man who was dwelling on the movement of her body. "Oh, don't think I can't face pain," she added almost defiantly. "But I don't care for it. That's why I grasp life while it's here!"

She had spoken impulsively, almost as though thinking aloud. Her hand brushed his. She rose and walked to a window, drawing the long curtain slightly aside to look out into the gloaming. But all she saw was her own reflection and the provocative gown gleaming back at her through the glass.

John watched her, waiting for her to come back. Why was she so long about it? Why was he waiting with such an intense desire for her to turn? A sudden panic seized him.

"Nonsense!" he thought, aghast.

That morning, blind with grief and saturated with its egotism, he had flung some things into a bag and had fled from London. An unexpected letter had toppled his small world over. It had come with the surprising unexpectedness of a poisoned arrow. It had contained poison, too—poison that had polluted the very springs of his faith. And in the first pangs of his agony he had headed for a station—any station—and had taken a ticket to a distant place—any place—so that he might escape the grotesque irony of immediate obligations. Any place would do, so long as it was an unfamiliar place, a place without associations. Somebody ahead of him in the ticket office had said, "Flensham." So he had said, "Flensham."

And this was where the somebody had unconsciously led him—to her own reflection standing out vividly and tormentingly in the darkness of a window!

"Nonsense—nonsense!" he repeated in his thoughts. "I'm just in a mess. This is reaction. It doesn't mean anything. Reaction, and my foot. Lord, how it's hurting!"

He concentrated on the pain, trying to trick himself. He rejoiced in its re-discovery, and saddled it with responsibility for his condition. Pain played the deuce with any one. It temporarily distorted values, and gave fictitious significance to unimportant things. That was why patients in hospitals so often fell in love with their nurses....

Nadine came back to him as abruptly as she had left him.

"What are you going to do?" she asked. "Stay here?" He stared at her. Her tone was almost harsh. "I mean—well, you've spoken so little about yourself, haven't you? Aren't you expected somewhere to-night?"

He shook his head.

"Where were you going when I met you at the station?"

"Didn't you ask that? Anywhere."

"That sounds morbid!"

"Don't judge by the sound. I'm fond of roaming."

"I see. And you roamed—here."

"Yes." He had a sense that they were going round and round in a circle, and he tried to smash his way out. "You know, I don't think my foot's half as bad as it seems." Yet a moment ago he had been insisting on the pain of it. "I believe I could get away all right."

"You think the foot could stand it?"

"I think so."

"But the question still remains—where do you want to get away to?"

They were moving back into the circle again. He became exasperated.

"Yes, and that's *my* question," he retorted.

"Sorry," she said.

He was appalled at himself. He had not intended to betray his exasperation. He was not exasperated any longer. He did not understand how he ever had been.

"No, *I'm* sorry," he muttered. "Really, you must forgive me. You've been terribly kind. I don't know what's the matter with me."

Nadine knew. It was her knowledge that had sent her to the window, and that had produced her rather lame effort to readjust the trouble. Something had happened very suddenly. She had sensed the exact moment. It was not the first time the moment had occurred in her experience.

Well—could it be helped? And did it matter? She thought of old Mrs. Morris upstairs. One day *she* might be like that! She thought of the hunt on the morrow, and of the hunted creature doomed to die, as every one at Bragley Court was doomed to die! But at this moment the hunted creature was not conscious of its fate, nor was any one at Bragley Court, saving Nadine Leveridge herself. She was always conscious of it, and of life's demand for compensation.

"Don't apologise, Mr. Foss, and don't worry," she said. "It will be all the same five hundred years hence. Meanwhile, since it's obvious you can't move, and would have nowhere particular to move to even if you could, remember that we are two very small dots in a very large universe, and finish your tea."

Chapter V

The 5.56

The 3.28 had brought two visitors to Bragley Court. The 5.56 brought four. The man at the window of the Black Stag watched them alight.

The 5.56 shared with the 12.10 the distinction of being a fast express, and was, therefore, favoured by the majority of Lord Aveling's guests. It was pleasant to arrive by the 12.10 in the morning, when the sun was at its highest and the sky was at its brightest; you reached your room at Bragley Court by half-past twelve, and your bag was unpacked and your brushes were out by the time the luncheon-gong sounded at half-past one. The 3.38 had its points, too, despite a tedious change, for there is always rather a jolly feeling when you arrive at a country house at tea-time. Tea is an occasion to look forward to after the dust and grit of travel; you flop into soft things and regain your belief in the harmony of life's rhythm.

But the 5.56 was the train-de-luxe. You could pass a reasonable portion of the day in London before catching it. You spent the minimum of time in it, and although you missed the yellow cups of Bragley Court, a smiling attendant brought you blue ones. And when, at 5.56 to the minute, the gravel sounded in your ears and the train slackened speed, you found Flensham station at its peak—the station-master at his most dignified, the porter at his most obliging, and Old Jim (who never troubled to meet the 3.28, his horse, like himself, being a veteran and needing afternoon rest) at his most hopeful. Not that Old Jim ever expected to get a fare to Bragley Court. His horseflesh was not of the Bragley breed, and Lord Aveling supplied cars for all his guests who did not bring their own. Still there were other destinations, and sometimes a passenger on the 5.56 was bound for one of them.

Of the four guests deposited on the platform on this particular evening, the last to enter the waiting Rolls was a tall, slightish man mid-way between thirty and forty. His name was Lionel Bultin, and he stood, silent and aloof, and purposely lingering, to watch a little incident.

His three companions were, as he had established in the restaurant car, Zena Wilding, the actress, and a married couple who lived an unenviable existence under the name of Chater. Bultin, a ruthless reader of character, had needed only two minutes to decide that an additional "e" slipped between the second and third letters of their name would have described the Chaters more accurately. When the husband looked straight at you he seemed to be seeing you round a corner. The wife hardly ever looked straight at you. She was a silent creature whose moroseness appeared to form her protection against a perpetual desire to scream.

Zena Wilding, on the other hand, was lively and talkative, and while she worried vivaciously about her luggage, she never missed an opportunity to advertise her dentist. Later on, the solemn station-master paused in the important business of writing "We could do—" to recollect her dazzling teeth before concluding "—with new fire-buckets." And the porter actually dreamt of the teeth, earnestly filling a freight train with tooth-paste to keep them white. But the dazzling teeth made no impression on Lionel Bultin, saving as possible matter for a theatrical paragraph. He felt no personal emotion about them. He had done with personal emotion ten years ago....

In order to understand Bultin's attitude, and the detachment with which his trained intelligence now absorbed an incident frightful with suppressed emotion, it is necessary to travel back those ten years to the day when, an eager and unsuccessful young journalist, he came to his great decision. In a not-very-attractive bed-sitting-room he had faced his mirror frankly, and had said:

"You're making a hash of things. Why is it?"

Yes, why was it? Why did people pay no attention to him? Why had an editor refused, for the third time, to see him that very day? Did eagerness and tenacity count for nothing? Willingness—obligingness—sensitiveness? Bultin possessed all these qualities, plus an average capacity to string words together. So why was he living in this faded bed-sitting-room? Why could he not go across to the restaurant opposite and order a wing of chicken? Why was he *hungry*?

And then, suddenly, his reflection had changed. The despair and the eagerness had left it. Something quite new had entered and, because he was intelligent as well as hungry, he studied it. The new thing was a queer, cold callousness. A callousness that, because it had lost its faith in humanity, was independent of humanity. He felt as though, all at once, his sensitive soul had died, giving a new functioning power to what remained.

"This means success or the river," he thought soberly.

He put on his hat and he went out, undecided. The river lay on his right, and the office of the inaccessible editor on his left. He turned to the left. The commissionaire whom he had interviewed thrice saw him coming, and exclaimed, "Can't you take 'No' for an answer?"

Bultin wrote something on a slip of paper. "Give that to your fool of an editor," he said, and left the office. He had written on the paper: "I could have given you a signed article by Bernard Shaw. Now you can sing for it. The above address will find me."

Next day the signed article appeared in a rival paper. The editor, a weak man who spent his life in fear of a dropping circulation, never learned that Bultin had not supplied the rival paper with the article. Two hours before Bultin had scribbled his rude note, a friend of his had sold it elsewhere. The editor sent for Bultin and offered him a commission. Bultin turned it down.

He managed to borrow fifty pounds. He began a life of curious isolation. He was ever present in journalistic and social circles, but he remained aloof in his attitude. His manner indicated personal circumstances that did not exist. You would have thought, if you had met Lionel Bultin during those weeks, that he had suddenly come into a large fortune, although he showed no generosity in spending it, and that he could now snap his fingers at life. A successful man attracts success.

Whether Bultin would have achieved his purpose without the assistance of a small social column is not certain. This column was the last remnant of his evaporating work at the time of his decision, and it was itself on the verge of evaporation. Now, however, it began to wake up. It ceased to be soft and kindly. Amazing bits about amazing people appeared in it. Startling bits. Rude bits. With still a few complimentary bits, as bait. All signed Bultin.

"What does Bultin say?" people started asking.

An actress in the Savoy grill-room—yes, Bultin now went there—left her table to tell him of a pearl necklace she had lost. Two or three weeks earlier he would have travelled five miles to the actress. Now she had travelled five yards to him. Twice the alleged value of the necklace was given exclusively in his column next day, with an account of how the actress had left her *pâté de fois gras* to tell him of the loss. It had really been tomato soup, and the necklace had never been lost at all; but such minor matters were unimportant. The important matter was that the concluding sentence of Bultin's paragraph was nearly, but not quite, libellous.

Bultin's column grew to two. Then to a full page. In a short while the fifty pounds was repaid. Bultin had killed himself, and never had a moment's financial anxiety afterwards. His carcass grew rich....

And, just as the actress in the Savoy grill-room had angled for his publicity, so Zena Wilding posed for him now on Flensham platform, striving to create a paragraph out of her luggage, her Paris hat, and her teeth.

"Oh, dear! Am I keeping everybody waiting?" she gushed, as Mr. and Mrs. Chater moved towards the car.

"Yes," answered Bultin. (His column should mention later how he had agreed with her.)

Then Zena forgot all about her luggage and her hat and her teeth. She also forgot Bultin. The man who had waited for hours in the Black Stag was standing before her.

She gave a gasp. For an instant she looked almost old. She stared at the man without moving, but Bultin gained an impression that she was arching her back like a cat. Then she turned swiftly, and dived towards the car. Mrs. Chater was just getting in.

"Is anything the matter?" inquired Mrs. Chater, apathetically.

"No, nothing!" cried Zena. "Which corner would you like?"

Mr. Chater turned, and saw the man. He also stared. But his manner was considerably more composed than Zena's. His expression of surprise changed to a smile, and he walked up to the man. The man had an unlit cigarette in his mouth.

"Want a light?" inquired Mr. Chater.

The man looked livid. Mr. Chater struck a match. The man blew it out.

"See you presently," he muttered.

"I wouldn't," answered Mr. Chater quietly.

Two seconds later, Mr. Chater was entering the car.

About to follow, Bultin changed his mind and strolled casually up to the man.

"You might as well," he remarked, taking out his lighter. "You're supposed to burn one end, you know."

The man switched round violently. Ten years previously Bultin would have dreamt of the expression in the man's eyes. Now he merely found it undoubtedly interesting.

"I am Lionel Bultin," he said. "I am spending the week-end at Bragley Court. I shall be there till Monday morning. I pay for material—provided, of course, that I use it."

For the second time that evening, the man escaped a brainstorm by the breadth of a hair. The first time it had nearly been caused by a penn'orth of mechanical music.

"Bragley Court," he repeated, suddenly calm. "You're going there, too, eh?" He bent forward and accepted the light. As he withdrew his head he added, "You'll get something to write about."

Chapter VI

Spottings of a Leopard

The drive to Bragley Court was stiff and uncomfortable. Bultin never did anything to put people at their ease, and Zena Wilding's forced vivacity was as unhelpful as Bultin's silence. The one subject that most vitally interested the majority of the party was studiously avoided.

"Don't you think there's always a sort of a thrill, going to a new country house?" exclaimed Zena, trying nervously to be brilliant. "Something like the curtain going up on a play?"

"Yes," answered Mrs. Chater dutifully.

It was not encouraging, but Zena prattled on:

"And then the guests—they're like the characters—and you wonder what's going to happen. Of course, nothing particular ever really does happen. Just as well! Suppose it did—a fire, or a burglary, or a murder! No, thank you, we'll leave that to the dramatists!"

She glanced at Bultin. She was speaking partly for his benefit, though partly also to drive her mind from the disturbing moment just before she had entered the car. If she made her conversation scintillating, Bultin might report it.

But Bultin was gazing out of the window, inventing headlines, although his ear did not miss a word Zena said, and it was Mr. Chater this time who broke the silence with a murmured:

"What? Yes, quite."

Mr. Chater was able to talk fluently on occasions, but this was not one of the occasions. He, also, was recalling the moment just before he had entered the car. Unlike Zena, however, he was not trying to forget it. He was dwelling on it, probing its meaning.

The actress made one more effort.

"I suppose I can't help seeing drama in everything," she said, forgetting that her drama rarely rose above the level of musical comedy. "Even when I was on the Riviera—do you know the Riviera?—it was there I met Lord Aveling— yes, even on my holiday I was always inventing plots about everything and everybody. Your mind just goes on working, you know, without your knowing it." She glanced again at Bultin. He was still staring out of the window. It was very disappointing. Well, she must give him some definite news—perhaps that would wake him up. "Yes, but one wants to get back to work. Of course, I enjoyed my holi- day immensely—after my illness—but it was far too long. Do you know, it seems years and years since I put on any make-up." Bultin did make a mental note of that phrase. "But—well, I don't believe it will be very long now. As a matter of fact—in strict confidence—I've got *the* play in my case at this moment!…Only perhaps you'd better not mention it just yet, Mr. Bultin?"

"I promise I won't," he answered.

The man was just a beast! She hoped earnestly that he would break his promise.

After that she gave up, and the journey continued in silence.

They reached their destination as Lord Aveling was greeting another guest who had just preceded them, and who had made the trip from London by car. "Earnshaw," Bultin identified. He also noticed that Lord Aveling was welcoming him effusively.

"Delighted you were able to get away, Sir James," said Aveling. "You're staying till Monday, of course?"

"Unless I'm called back," replied the Liberal member, his large rich voice filling the hall. He gazed about him as he spoke, leisurely and unflurriedly. He had all the solid assurance of a well-groomed, well-fed man. "Land question, you know."

"It's the eternal question," smiled Aveling. "I expect we'll talk about it. State or private ownership. Communism or—common sense, eh? No middle course these days."

The Liberal member looked at his host sharply. He, too, was doubting the wisdom of the middle course. Moderation was in a disconcerting minority at the moment. But it was not this reflection that had arrested him. It was "Communism or Common Sense." He revolved the words in his mind. A slogan there, somewhere. Communism or Common Sense. Communism or Common Sensism. House of Commonism....

The Honourable Anne appeared on the stairs. Slogans vanished as he strode forward to meet her. Meanwhile Lord Aveling's polished voice droned on:

"Ah, Miss Wilding! How are you? I hope the journey was not tiring?" He took the actress's hand and held it for an instant. "We have something to chat about, have we not? Ah, Bultin—how is the world treating you? Or perhaps we should say, how are you treating the world? Have you brought your large note-book? Be careful of this man, Miss Wilding! He can make or ruin one in a single paragraph. We all try to keep on the right side of Mr. Bultin."

Bultin smiled faintly. He knew that, behind his polished badinage, Lord Aveling was just a little anxious about him. This week-end was a sort of bribe. The tobacco and beads for the naughty Indian with the scalping-knife.

Then Lord Aveling turned to the last of his guests to enter through the front door. Sir James turned also with a sudden sense of responsibility. He was still leisurely and unflurried, but a little of the rich warmth left his tone as he said:

"How well we have arranged this! I arrive just in time to perform the introductions. Mr. and Mrs. Chater, Lord Aveling."

John Foss had said he was not superstitious, but he had been watching the front door from his couch, and counting. Zena Wilding, ten. Lionel Bultin, eleven. Who would enter first of the last couple?…The man—no, he had paused on the threshold. The woman preceded him. Mrs. Chater, twelve. Mr. Chater, thirteen.…

The new guests dissolved to their respective rooms. Dinner was at eight, and bags had to be unpacked and clothes changed. Lionel Bultin followed a servant up the soft stair-carpet to a room on the second floor. The artist, Leicester Pratt, wagged a hand from an easy-chair as he entered.

"Hallo, Lionel," said Pratt. "We're to be stable lads together. I hope you don't mind? There's no way out, if you do. It was my idea."

Bultin did not mind. His invitation to Bragley Court had also been Pratt's idea. It was Leicester Pratt who had lent Bultin fifty pounds ten years ago, at the critical moment of the journalist's career. Pratt was then an unknown artist, doing infinitely better work than he was doing to-day. Pratt had discovered Bultin, and in return Bultin had discovered Pratt. No two men had helped each other more, or understood each other better.

"Well?" queried Bultin, after five minutes of silence.

Pratt laughed.

"You know, I'm quite a little child at heart, Lionel," he answered. "I love to call you Lionel, and even more I love to make you say, 'Well?' I believe I'm the only person who can do it outside the King and Mussolini. Lionel Bultin, purveyor of world news, world gossip, world washing, authority on Eden's size in collars and Greta Garbo's lip-stick, asking *me* for information! Admit it's a score!"

"I don't ask even little children twice," observed Bultin, removing one of Pratt's coats from a hook so that he could use the hook for one of his own.

"You'd ask *this* child twice, if it were necessary," retorted Pratt. "You see, I have the advantage of not being a sentimentalist. You've grown so fond of life that you will woo it with any weapon. I dislike life so much that I'm without fear. Once life begins bargaining for my heart, I've done with the jade! Yes, and here's an interesting thing," he added. "You couldn't commit suicide if you tried. If ever I decide to, I won't hesitate. Posthumous opinion can find me out, if it's amused—I shan't be here."

"The little child is objectionably precocious," commented Bultin, quite unmoved. He rather enjoyed being thought a sentimentalist. "Get on with it."

"I understood you never asked twice!" jeered Pratt. "'Get on with it,' is your second 'Well?' camouflaged. All right. Here goes. News from the advance guard, for Bultin's column, 'How the Wind Blows,' preferred by ninety-nine per cent. of the population to Hamlet, the Bible, and Omar Khayyám. Paragraph One. 'Miss Zena Wilding, age thirty-two by the kindness of her friends, forty-two by the unkindness of her enemies, and thirty-eight by the justice of God—'"

"Thirty-seven," interposed Bultin.

"'—is an interesting visitor at Bragley Court this weekend. She has long awaited the really big theatrical chance she so thoroughly does not deserve. My little leopard informs me that, if she is very good, but perhaps not too good, she may receive the promise of the necessary backing by Monday next.'"

"I already knew that," said Bultin.

"Your comment was inevitable," replied Pratt.

"She first met the backing on the Riviera," said Bultin, "where she went to recuperate after a serious illness. Cause and nature of illness not known."

"And possibly not for publication when known," added Pratt. "Paragraph Two. 'The celebrated artist, Leicester Pratt, who has the world of portraiture temporarily at his feet, who calls a scarcely less celebrated journalist by his Christian name, and whose bow ties become increasingly flowing, has been at Bragley Court for several days, and is now completing a portrait designed for next year's Royal Academy of Lord Aveling's only daughter, the Honourable Anne Aveling.' Kindly turn *that* paragraph into a column."

"Does this window look out on the back?" said Bultin.

"It looks out on the studio," answered Pratt, "where the aforementioned masterpiece is in process. Paragraph Three. I think you'll like this one better. 'It is interesting to find Sir James Earnshaw among the guests at Bragley Court. It is well known that he does not hunt stags for the pleasure of it. Is he hunting anything else? My little leopard informs me that, if Sir James is to survive politically, he must turn Labour or Conservative, and he would be given the hand of the Honourable Anne Aveling if he decided to survive as a Conservative. This would not outrage Sir James's private political convictions, because he hasn't any, and then Lord Aveling might himself survive as a Marquis instead of a mere Baron, in virtue of the additional vote he brought to the Conservative Party.'"

Bultin condescended to turn away from a wardrobe he had been examining, and fix Pratt with a rather fish-like eye.

"Really?" he said.

"Really," nodded Pratt. "Thank you for your passionate interest. I charge 3/10 for that one. But you can have the next paragraph for nothing. 'Miss Edyth Fermoy-Jones is studying Nobility at first-hand. This is a pity, because we shall now lose those delicate flights of fancy that have illuminated so many of her previous volumes on High Life, and which once caused a Countess to bathe regularly in expensive hock. My little leopard tells me that her next novel will open with an accident to a young man at a railway station. A very beautiful widow will convey the young man to an ancestral home, will fall in love with him, and will discover that he is really a necklace thief. When a celebrated artist is murdered for painting a mole on the neck of a débutante, the young man will be arrested for the crime, and only the beautiful widow will know that his heart was too pure to devise anything worse than stealing necklaces.'"

"Will it come out that the real murderer of the artist was a famous journalist?" inquired Bultin.

Leicester Pratt laughed, and ran on:

"But the next paragraph is worth another 3/10. I might even work you up to four bob. 'If Lord Aveling, already secretly harassed for funds, becomes a Marquis, how will he meet enhanced expenses? Perhaps—my little leopard tells me—Mr. and Mrs. Arthur Rowe, who have made a fortune from pork and who are anxious to emerge from the sausage-skin that has encased them so long, could supply the answer. They and their charming daughter, Ruth, have been staying for some days at Bragley Court, and if Ruth were launched into Society with a Capital S, it is possible that Lord Aveling would be able to support a marquisate.

And, incidentally, to justify the expense of backing a show, while waiting.'"

Bultin refused to register any gratitude.

"Who is the attractive widow?" he asked.

"Nadine Leveridge," sighed Pratt, in mock disappointment. "Well, if I can't interest you above-stairs, let me try below-stairs. Leopards also prowl in basements. Do not be surprised if you are given bamboo-shoots for dinner to-night. We have a Chinese cook. No good? I'll try again. We have something in the domestic line more attractive than a Chinese cook—a very pretty maid. Name, Bessie. Delightful figure. Make a good model. But when this was suggested to her, she was filled with charming confusion." He rose and stretched himself. "I shall waste no more time over you, Lionel. You're not worth it. I shall take a stroll before dressing."

"Do," said Bultin. "Since you can't tell me anything about the most interesting people here."

"Who?"

"Mr. and Mrs. Chater."

"Ah, the Chaters," answered Pratt. "Yes, there I'm beaten. The little leopard knows nothing about the Chaters."

"Nor does Lord Aveling," replied Bultin. "But James Earnshaw does. And, unless I am reaching my dotage, the Chaters know something about James Earnshaw. Which is my bed?"

"That one over there."

"Good. I'll have the other one."

Pratt laughed and left the room. Outside he paused. Harold Taverley, the one man he had not mentioned, was entering his room opposite, and threw him a smile.

"Why does that man always make me see red?" wondered Pratt.

He went downstairs thoughtfully.

Chapter VII

Whitewash and Paint

A narrow passage led from the back of the lounge-hall into the grounds, and as Leicester Pratt passed out into a sheltered lawn, its dark surface streaked with slits of light from upper windows—one window being that of his bedroom—he noticed a thin coil of smoke spiralling upwards. Then Nadine Leveridge gleamed at him out of a shadow.

She was a creature of dazzling white, softened by the deep green of her dress. Her shoulders were perfectly formed and perfectly revealed. One was tempted to envy the narrow green strips curving with such apparent insecurity over them. A double rope of pearls made a loop in front of the simple green bodice. A silk wrap, also of green, but deeper and more brilliant in hue, partially covered one shoulder.

"Nadine Leveridge is Life's relentless weapon," thought Pratt. "A woman for fools to fear."

Pratt did not fear her. He could even stand and regard her, deliberately studying her subtle challenges with the impertinent privilege of an artist.

"You've dressed early," he said. She nodded. "Not afraid of the cold?"

"Not a bit."

He felt for his cigarette-case, and found he had left it in his room.

"I'm sorry I can't oblige," remarked Nadine. "Mr. Taverley gave me this."

She held up her cigarette. Pratt noticed that it was a State Express 555.

"Don't move for a moment," he said. She stood motionless, her eyebrows raised a little. Only the cigarette smoke continued its movement. "The lady with the cigarette. The lady in green. Modern Eve. Woman. Anything you damn like. When do I paint her?"

"She'd have to pawn her pearls to pay your price," smiled Nadine, puffing the cigarette again.

"That's terribly material."

"Goes against the grain?"

Now Pratt smiled.

"You must hate meeting pieces of wood like Bultin and me," he observed.

"Nonsense—nobody's wood!" retorted Nadine. "Some people build wooden walls around themselves, that's all. Bultin does, certainly."

"Yes, I agree. He's chained himself inside in case he should get out and collapse. But—me?"

"Something could move you."

"What?"

"I've no idea. But *I* couldn't. That's why I don't think I'll pawn my pearls, thank you. Any one who paints me must be an out-and-out idealist."

"An idealist is merely another sort of man who builds a wall round his passions."

"And whose passions are the most ardent when the wall goes?" replied Nadine. "Yes, I know all about that! But he begins with a kind heart, and I only allow artists with kind hearts to paint me. I've seen your Twentieth-Century Madonna!"

"I should never have thought *you* feared the truth, Nadine," reproved Pratt.

"I don't. But no artist can paint the whole truth. He just paints his half—and the other half can't answer back from the canvas. The half I fear is your half—all by its little lonesome!"

"Touché," murmured Pratt, "although I am not admitting there is any other half."

"Didn't you paint the other half when you were twenty? I remember a picture called 'Song of Youth.'"

"My God, spare me!" he winced. "Must that ghastly song follow me to the grave? And anyway," he added, "how on earth do *you* remember that ancient atrocity? From your appearance, your memory shouldn't take you back so far."

"I'm in shadow."

"Kindly step out of it."

She hesitated, then did so.

"I repeat my astonishment," said Pratt, staring at her. "You look twenty yourself! And now, I suppose, you will charge me with gallantry? No, I couldn't stand that! Not immediately after the resuscitation of my 'Song of Youth!' Excuse me, before I become utterly whitewashed!"

"I'll excuse you," answered Nadine, throwing her cigarette away, "but I don't think I'm exactly the kind of person to whitewash anybody."

"Thank God!" said Pratt devoutly.

He watched her pass back to the house, then stepped on to the dark lawn. It was thirty strides across. Beyond, a flagged path led between bushes to the studio.

As he reached the building he felt in his pocket for the key. There had been no afternoon sitting that day, for horses had supplanted canvas; and there was not much chance of a sitting on the morrow, either. A stag was to be routed out of Flensham Forest, to perform its entertaining death-run. Well, he could add a few touches to the picture by himself, and finish the thing on Sunday. He'd have to get it out of the way by then, if Ruth Rowe's was to follow.

"Where the devil—?" he murmured.

Then he saw the key in the door, and recalled that he must have left it there after his visit with Mr. Rowe before tea. It was then that the picture of Ruth had been decided on.

He turned the key and entered the large room. Ruth's picture would be dull compared with Anne's. There was little to paint about Ruth. There were fathomless depths to reveal in Anne. He knew them. He could pierce through right down to the bed. Yes, he liked this picture—there was something definitely challenging in it. "No whitewashing, my child—we'll show 'em—a bit of real collaboration. As a rule, I'm the only one that understands, but you understand, too. That's what makes it!"

And Earnshaw's presence here this week-end added its touch of ironic justification. Anne could sell her soul, like the rest of them—or the mythical thing that was called a soul!

He switched on the light, and turned to the picture of the Honourable Anne Aveling.

It was almost obliterated by a long, broad smudge of paint. The smudge, crimson lake, began at Anne's right ear, and descended diagonally across the dark-green riding habit.

"Something could move you!" Nadine's words screamed through his ears, as though repeated by an invisible loud speaker turned full on. He found himself trembling. He fought against vulnerable emotion.

"Somebody's gone mad here," he thought. "All in a moment."

He recalled the moment when *he* had seen red in the passage outside his bedroom. Yes…it could happen.

He turned away from the canvas, to control himself. He stared round the studio. On another easel was a large painting of a stag, done by Anne herself. It was not good, saving for the terrible, dull fear she had somehow planted in the stag's eyes—a fear she should not have known about, since she hunted. He concentrated on the stag's eyes for a few seconds, then turned his own eyes back to the ruined canvas. The fit of trembling had passed.

"Queer game," he said aloud. "I wonder whether I shall ever have the pleasure of painting the person who did this?"

He glanced at his watch. Five minute to seven. He left the studio abruptly, locked the door, and put the key in his pocket. A spent cigarette-end loomed dully from the ground. He picked it up.

Some one was moving in the path. He dashed forward and grabbed. Sheer instinct had caused the sudden action. A hand banged him in the chest, and he staggered. When he had recovered, he was alone.

As he came to the end of the flagged path a figure met him off the edge of the lawn.

"Good-evening," said the figure.

Pratt regarded the face that rose abruptly before his, and smiled.

"Good-evening, Mr. Chater," he answered.

"That's a good guess," replied Chater. "We've not met."

"No, that's how I guessed," responded Pratt. "Process of elimination. You came on the 5.56, didn't you?"

"That's right."

"You've not been here before?"

"No, my first visit. Rather a nice place, isn't it? I'm just having a stroll round."

"I'm afraid you won't see much in this darkness."

"Enough to get one's bearings. Where does this lead? Is that building over there the stables?"

He was gazing along the flagged path.

"No, that's a studio," answered Pratt.

"Oh, yes, there's an artist here, isn't there?"

"Well—he calls himself an artist. Are you interested in art, by any chance?"

"Me? Not particularly. Who's the fellow?"

"What fellow?"

"The artist?"

"Leicester Pratt."

"Oh, Leicester Pratt! He's rather the craze just now, isn't he?"

"Some people like his work."

"And some don't?"

"They all pay big prices for it."

"Then I don't suppose *he* worries! Is he painting anybody here?"

Pratt paused for a second before replying.

"I have just been looking at a picture he is painting of somebody here."

"Good?"

"He thinks so."

"Who's it of?"

"Lord Aveling's daughter."

"Oh, not his wife."

The remark was made carelessly, but Pratt realised that his face was being watched, and he took great pains that it should convey nothing as he answered dryly:

"I said his daughter."

"So you did," smiled Chater. "Rather an attractive girl, though I've only seen her for a moment. Isn't she just going to be engaged or something?"

"Do I follow you?"

"Eh?"

"The 'something?'"

Chater's smile augmented to a laugh, and his teeth gleamed in the dusk.

"Don't mean to insinuate anything," he said. "It's Earnshaw, isn't it?" As Pratt did not respond, he added, "Hope I'm not asking too many questions; but when you're a sort of stranger—well, it's helpful to know things. Often saves you from making a *faux pas*. Curiosity's not one of my natural vices."

"That idea would never occur to me, Mr. Chater," observed Pratt ironically.

The irony made no impression.

"I admit I would rather like to see that picture, though," Chater went on. "Is one allowed in the studio?"

"I'm afraid it's locked," replied Pratt.

"Locked? Then how did *you* get in?" inquired Chater.

"I have the key," said Pratt, "and I locked it."

"That sounds as if you're Leicester Pratt."

"I am."

"You might have warned me. Now I shall spend the rest of the evening trying to recall our conversation to see if I've put my foot in it! Or p'r'aps you'll save me the trouble? *Have* I?"

There was something cheap, almost insulting, in Chater's coolness, which appeared to have been deliberately acquired, whereas the *sang froid* of Pratt was a natural inheritance. The artist answered:

"You have not even put your foot in my studio. Or—have you?"

"What, put my foot in your studio?" exclaimed Chater. "How could I have, if it's locked?"

"It wasn't locked ten minutes ago."

Chater's expression changed slightly. It was still cool, but a watchful quality entered into it.

"Ten minutes ago I was saying good-evening to a maid," he said.

A clock struck seven as he spoke. It was a clock over the stables.

"I see," murmured Pratt. "Then you have not been out here ten minutes?"

"I'd just come out when I met you."

"Did you meet anybody else?"

"Excuse me, Mr. Pratt, but what's all this about?"

Pratt shrugged his shoulders.

"Nothing important," he replied. "See you at dinner."

Chater turned his head as Pratt began to resume his way.

"Do we like each other?" he asked.

"Not a bit," answered Pratt.

That was also Chater's conviction as, after watching the artist disappear into the house, he himself turned back to the flagged path and walked towards the studio. If Pratt had not locked the studio door, he would not have seen the thirteenth guest at dinner.

Bultin was fixing an over-large white tie round his collar when Pratt rejoined him. Bultin liked large things. His soft felt hat was of Italian dimensions, although it came from a shop in Piccadilly.

"Enjoy your walk?" asked Bultin, without turning his head.

"Immensely," answered Pratt, throwing off his coat, "though not quite as much as Edyth Fermoy-Jones would have enjoyed it in my place. 'Why?' the famous journalist refused to inquire. Because, my dear Lionel, Edyth Fermoy-Jones would have made a most sensational discovery, and would have torn up the first chapter of that novel of hers."

"The one thing I have never learned to do without an effort," said Bultin, "is to tie a white tie."

"And she would have started her story afresh, you vile pretender! Yes, Lionel, I made a mistake when I described her plot to you just now. It will certainly contain the mar- vellous necklace round the neck of the attractive widow—a double rope of pearls worth—you like to quote figures, don't you?—worth every penny of ten thousand pounds. You can make it twenty, if you like. Edyth Fermoy-Jones will make it fifty. But it won't be stolen! Not, at least, for several chapters—till her editor has put the wind up her by shouting for more drama. No, a picture will be mutilated, instead. Less hackneyed idea, isn't it? With first-rate possibilities for development, and an unimpeachable setting. Studio—model's screen—artist's lay figure—strange pictures on large easels—somebody hiding behind one of 'em—" He paused, arrested by a thought, then continued: "The mutilated picture in Miss Fermoy-Jones's studio will be of a baron's daughter. Value—no, price—one thousand guineas. Smeared over with paint, my boy. Smeared over with paint."

"I thought that was the fate of all pictures," remarked Bultin.

"The fate is bearable when there is only one artist," answered Pratt. "But here there are two. The first artist's smear has been smeared out by the second. I wonder how Epstein feels when people daub his statues? Scornful? Callous? Cynical? Or just bloody angry? I must ask him."

Bultin's nose for a true scent was as accurate as any hound's. He paused for a moment in his struggle with his tie.

"Like that?" he said quietly.

"I don't suppose, Lionel," replied Pratt, kicking off his shoes, "there's a soul alive without his vulnerable spot. An elephant's got one behind his ear. I've got one behind my paint. Where's yours?"

"You'll have to paint me, as you paint other people, to find out," answered Bultin, almost humanly.

"Perhaps I've found out already, without using my brushes."

"Or perhaps I haven't got one? Or perhaps the only individual who will ever find it out is the unpleasant old man with the scythe."

"Death," mused Pratt. "I'm not thinking of Death. That's miles away...."

He stopped abruptly. Bultin loosened his tie, pulled it off, and began again.

"Are you sure, Leicester?" he inquired. "Are you quite sure—with your mutilated picture only a few *yards* away? There may be murder committed in Miss Fermoy-Jones's novel yet—eh? By an artist?"

"I don't kill," said Pratt. Then he recalled the moment when he had seen red in the passage, and again when he had found himself trembling in the studio. He held up his hand. It was perfectly steady. He smiled. "No; I don't kill. The murder may appear in Miss Fermoy-Jones's shocker, but it won't be reported in Monday's newspaper. I'm afraid I won't be giving you *that* paragraph. Just the same, Lionel," he went on contemplatively, "there's a lot beneath a quiet surface. The person who spoilt my picture may have been a quiet sort of a person. He may have been more surprised than any one at his action. A sudden moment of passion, eh? A sudden dizziness? It can happen." He raised a slender finger. "Listen! Dead quiet, isn't it? Not a sound! But if we could *really* hear, Lionel? Storms brewing in the silence? There's silence in the passage outside this door here—silence in the hall below—silence on the lawn, silence in the studio—silence in a room where an invalid lies. A brooding silence, my boy—that's not going to last!"

Bultin looked at Pratt, whose hand now dropped into a pocket to emerge with two small objects. One was a cigarette-end. State Express 555. The other was the key to the studio.

"Damn this tie," said Bultin, and chose another.

Chapter VIII

How Things Happen

John looked up quickly as Nadine entered the ante-room, and there was something apprehensive in his eye.

A feeling of peace had come to him when, shortly before dinner, his couch had been rolled in here from the hall and he had escaped temporarily from social responsibilities. Nadine, dressed early, had herself supervised the removal and the arranging of the room, assuming responsibility for his comfort, but she had only lingered for a moment or two afterwards. He gained an impression—it was correct—that she had originally intended to stay longer, and had then abruptly changed her mind.

A perfect dinner had followed. Its character gave no hint that it had been designed and cooked by a Chinaman. He had had one visitor during the meal. Anne had left her table to make sure that everything was all right. "I suppose I really ought to have watched you being shoved in here," she had said, "but I'm afraid I never do half the things I ought to do, and anyway Mrs. Leveridge was looking after you, wasn't she? She's terribly nice, isn't she? I love her. Be sure to give a view-halloa if you want anything, won't you?" The idea that any one in Bragley Court should have to shout for service made John smile.

The dark lawn outside the window sheltered by the long ballroom wing—had the ballroom been a lecture-hall and the ante-room less luxuriously furnished, he might have fancied himself back in college, staring out into the dark quadrangle where studious figures flitted not always with studious thoughts—had contributed to the sense of mental repose.

Then the peace had been broken. Guests, impelled by kindness or curiosity, had paid him short visits, or popped their heads in to give him a word or a smile. Apart from Harold Taverley, the men had fought rather shy of him, but the women had formed an intermittent procession. Mrs. Rowe had introduced her daughter, Ruth, who had been thoroughly unmodern and had blushed rather painfully. Miss Fermoy-Jones, on the other hand, had been quite unblushing, and during ten boring minutes had contrived to mention the titles of six of the sixteen mystery novels she had written. "Of course, they're terrible stuff, really," she had gushed, when she had become mistakenly convinced that she would not be believed, "but if people demand a thing, what are you to do? And just as you can write a bad psychological novel, I suppose you can write a good detective story. Lift your readers up, I say, and it doesn't really matter where you start from—if you understand what I mean, Mr. Foss. But I mustn't make your head ache by talking literature!" Lady Aveling had introduced Zena Wilding. Maybe she had hoped Zena would stay, but this interview had ended rather abruptly when the actress had suddenly noticed Lord Aveling in the doorway, and had whispered confidentially, "I'm so sorry, I've got to go and talk shop, but perhaps I'll see you again later." Anne, too, had paid him a second visit.

But Nadine Leveridge had kept away, and during the intervals of the procession John had visualised her in the ballroom, from which music faintly floated. He visualised her with painful clearness and struggled not to....And he was struggling not to now, when she appeared, and caught his expression.

If she had been dancing, there was little sign of it.

She looked as neat as when he had last seen her, and the double row of pearls lay against smooth, cool skin.

"Shall I go?" she asked with disarming bluntness.

"Go? Good Lord, no!" he exclaimed. "Why on earth?"

"You look worried." His mind raced for the right answer, but her mind raced his. "I expect your foot's still giving you the devil."

"Just a bit."

"So I will go. You'd rather be alone. I know you've had a string of visitors. Good-night."

"I say—you're not—wait a minute—you're not really going, are you?"

"You're quite sure you don't want me to?"

"I should hate you to!"

"Well, after all, I didn't really come here just to turn round and go back again," she smiled.

She entered the room and walked towards the window. A dog across the dark lawn was barking.

"Haig's a bit restless to-night," she remarked. "Haig is our watch-dog, and Lord Aveling's method of keeping the Great War green. Though why anybody wants to keep a war green I've never learned." She pulled the long curtains across the window, shutting out the lawn and muffling Haig's war-cry. Then she rolled a large green silk pouffe towards the couch and sat beside him. "What do we talk about, Mr. Foss? Things that matter, or things that don't?"

"I'll leave the choice to you," he hedged. "But perhaps cabbages and kings would be the safest."

"Safest?"

He turned red. What a fool he was! What a blundering ass! Usually he was rather good at conversation, but now he could not even talk of cabbages and kings without putting his foot in it. He did not realise that there are some women with whom it is almost impossible for a man to talk insignificantly. Beneath their trivial words they are telling him all the while that they like him or dislike him, love him or loathe him. The personal equation is all that lives behind their conversation.

"Have a cigarette, and don't worry," said Nadine. She produced a tiny gold case and held it out to him. "Forgive their idiotic size."

She struck a match. As the light flickered on her features, their perfection almost hurt him. Of course, it was beauty-parlour perfection. Therefore, not really perfection at all. He held on to that thought while he advanced his head to the light. She blew the match out as soon as he had used it, then struck another and lit her own cigarette from a greater distance.

They smoked for a few moments in silence. He had an agonising sensation that valuable seconds were slipping away, dropping irreclaimably into the void of time. Suddenly she raised her head.

"Yes,—I remember—one can just hear the music from this room," she exclaimed. "Has it tantalised you, as it tantalised *me* when I was lying on that couch two years ago?"

"I'm not a great dancer," he answered, "but I like it."

"You're cut out for the diplomatic service," she smiled, "you answer questions so tactfully! *I* could hardly lie still! There were better dancers that time than this. Apart from Mr. Taverley—and even he trod on my foot once"—She

advanced a shoe and regarded the gold-sandalled toe—
"there's not a good dancer here. Well, Lord Aveling's not
bad—but the rest! Sir James dances with a sort of pompous
caution. Mr. Pratt seems to have the one object of prevent-
ing you from knowing what steps he's going to do next. I
can usually follow anybody, but he beats me. I'm sure it's
on purpose. Of course, his bosom companion, Mr. Bultin,
doesn't dance at all. Or, if he does, he won't. He just watches
with a kind of insulting boredom. So I escaped him. Also
Mr. Rowe. But Mr. Chater—oh, my God! We almost came
to blows!"

"How does Mr. Chater dance?" inquired John, feeling
that all this conversation was mere prelude. "I can't imagine
him dancing attractively."

"Why not?"

"I don't know."

"Well, you're right, anyway. He—how can one describe
it?—he seems to press, and yet he doesn't. I think it's because
he is pressing with his mind. He was asking questions—quite
quietly and casually—all the time we danced." She laughed.
"He even asked a question about us."

"What—you and me?"

"You and me. He wanted to know whether we'd known
each other a long while."

"Confound the fellow! It wasn't his business!"

"So I implied. Although he did it quite nicely. Shall I tell
you what he reminds me of? A fairly intelligent worm—and
after talking with fairly intelligent worms, I always feel I
want a bath!"

"I suppose it was when you implied that it wasn't his
business that you nearly came to blows?" asked John.

"No—we just survived that one. It was when he said,
'Did I hear somebody say your husband's in the army?'"

"I—see," murmured John.

"I believe you do," she answered.

A wave of anger swept through him.

"The man's a cad!" he exclaimed. "What's he doing here?"

"That's what I'm wondering, Mr. Foss," replied Nadine thoughtfully. "Lord Aveling sometimes collects queer folk, but he's rather excelled himself this week-end—I've not come across Mr. Chater's type here before. By the way—do *you* know my husband isn't in the army?"

John nodded, and hoped he was not flushing as he recalled the information Taverley had given him.

"Would it be cricket to ask who told you?"

"But you know that, don't you?"

"Yes, of course. Harold Taverley. He was one of my husband's best friends."

"He still is."

She looked at him quizzically, then smiled.

"You put that rather nicely," she said. "And is Harold Taverley still my friend? No, never mind. I'm asking unfair questions." She paused. She gave a queer little sigh. "Well, we've exhausted the cabbages and kings!"

She checked a movement to rise from the pouffe, and hunched her shoulders instead. The green wrap slipped from her back. As she half-turned to pick it up, a bare shoulder touched his sleeve.

"Your first impulse was right," he said.

"What impulse?" she answered.

"Weren't you going?"

"Yes. And then I decided not to."

"Well—I think you'd better!"

"You're not afraid of Mr. Chater?"

"Hell, no! I beg your pardon."

"I like honest swearing, and hell's a good word. Mr. Leveridge used it constantly. Are you afraid of me?"

"That's possible. But more of myself. So, you see, you'd really better go."

"It wouldn't do any good."

"What do you mean?"

"You'd only want me back again."

He took a breath. He could not decide at that instant whether she were wonderful or hateful.

"Suppose that's true?" he demanded.

"There's no need to suppose it," she replied smoothly. "It is true. I'm sorry I brought you here. That's one thing I wanted to say. But, as I have, let's face it and talk it out, shall we? It's only when you don't face facts that they become exaggeratedly distorted—or fruitless."

He decided that she was wonderful. Already the idea of facing facts and of avoiding conventional subterfuges brought some ease to his mind, although he had no notion where the process was going to lead.

"Then let me make an admission," he said. "It may—explain things a bit. My attitude, I mean. You've come upon me at a pretty bad time, Mrs. Leveridge." He said "Mrs. Leveridge" for the conventional protection of it. "There's no need to tell you things that just concern myself—that wouldn't interest you. But please accept them as an explanation of my mood and of any silly blundering. I dare say you were right not to act upon that first impulse of yours to go. Yes, I'm sure you were. Something had to be said—you didn't know quite what—but now I hope I've said it. If I have, you're released to go back to the ballroom."

"I haven't implied any burning desire to go back to the ballroom," she reminded him.

"Well—anywhere else."

"Anywhere but here? Because, if I don't, my seconds are numbered, and you will leap up, despite your foot, and throw your arms round my neck?"

"Lord! I give it up!" he muttered.

"No, don't give it up—stick to it," replied Nadine soberly, "only try playing it my way. I know a lot more about men than you do about women, which is generally the case, although men can rarely bring themselves to believe it—and I know a lot about *you*. No, don't interrupt. I'll tell you what I know. Not dates and facts and things. I don't know the year you were born in, for instance, or the house you live in. I don't know your particular sport, though I'm sure you've got one and it isn't hunting. You're not fond of killing things, and would only do it happily for England. You look as if you'd got your fair share of *that* particular folly. I don't know—" She paused suddenly. "Want me to go on? Now I'm warning *you*!"

He nodded. She pressed her cigarette-end into an ashtray, and continued:

"I don't know the name of the particular trouble that sent you scurrying out of London to a remote place like Flensham, without even a definite address for the night.... By the way, I'm quite aware that you were behind me at the ticket office in London, and you can try and work *that* out if it has any significance and if it amuses you....But I *do* know that, whatever her name is, you didn't treat her shabbily. And you can think, if you want to, that it was because of that knowledge—just instinctive then, of course—just a feeling—that I stuck to you rather more than I might have done after your accident. I don't mean—since we're being frank—that the adventure of it all didn't attract me. But I soon realised that you weren't chasing me."

He stared at her. She laughed.

"It's funny how little men believe in a woman's instinct," she said, "and yet how much they owe to it! Do you really suppose that—well, do you suppose that if a man like Mr.

Chater had tumbled out of that train, I'd have troubled to lug *him* along here like this?"

"I'm sure you would have!" he exclaimed impulsively. "You'd never have left him—or anybody else—in a hole!"

"For heaven's sake, don't start idealising me!" she begged, good-naturedly. "I'm not idealising *you*. I'm just suggesting that you're rather straight—as men go. No, I wouldn't have left Mr. Chater in a hole—though I would *now*, and help to pile the earth on top! I'd have taken him to the doctor's, and I'd have parked him there. Or even if I'm underrating the Good Samaritan in my nature—even if I had brought him here—I wouldn't have deserted the ballroom for him, and smoked a cigarette with him, and have thrown the cabbages and kings overboard. Am I mixing my metaphors?" She paused, and the light he had seen in her eyes before, and which he found himself instinctively watching for, sent a queer sensation through him. "So perhaps I've as much necessity to warn you, Mr. Foss, as you have to warn me?"

She looked at him with provocative inquiry. He shoved aside a sudden wonder whether, after all—behind everything—she were laughing at him. He knew the wonder was not worthy, or genuine, and that it was merely another protective device. He decided that the most protective thing to do would be to go on idealising her.

"I believe I'm a little bit out of my depth," he said.

"Most of us are," she answered.

"Yes, perhaps. Life's a puzzle. But what I meant was—I may as well admit it—I haven't had time yet to become a man of much experience." Was he talking idiotically? Like a small boy? He had no notion, but he plunged on, "Things still seem rather wonderful to me, you know. Probably I'll grow out of that, only I don't want to. I thought I'd grown out of it this morning. Now—I'm not quite sure." He stopped, arrested by a thought. Instinctively she bent a little closer, following his mind rather than hers. He continued hurriedly, "That was an extraordinary guess of yours just now. About my trouble. I mean. I don't know which is more extraordinary—your guessing it, or my not minding. I didn't think I could ever talk about it to anybody. When a fellow's been turned down—"

"Don't say more than you mean to—"

"No, it's all right. Well, he generally keeps it pretty well inside him. Or so I should imagine. Doesn't want people to be sorry for him. Gets into a sort of—mental loneliness that no one must disturb. You know, I believe it's a sort of silly, self-pitying exaltation. But, whatever it is—I say, I'm getting a bit tied up! What's happening to me? I'm just talking rot!"

Something almost uncontrollable surged through him, surprising him by its force. He stared at her, keeping very still. His forehead became damp in a moment. Then he found Nadine's lips against his.

Nadine had kissed many men in her life, but she had never kissed any man as she now kissed John Foss. There was not only passion, there was something maternal in her kiss.

"I didn't mean to do that," she said. "I'm sorry, John."

She turned her head suddenly. Mr. Chater stood in the doorway.

"I beg your pardon," he said. "I was looking for Lord Aveling."

He closed the door again, and was gone.

"Well?" asked Nadine. "What do we do to Mr. Chater?"

Chapter IX

Largely Concerning Chater

"That man's dangerous," said Nadine. "Let's be practical. Two points stick out. One, I've been a beast. Two, Mr. Chater knows all about it."

"Do you think I care a damn about Mr. Chater?" replied John, through the whirl of his mind.

"Don't you?"

"Why should I?"

Nadine smiled rather ironically, and he misinterpreted her expression.

"No, I'm the beast," he exclaimed. "I meant I didn't care a damn about Mr. Chater for myself—I forgot about you."

"I wasn't thinking of that," she answered. "You needn't worry about me. I'm case-hardened—"

"*Don't!*"

"What?"

He looked at her almost angrily.

"I can't bear it when you talk about yourself as though—as though you were—"

"The world's worst woman? No, John, I'm not that. I generally play the game—however dangerous—and I generally choose players who know all about the risks. I'm being quite honest with you. Virtues and vices alike. But just sit on that impulse to idealise me. Men like you do that much too easily. The reason I said I was a beast was because I've taken you at a disadvantage and got you into a mess."

"I don't admit that!"

"No, you wouldn't. You're even better than your old school tie."

"Are you idealising *me*?"

"Heavens, no! I could tell you something that would make you wince! But I want to get you out of the mess. If I could do it by saying good-night and walking out of the room, I'd leave you this moment."

"That wouldn't help," he agreed.

"What will?" she asked. "Have you any suggestion?"

"Yes."

"Is it a good one?"

"It's the only one—and if you know me as well as you think you do, you'll realise it."

"Go on, then."

"It's the continuation of your honesty with me. You can't do the David Garrick stunt, you know."

"David Garrick?"

"He got drunk to cure Ada Ingot of her love for him."

"I won't get drunk," she smiled. "But I still don't see your solution?"

"I think it resolves itself into the answer to a simple question."

"That sounds horribly risky!"

"Yes—perhaps. But this time I *do* know all about the risk, so you'll be playing fair."

"You're not going to ask me what I know about you that would make you wince?"

"No. You can tell me that voluntarily, if ever you want to. May I put the question?"

"Yes."

"Well, here goes. It'll show you, anyhow, that I'm not idealising you." She wondered. "When you kissed me just now, did you feel as though you were beginning another 'affair'?"

For an instant she almost decided to cheat. But for his reference to David Garrick, she might have. That reference had weakened her defences, however, for she doubted now, as she saw his eyes watching her for every informative little sign, whether she could cheat him. For once in her life, she had the sense that she was being beaten.

"Would you like to withdraw the question?"

She gave him that chance, but he did not take it. He shook his head.

"No, I didn't feel I was beginning an affair," she answered. "So now where are we?"

He found, to his dismay, that he did not know. The exact significance of a kiss has baffled countless intelligences. His expression gave him away, and as she felt her power returning she was urged by an intense desire to use it kindly.

"Listen, John," she said. "And you can call me Nadine. *That* doesn't mean anything these days. I'm not a silly, impulsive woman, though a few fools sometimes imagine I am, but I do react quickly to a situation when it develops. That's my true nature. I even remember the day when I found it out—consciously, I mean. A pretty foul beast kissed me, and spoilt his chance of a repetition by saying, 'If you can't be good, be careful.' I slapped his face, but I took his advice. I asked myself whether I was 'good.' I refused to hedge. I found I wasn't. But—you may or you may not understand this—I refused to desert myself—to become twisted, or dull, or insignificant—by living the life of some one else. It wouldn't have been life to a person like me. It would have been death. So I decided to be careful, to stick to a few rules I made, and have generally kept to, and to go through with it."

She paused suddenly. Then gave a little shrug, and continued:

"Rather funny, telling you all this after only a few hours' acquaintance, but somehow I feel I owe it to you. And then one of my rules is to be frank—although I admit my frankness with you has been unusually rapid....I wonder why?"

He restrained an impulse to make a suggestion. Her self-analysis fascinated him, and he did not want to interrupt it. His eyes were on the contours of her shoulder, but his attention was on the contours of her mind.

"I expect you've had something to do with it. You're not very easy to lie to. Where is all this getting us to? Perhaps nowhere, after all. I kissed you, John, because I suddenly wanted to—"

"And because you knew I wanted you to," he interrupted her then.

"Yes. But—this is what I want to say—and what I want you to believe. That moment wasn't as important as it seemed to you, and as it may go on seeming to you for a little while. You see, you take life very seriously—don't you?" He nodded. "And everything's important to you, particularly in your present mood. That's why I feel so mean, and want to get this in its right proportion....No good! I'm making a horrible hash of it! I wish, for your sake, that you didn't have to stay here over the week-end."

She stared at his foot, annoyed with herself for making a hash of it.

"Well, I'm glad I'm staying," John answered abruptly, "if it's not going to make any difficulty for you. I mean—that fellow Chater—"

"Oh, he can't hurt me!"

"If he does, I'll murder him!"

"Please don't! I'd hate to appear as a witness at the trial!" Her voice grew lighter. "After all, John, I don't think a kiss between two unattached people at a week-end party is going to excite a blackmailer!"

"Blackmailer?" repeated John with a frown.

"The word slipped out," she responded.

"But you seemed to mean it."

"Well, he does rather strike me as that type, though legally one isn't supposed to say so without proof."

"Perhaps you've got the proof?"

"No."

"You know more than you've told me, though?"

Nadine hesitated as a small incident flashed into her mind. She had tried to dismiss it, but somehow it had stuck.

"Nothing much," she said, "only if you *have* any dark secrets, John, I wouldn't leave them about when Mr. Chater's around."

"Please tell me," he urged. "I've a hunch about that chap—and also a special cause for curiosity. If he *is* going to be a nuisance, I'd like to know all that's going about him."

She looked at him curiously, then laughed.

"If I satisfy your curiosity, will you tell me the cause of it?" she bargained. "Fifty-fifty."

"Right," he laughed back. She was trying to steer their moods away from the personal equation, and he responded to her lead. "You first."

"Well—it happened before dinner, just after I'd seen you moved into here," she said. "When I left you I walked into a little comedy. Or tragedy. Miss Wilding—you've met her, haven't you?"

John nodded. "She came in here a little while ago, shortly before you did," he answered. "Then she went off with Lord Aveling—I think to read a play to him or something."

"Did she?" Nadine looked thoughtful for a moment, then proceeded: "She was coming down the stairs. I'd dressed, but she hadn't. Thomas—that's one of the butlers, the only one I don't like—he nearly knocked my champagne glass over at dinner—Thomas darted out of a shadow, and gave her an envelope. Then, while Miss Wilding was looking at the envelope, Mr. Chater came running from somewhere—very quietly, like a cat—and bumped into her. She dropped the envelope, and he picked it up and returned it to her, full of apologies. I noticed that he looked at the writing on the envelope before he gave it back."

"It doesn't sound too good," remarked John, "but there needn't have been anything in it."

"Possibly there wasn't," answered Nadine. "But Miss Wilding looked very red when she turned and went upstairs again, and Mr. Chater would have turned and followed her if I hadn't asked him for a light."

"I see. Did he give you the light?"

"Most unwillingly."

"And then?"

"He said, 'Chilly evening, isn't it?' and went upstairs after Miss Wilding....This sounds horribly like gossip, doesn't it? I don't usually poke my nose into other people's affairs. But—well, you asked for it."

"Thank you for telling me."

"Oh, no, I want my payment!"

John looked a little ashamed of himself.

"Well, I'm only telling you *this* because you're asking for it," he said. "If there's nothing in your information, there's less than nothing in mine. Are you superstitious?"

"I'm wearing green."

"Then it won't worry you to know that there are thirteen guests sleeping here to-night."

"No, are there?" she exclaimed, and the tone of her voice rather belied her implication of immunity. "Have you counted?"

"Mr. Taverley did it for me."

"I—I hope *you're* not superstitious?" she asked, after a little pause.

"No more than you are," he smiled. "But even if I were, I'd be safe according to Mr. Taverley's theory. He said that, if any bad luck came, it would come to the thirteenth guest to arrive through the front door."

"Who was the thirteenth?"

"Our friend Mr. Chater. And I'll tell you something, Nadine. There—I've said it. If our friend Mr. Chater plays any of his alleged tricks on you, he'll have the worst luck he's ever had in his life. You can remember that!"

She looked at him seriously, then rose from the pouffe on which she had been sitting.

"Be very careful, John," she said, holding out her hand. "I should never forgive myself if anything bad happened to you. I think it's time to say good-night."

He took her hand and pressed it.

"Good-night," he replied. "I'm under no delusions about anything. But I mean what I said. Like hell."

Chapter X

Movements in the Night

Many things stirred that night. The golden retriever, Haig, restless in his kennel near the locked studio and sniffing sensitively with his cool black nose, was not alone in sensing uneasy happenings. The stag destined to be roused by harbourers on the morrow from his entanglement of fern and briar, lifted his head from the ground as though momentarily conscious of his new danger as well as his new dignity. He was in his fifth year, and had just emerged from the raw designation of young male deer. Then he lowered his head to invisibility again, with antlers laid back almost parallel with his body. The cock-pheasant in the little wood near Bragley Court suddenly fluttered for no reason his sleepy mind could fathom. No stoat was near. Had Death itself, that unbelievable conception, cast a transitory shadow over the bird's wing while seeking a location for its next victim? The sly old fox, back in his burrow at Mile Bottom after a pleasant meal of mice and beetles, took longer than usual to settle in his earthy den. He missed the badger whose house he had stolen. It was a pity the badger had not taken it kindly, and that they had quarrelled over the possession of a hen. They might have been pals.

But it was Haig's uneasiness that awakened John Foss to his own. The dog barked suddenly, shooting him out of a dream he could not remember. He tried to return to it, for he felt it had been pleasant, but a low growling held him to reality, and by the time the growling had ceased the reality had got him, and the dream had slipped irreclaimably away. In its place was a dull pain in his foot.

"Damn!" he thought. "Must have lain on it."

A clock in the hall sounded a single chime. One a.m.? Or half-past something? He struck a match and consulted his wrist-watch. Half-past midnight.

The time surprised him. It was only an hour since Nadine had left him. He had thought it was later. He lay with his eyes closed for a little while, recalling her departure; how she had looked as she walked to the door, the faint rustle of her soft green dress, the turn and the smile at the door. And then the strange silence afterwards. The music had no longer sounded from the ballroom. The hall beyond the door had been quiet, saving at odd moments when people had passed through it on their way to bed. He had heard Mr. Rowe's voice: "To-morrow we must talk about Ruth's picture." Presumably the remark had been made to Leicester Pratt, but the artist had made no audible reply. A little later, Miss Fermoy-Jones's: "I don't expect it to sell better than *Horse-flesh*. Even I don't often exceed thirty-one editions. Yes, my dear, thirty-one. I believe it's only been beaten by *The Good Companions, Jew Suss* and *If Winter Comes*. Oh, and of course that obscene thing, *All Quiet on the Western Front*. But, well, it's a better book. More along the lines of *Wings Over Cities*. Have you read that one?..." The silence had seemed thrice-blessed as her voice had faded away up the staircase. And Mrs. Chater's: "Well, I've had enough, you can come up when you like." And, the last of them, Taverley's: "Good-night, Anne. You look tired." And Anne's: "Am, a bit. Good-night."

And then John had drifted off. And now he was trying to drift off again, with less success.

"What *is* the matter with that dog?" he thought, as Haig barked once more.

A door opened somewhere. Or was he imagining it? No, for here were footsteps, softly crossing the hall. "Last up," he reflected, as he followed them in his imagination to the staircase. "Wonder which?" But the footsteps did not go to the staircase. They came to his door. He sat up abruptly.

"Just five minutes!" came Lord Aveling's voice quietly.

The door-handle turned.

"No—really—isn't it rather late?"

That was Zena Wilding, in an anxious whisper.

"But I'd like you to see it," answered Lord Aveling. "Han dynasty. Genuine. Two thousand years old. They imitated it in Delft—"

The door opened an inch or two, then suddenly closed.

"Can't—I forgot!" came the mutter. "Of course, Foss is in there!"

"Never mind, to-morrow!" answered Zena Wilding, and John detected the relief in her voice. "I'd adore to see it then."

"You shall, my dear. And we'll talk some more about your play. Although I think I may say to-night—I have almost made up my mind to—"

"No, do you really mean it?"

"Would it make you happy?"

John stuffed his fingers in his ears. Something in Lord Aveling's tone had made him do it. He kept them there for a minute. Then he took them out.

But he took them out a second too soon. He heard Zena whisper—"Please—good-night!"

Then, silence.

"This won't do!" decided John unhappily. "I *must* get to sleep! Meanwhile, it's strictly understood, I've been dreaming!"

He closed his eyes tightly. He pretended not to hear the dog growling. He pretended so well that sleep began to come to him at last. But it was not peaceful sleep. Footsteps drifted through it, and Nadine's green wrap. The wrap became a large green silk boat in which he was floating first with Nadine, then with Zena Wilding, and finally with Edyth Fermoy-Jones. "Mr. Pratt has been painting my picture," barked Edyth Fermoy-Jones, like a dog, "and it will ruin my circulation. I must smash it!" A butler brought the picture on a tray. The picture was framed, behind glass, and the enraged authoress struck it with her fist. The glass splintered all around them, and John dodged and sat up.

He was no longer in a green silk boat. He was on his couch, staring ahead of him into the darkness.

"Did I dream that glass?" he wondered. "And Edyth Fermoy-Jones's bark?"

A few moments later he knew he had not dreamt the bark, for it was repeated. Once—twice—thrice, each time a little more distant. Then, a final bark....

A door opened. It was not the one Lord Aveling had opened; he had heard that through his own door. He heard this through his window. In a few moments there came a gasp, obviously feminine. Then steps flying across the hall. Then other steps—slower, deliberate, stealthy. And then an exclamation.

"Hallo!"

Chater's voice.

"Eh?"

He did not recognise the second speaker, but it was another male voice.

"What are you doing here?"

"Well, sir, I—I thought I—" The tone suddenly changed. "There's a door open somewhere!"

"Oh?"

"A draught—from over there—"

"Here, wait a moment!"

The order was not obeyed. A short silence was broken by the sound of hurrying feet. Then the second speaker returned.

"Did you open that door, sir?"

"I? No, certainly not!"

"Then, might I ask why *you've* come down?"

The question was asked with timid challenge.

"Well, I've no reason for not telling you," came Chater's response, after a pause. "I came down because I thought I heard noises."

"Ah—I see, sir."

"And why did you come down?"

"For the same reason, sir."

But John would have sworn they were both lying.

"Apparently we were right," said Chater. "Or have you any other explanation of the open door?"

"I may have forgotten to lock it."

"Is that your job?"

"Yes, sir."

"What's your name?"

"Thomas, sir."

"Thomas. I'll make a note of it. Well, Thomas, even an unlocked door doesn't open of its own accord."

"The latch is defective. It might have blown open."

"It might. And it mightn't. Now suppose you tell me the *real* reason you're here?"

"I have told you!" exclaimed Thomas, the anxiety in his voice disputing his statement. "I thought I heard noises—as you say you did yourself—"

"All right, all right! Don't raise your voice like that! Suppose we did hear noises? Is there a burglar in the house? If so, why aren't we searching for him? But perhaps it isn't a him, Thomas? Perhaps it's a lady? Or, more correctly speaking, a maid. Tell me, does Bessie sleep in the house, or in some annexe or other outside?"

Thomas did not reply. John missed the flush that came into the butler's pale cheeks, and the expression of astonishment that gradually changed into mute fury. But he gathered that something emotional was happening when Chater's smooth voice droned on:

"Attend to me, my man. I'm asking no questions, but that may be because I don't need to. You didn't come here to find any burglar. And it won't help your career if anybody inquires to-morrow what you *did* come here for. So your policy is to go right back to your room, this minute, and not to let any one know that you ever left it. Whether I'll assist you will depend upon what I decide—and how you behave."

"What do you mean?" muttered the butler.

"Ought to be clear," answered Chater. "I know all I need to know to smash you—*and* Bessie. So if I have any little jobs for you, you'll be a good boy and do them. Well, what are you waiting for? Whoa, steady!"

Then John heard heavy breathing, and a sharp, stifled cry of pain.

"Want it broken?" inquired Chater's voice.

"Let go!" gasped Thomas.

"I wonder what Bessie would think of you if she could see you at this moment," answered Chater. "She'd lose her good opinion of you, I'm afraid—and gain it, perhaps, for some one else. She's a pretty girl.... You know, I'm quite ready to break it, if you want me to.... Ah, that's more sensible. Now get out!"

John heard the butler's footsteps receding towards the servants' quarters. Then, after a pause, he heard Chater moving. Chater did not move towards the main staircase, but towards the passage that led to the back lawn. It was the door to this lawn, John concluded, that had been under discussion, and that he had heard opening shortly before Chater and the butler had met.

A long silence followed. John waited, his nerves frayed, for Chater's returning footsteps. The clock in the hall chimed once. Was that one, or half-past? He had lost count of time. About to switch on the lamp—not that the time mattered, but he wanted to do something to break this uncomfortable silence—he paused abruptly. Ah—Chater's footsteps, at last.

"He's been the devil of a time," thought John. "What's his latest mischief?"

He listened to the soft tread. In the back passage—on the hall carpet—towards the staircase—no, some other direction—silence. Quite a long silence.

"What's he doing?" wondered John.

The silence continued. Then, suddenly, the steps were heard again, crossing the hall and mounting the stairs.

"Where did he go that time?" murmured John. "Nocturnal prowling, to see what else he can pick up?"

Now John switched on the light and again consulted his wrist-watch. Twenty-five minutes to two.

Well, the hall was empty at last, and now he could try once more to go to sleep. If he kept awake much longer he'd be a wreck in the morning. He began counting sheep. No good. They all had Chater's face. He concentrated on another face. Perhaps Nadine could send him off. He visualised her hair and her eyes and her lips, deliberately and unashamedly. His mind was full of little pricks, of other people's affairs, of fragments of disturbing knowledge that seemed to saddle him, somehow, with responsibility, though he had no idea how to discharge the responsibility, or who would thank him—and he wanted to escape from them to one unshifting point. And the pleasantest point he could escape to was Nadine. He wondered what it would feel like to lie in her arms....

"Some one *is* in the hall still!" he thought suddenly. "What the blazes—!"

Chater's face drove Nadine's away. Indignation surged through him. Why didn't the fellow go to bed? He must have come down again, and probably his ear was at the keyhole.

"Well, I've had enough of it!" decided John. "I'll give the poisonous blighter a shock!"

He rolled carefully off his couch. He wrenched his foot a little, but just managed to keep back his groan. Then he rose, and using the support of furniture *en route* he hopped to the door. With his hand on the knob he paused to listen. Yes, somebody was undoubtedly there. He turned the knob, and threw the door open.

Moonlight came through a high window above the stairs, making a bright patch on the hall carpet. In the patch, her head turned towards him, and her right hand pressing the folds of her soft cerise dressing-gown, stood Anne.

Even in the surprise of the moment the thought flashed through John's mind that this was how she should have been painted. There was no trace of hardness now around her mouth. Her lips were slightly parted, and there was an expression in her eyes he could not define. It was as though her softness had been surprised and caught, and while she would not have revealed it voluntarily, something courageous in her refused to hide it again at once. The lines of her dressing-gown accentuated her slim boyish figure without detracting from her feminine appeal.

But it was something else that caused John to break the little silence suddenly and to speak first. He sensed not only her courage, but her need for it. Behind her poise, he was certain, lay fear. He wanted to eliminate himself from her oppressions.

"I'm awfully sorry," he said. "I thought I heard something."

His voice brought back her movement. She turned to him fully, and smiled.

"You did," she answered. "You heard me. I'm the one to apologise."

"Not a bit."

"Did I wake you?"

"I'm not sure. I think I was in that state known as betwixt and between."

He felt that she was grateful to him for his easy, uncurious attitude, even though he also felt she rewarded him with a lie.

"I came down to get a book," she said.

"You read late," he replied.

"Yes. When I can't sleep. How did you get here? Did you hop?" He nodded. "I'll help you back."

"I can manage."

"Don't be silly."

She came to the door, and assisted him back to the couch. When he was settled, she stood regarding him for a second.

"This is rotten luck on you," she said.

"I'll get over it," he answered. "I'm not invalided for life, you know."

"No—not for life," she repeated slowly. This was one of the many moments he recalled later. Then she added, her speech quickening, "But it was disgusting of me disturbing you like this. If you tell any one, I'll get into hot water."

He recognised the request behind the statement.

"Count on me," he smiled. "Good-night."

"Good-night."

A few seconds later he listened to her footsteps fading up the stairs. She had not stopped to get her book.

Chapter XI

Haig

"*Must* you get up so early?" asked Bultin sleepily.

"It's seven o'clock," replied Pratt, as he crossed to the window and pulled up the blind. "And what a morning!"

"But the fires aren't lit," protested Bultin.

"One doesn't get up before breakfast to sit by a fire," retorted Pratt. "One gets up to take a stroll."

"One does," murmured Bultin, turning away from the light, "but two don't. For God's sake, pull down that blind!"

Pratt smiled, gazed out for a moment at the lawn, and then satisfied his friend's craving for continued dimness. The blind came down again. Fifteen minutes later he was out on the lawn.

A low white mist was slowly rolling off it. The air was autumn-crisp. Raising his eyes, he rested them on russet bushes, then raised them higher to the sky. It was cloudless, and an early lark was singing the song men envy.

"The illusion of joy and beauty," reflected Pratt.

Yet it was odd how moments came when intelligence fled and one could enjoy the illusion!

He walked across the lawn, his eyes no longer on the sky but on his boots moist with mist. The movement of the boots had a restless purpose that contrasted with the mist's leisurely drift. He reached the russet bushes, and walked through them to the studio. He was making for the door, when a window caught his attention and diverted his direction. It was smashed.

He stared at the splintered glass beneath the window. He lifted his eyes to the sky for a moment and asked, "What about this, blithe spirit?" and then stared at the glass again. Somebody had broken into the studio. No—in that case, most of the glass would be inside. "Some one has broken out of the studio," he corrected his thought. "But how did they break in, to break out?"

Now he walked to the door, and producing the key unlocked it. The studio seemed as he had left it on the previous evening. There was the ruined picture of Anne, with its long smudge of crimson paint. It pleased him that he could look at it calmly. There were all the other pictures and easels, including Anne's own large painting of the stag. And the studio furniture. Nothing looked altered....No, wait a moment....

He crossed to the picture of the stag. "As bad as it is big," he murmured. If the criticism were just, the picture was unusually bad, for the canvas almost obliterated the large easel on which it stood, leaving only a few inches of pedestal visible beneath it. He walked behind the canvas.

"Possible," he murmured. "Possible."

He stood for a few moments pondering, his eyes scanning the ground. Then he turned in the direction of the picture of Anne, moved a pace to the side, and stooped. He stooped until the top of the canvas he was behind rose in his line of vision, and obliterated the picture of Anne.

"Yes, quite possible," he said. "And—then?"

He rose, and walked to the broken window. It was a small window in a wall, though not too small for a man to pass through. The larger window in the sloping roof, facing north, was intact. He examined the edges of broken glass, put his head gingerly out, and brought it in again. Then he left the studio, locking it as before, and dropping the key in his pocket.

He walked round the studio. The path continued at the back towards a little wood. He walked towards the wood, his eye attracted by something. It was a brown heap a few yards off the path, lying under a bush. Reaching it, he stooped and touched it. It did not move.

On his way back to the house he passed a gardener.

"I'm afraid one of your dogs has had an accident," he said. "It's on the left of the path to the wood at the back of the studio. You'd better go and have a look."

Bultin grunted as Pratt re-entered the bedroom, but did not turn.

"I hoped you'd stay out longer," he muttered.

"I was out quite long enough," answered Pratt, throwing himself into an arm-chair. "Are you interested in dead dogs?"

Bultin turned, and opened an eye.

"Should I be?" he inquired.

"I asked if you were," retorted Pratt.

Bultin considered. Then he closed the eye and murmured, "Not particularly."

Pratt lit a cigarette.

"You're a horrible bedroom companion," said Bultin. "Getting up at unearthly hours. Filling the room with foul smoke. And talking of dead dogs. Is that the way you work up your breakfast appetite?"

Pratt continued to puff the foul smoke without responding.

"Well?" smiled Bultin.

"It's name is, or was, Haig," remarked Pratt. "A golden retriever. It is lying at this moment under a hedge, and it has a nasty wound in its side."

"You mean, some one's killed it?"

"Without doubt."

"Probably a poacher."

"That may be the theory."

"But it's not your theory?"

"No, it's not my theory."

"Perhaps I'd better get up," sighed Bultin, rising regretfully from his pillow and sticking a leg out of bed. "What's your theory?"

"I'm not sure that I have one," admitted Pratt.

"Your guess, then?"

"Well, I'm wondering whether the person who killed the dog is the person who ruined my picture."

"The connection being?"

"A broken window."

"Where?"

"Getting interested?"

"Not enough to telephone my editor."

"I'll wager you a hundred cigars you'll be phoning before the day's finished!" exclaimed Pratt suddenly.

"I'm not a betting man," replied Bultin. "Where is this broken window?"

"The studio."

"Really?"

"Yes. Somebody smashed his way out. And shall I tell you why?"

"I have a brain."

"Use it."

"Because he wanted to get out."

"Don't be irritating, Lionel," pleaded Pratt. "If you wanted to get out of this room, what would you do? You would go out of the door. But this person smashed his way out of the window because he couldn't get out of the door. I'd locked it."

"When?"

"Yes, let's get the details straight. You'll need them later for a front-page splash. I went to the studio three times yesterday. First, in the morning, when Anne gave me a sitting. I wanted her for the afternoon, but she went riding with Taverley. I took Rowe across, however—that was the second time—to show him the picture—"

"Bait for his future patronage."

"He's nibbled the bait. But that's not what we're talking about. The second time was just before tea. Say, half-past four. Perhaps a few minutes after. When we passed through the hall, Taverley was talking to Foss, and we had a few words." He paused for an instant. "Nobody was in the studio during that second visit—I'm sure of that. We went all round it. But—now we're coming to it—I left the key in the door, through an oversight. So somebody could have gone in between the second and third visit. The third visit was after you arrived, and after our chat. Do you remember the time I left you?"

"Nineteen minutes to seven."

"How on earth do you know?" asked Pratt, surprised.

"I don't know," replied Bultin, "but I'm a journalist."

"I see!" laughed Pratt. "Sailors don't care, and journalists always know. Anyhow, you must nearly have hit the mark. I was delayed on my way to the studio—passed Taverley in passage—spoke to Nadine Leveridge on the lawn—and got to the studio, and found the picture ruined, at about ten to seven. And a minute or two later I left the studio for the last time, locking the door."

"And locking the somebody in?"

"That seems obvious."

"And the some one got in—let's call him Z—between 4.30 and 6.50."

"Make it 6.40. That gives him the maximum time to have done his dirty work."

"Are you sure the window wasn't broken at your third visit?"

"I'd have noticed it."

"You didn't notice Z."

"Touché. But I've found out why."

"Where was he?"

"Behind another canvas. A very large one. I've tested my theory, and found that he could have remained concealed by stooping."

"Did you find any clues?"

"No."

"Well, continue. What did Z do after you locked him in?"

"Yes, that's a pretty point," said Pratt. "If he killed the dog, he didn't get out at once."

"Why not?"

"Because I know Haig's bark. He was barking late last night."

"Was that the dog I cursed?"

"The very one."

"Then he was alive after midnight."

"Yes."

"If you're sure it was Haig who barked."

"Positive."

"And if you're sure it's Haig who's dead."

"Equally positive."

"And if you're sure it was Z who killed him."

"Of that I'm not positive. But the bark and the broken window fit. A dog would bark if he heard the splinter of glass, and the man he barked at might not like it."

"So all we've got to find out," said Bultin, "is why our friend Z stayed in the studio from 6.50 till after midnight. A trifle like that needn't worry us."

Pratt smiled.

"We'll find it out, Lionel," he answered. "You shall have it for your front page."

"I doubt whether a dead dog would make a good head-line," commented Bultin.

"It all depends where the dead dog leads."

"Where is it going to lead?"

"I don't know yet. That was an unintelligent question. But then you are unintelligent. You merely know how to fatten on other people's knowledge. Listen. I find my picture ruined. I, a famous artist. And the picture, of an interesting young lady whose photograph has appeared in the *Tatler*, the *Sketch*, and the *Bystander*. Wouldn't another photograph of her ruined portrait be worthy of your front page? Though you sha'n't have it yet. Libretto, 'Who Did It?' And who *did*? A well-known cricketer, who returned to his room shortly before I visited the studio, and whose cigarette-end I found outside the studio? The key was in the door then. Any one could have entered."

"Why should Taverley do it?"

"Have I ever told you that sometimes I see red when I meet Taverley? Perhaps he sees the reflection. It's interesting. Chemically, we do not mix. He loathes my picture of Anne, though he has not mentioned the fact aloud....Or Nadine Leveridge, who dressed early, and was smoking—one of Taverley's cigarettes, by the way—on the lawn when I left the house to cross it? Or Chater, who was on the lawn when I crossed back again, and whom I would rather like to paint in the shape of a toad? Or the unknown person I had a tussle with in the dark, after leaving and locking the studio? Or the other unknown person who, during that tussle, was a prisoner in the studio? You said just now, Lionel, that all we had to find out was why Z stayed in the studio from 6.50 till after midnight. We have got to find something more important than that. We have got to find Z. Are you going to the Meet this morning?"

"I'd thought of it."

"I'm not. I'm going to hunt something on two legs, not four, nearer home. More in your line, I think."

Bultin considered, or pretended to. He had already made up his mind.

"I could have a toothache," he remarked.

"Choose your pack," answered Pratt. "Both hunts may end in a kill."

"I'll have a toothache," said Bultin.

Chapter XII

Undeveloped Details

Breakfast at Bragley Court was a come-as-you-please affair. You could stay in your bedroom and have the meal brought to you on a neat tray, or you could descend to the large dining-room and eat at the long oval table. This morning only two remained in their rooms—Nadine Leveridge and Zena Wilding. The rest, with the exception of Anne, were already seated when Pratt and Bultin appeared.

"Where's Anne?" Lord Aveling was saying. He looked very dapper in his riding kit. "Didn't she go out with you, Harold?"

"Yes," answered Taverley. "She made me chase her new mare. A beauty."

"Ah, you like her?"

"Magnificent. It was all I could do to hang on her heels."

"It's all I can do to hang round their necks," observed Miss Fermoy-Jones, with rather unexpected humour. She considered it a literary duty to scintillate over breakfast, and performed the duty with difficulty. "I'm glad I'm going in the car. Who will be with me?"

"We will," answered the Sausage King, deserting his kind for tomatoes-on-toast. "The whole Rowe."

He laughed loudly at his joke. He always did, in case others did not.

"I am afraid you will miss most of the sport," said Lord Aveling, "but the chauffeur is a genius, and will keep you in touch as far as he can."

"Well, I'm always happy when I'm getting local colour," replied the authoress. "Are you a keen huntsman, Sir James?"

She turned to the Liberal member, whose eyes were wandering towards the door.

"Eh? Oh, I ride with the tide," Earnshaw responded. He nodded to Pratt and Bultin. "How about Art and Journalism?"

"Art merely hunts commissions," replied Pratt, "and Journalism has a toothache. Ergo, the Professions will stay at home."

"Toothache!" exclaimed Lord Aveling. His voice was concerned, giving the impression that, as host, he was responsible. "I hope it is not bad?"

"I shall live," answered Bultin. "Some animal will not."

A little silence was broken by Mrs. Rowe, who made one of her rare remarks. She only made it because the silence seemed rather strained, and she thought it might help. Somehow, everything seemed a little strained this morning; she didn't know why. Perhaps it always happened just before a meet.

"Of course, I know it's very wrong of me," she said, "but I always hope the fox will get away."

"Stag, mother!" whispered Ruth, as though her mother had dropped an H.

"Oh, well, whichever it is," murmured Mrs. Rowe.

"It will be foxes next month," said Lady Aveling, coming to Mrs. Rowe's aid. "As a matter of fact, to-day is the last day for stags. But you needn't feel sorry for them, Mrs. Rowe—they injure crops and damage trees, and are really a thorough nuisance."

"Then why have a last day for hunting 'em?" inquired Mr. Rowe. "Why not get rid of the lot?"

"That, Mr. Rowe," replied Pratt, since no one else volunteered an answer, "is a question no true Britisher ever asks."

"I beg your pardon?"

"Personally I am less interested in stags and foxes than dogs," went on Pratt, his voice becoming solemn. "I suppose my discovery has been reported to you, Lord Aveling?"

Lord Aveling frowned.

"You mean—Haig?" Pratt nodded. "We were talking about it before you came down. A real tragedy."

"Have they found out how it happened?"

His eyes strayed towards Chater, while Lord Aveling replied:

"Probably the work of a poacher."

"I see—making too much noise. But how did the dog get out of the kennel?"

Suddenly conscious of Pratt's gaze, Chater raised his head.

"Mightn't it have got out while the poacher was trying to get in?" he suggested.

"Why should the poacher try to get in?" asked Pratt.

"To knock it on the head."

"No, he used a knife," said Pratt.

A little shudder ran round the table. Mrs. Chater was the only member of the company who remained entirely motionless. Bultin turned his head and watched her as she stared at her plate with static accusation. "She wants to smash it," thought Bultin, almost pityingly. Edyth Fermoy-Jones's eyes goggled, and Mrs. Rowe gave a little gasp.

"Knife!" she murmured.

"I hadn't heard that," said Earnshaw.

"There are other things that haven't been heard," remarked Pratt. "One of the studio windows has been smashed."

Now Lord Aveling looked astonished.

"That wasn't reported to me!" he exclaimed.

"Then I'm first with the news," answered Pratt.

"I suppose the poacher—or whoever he was—was breaking into the studio when the dog began barking," suggested Earnshaw. "Was the studio door locked?"

"I have the only key," nodded Pratt.

"You've been in this morning, of course?"

"Yes."

Bultin found Pratt's boot pressing his toe under the table. "Well, what did you find?"

"Apart from the broken window," replied Pratt, "everything was just as I'd left it the night before."

The statement was accompanied by a perfect example of silent teamwork. While Pratt's eyes casually combed one side of the breakfast-table, Bultin's combed the other.

"Then no one had designs on your latest work of art, Pratt," observed Taverley.

Pratt gave no indication of the degree to which the remark interested him. It was Chater who replied:

"Vandalism? The knife really meant for the picture?"

"Yes, now that *is* an idea!" exclaimed Edyth Fermoy-Jones. "Perhaps it wasn't a poacher, after all, but some jealous brother artist! Have you a rival, Mr. Pratt? I believe I'm getting a plot!"

Lord Aveling interposed definitely.

"Do not let this spoil our day," he said. "Shall we change to a more cheerful subject?"

"Yes, I agree, my Lord," answered Chater. "Is it true you are backing a play?"

Earnshaw, whose eyes had been wandering towards the door again, suddenly turned them on Chater, as though an idea had struck him, and as he did so the person he had been watching for entered. She was wearing her dark-green riding habit, and she looked very different from the feminine creature John Foss had surprised on the night before. Her mouth was tightly set, and her attitude was almost aggressively assertive.

"Sorry I'm so late," she exclaimed. "I expect the tea will be black!"

"What kept you, dear?" asked Lady Aveling vaguely.

"I just popped in to see Grandma," answered Anne.

"How was she?"

"Not too good. Coffee, please, Bessie. Well, everybody, it's going to be a perfect day."

Her mood cut across the moods of others. They accepted it, and followed it. Conversation veered away from uneasy subjects, and became appropriately centralised in the hunt.

In the ante-room John was finishing his breakfast alone. He had awakened late, to his annoyance—he hated oversleeping—and the first hour had been devoted to the rather tedious business of medical attention and a few kind inquiries. The particular kind inquiry he was waiting for had not yet materialised, and as he concluded his lonely repast his gaze continually travelled to the door.

His mood was not contented. Apart from the annoyance of being tied to one spot, he felt decentralised. He did not belong to the spot he was tied to, and he was worried also by knowledge that did not belong to him. He ached, with a stranger's aching, to talk to somebody he knew intimately. There was one person here whom, in a sense, he did feel he knew intimately, despite the shortness of their acquaintance, but perfect ease of intercourse was denied by her physical beauty. That did not belong to him, either. He wished Nadine had been plain, so that he could have enjoyed her companionship with a free mind and conscience. Yet had she been plain, would that companionship have been so keenly desired? He refused to face the question.

The door opened. He concealed his disappointment as Lady Aveling stood in the doorway.

"How are you feeling?" she asked.

The interminable question! Lady Aveling had herself asked it once before that morning.

"Fine," answered John. "Don't worry about me, please."

"It must be very tantalising for you. I suppose you ride?"

"Never been on a horse in my life. Perhaps that's lucky."

"Why?"

"What you don't know, you don't miss. I'll be quite happy with all these books."

Lord Aveling had brought him half a dozen.

"You like reading?"

It was all very polite. He felt she was not really in the least interested, and did not see why she should be.

"Rather. And there's one of Masefield's."

"Yes, I like him, too. His novels are always so…well, be sure to ask for anything you want. The bell's by you. And I'll tell Mr. Pratt and Mr. Bultin to come and talk to you— they're staying behind. Oh, no, perhaps not Mr. Bultin—he's got a toothache."

She recalled that the journalist had only made one remark during breakfast.

Some one passed behind her. "Don't be long, Anne," she called over her shoulder. "We start in a quarter of an hour."

"What time is the meet?" asked John.

"Eleven. We're leaving at ten-thirty."

She smiled and departed. John watched for the door to open again. It opened in two minutes.

"How's the patient?" boomed Mr. Rowe.

"First-rate," replied John.

"That's good," said Mr. Rowe. "I'm not sure that I don't envy you! You've a nice fire."

Bessie, the maid, passed behind Mr. Rowe as he spoke. She was carrying a tray on which John noticed a blue glass jug of water. He did not know that he had noticed it till later. The glint of translucent colour only lived in his vision for an instant, then vanished towards the staircase.

"Well, be good," concluded Mr. Rowe, seeking an effective peroration. "Not much chance of being anything else, eh? Ha, ha!"

About to close the door, he suddenly stood aside.

"Ah, good-morning, Mrs. Leveridge!" he exclaimed. "All dressed up and somewhere to go, eh? Well, I must say, if you'll take it from an old man, riding togs suit you!"

He melted away as Nadine entered. The atmosphere of the room changed to the man on the couch. Before, it had been dead. Now it was electrically alive. He forgot his foot for a moment and made a movement to rise, then lay back again with the sensation that he was behaving like a schoolboy.

"Please don't ask me how I'm feeling," he begged. "I couldn't stand it!"

"You've answered me without my having to ask," she laughed. "You're better."

"How do you know that?"

"Your sense of humour."

"Nonsense!" he retorted. "That's heroism. Well, I won't pay you a compliment. You've just had one."

"Two's company."

"All right. You look wonderful. And you've no right to, because riding clothes are really hideous. How did you sleep?"

"I always sleep well. How did you?"

"Too well the last part—rottenly the first."

"Foot?"

"No."

"Me?"

"Not even that!"

"I'm glad. What kept you awake, then?"

He hesitated. He wanted to tell her. He couldn't make up his mind.

"How long before you start?" he asked.

"Almost at once."

"I hoped you'd come and say good-morning earlier. When will you be back?"

"That depends on the stag."

"Assume the stag behaves like a nice, normal creature?"

"Assume that, and it won't! The meet's at eleven, but we may not get away till half-past, or even twelve—you never know."

"And when you do get away, how long is the run?"

"That also depends on the stag. The run may be ten miles or twenty, and north, south, east or west! We ought to be back well before tea. But if you've anything special to tell me—"

"Ah! Our interesting invalid!" exclaimed Edyth Fermoy-Jones behind her. "Are you feeling better? That's one advantage of my profession—no matter how ill you are, you can always write. Unless, of course, you are unconscious. Do you know, Mr. Foss, I wrote the whole of *Steep Hill* while recovering from appendicitis."

She shoved her generous frame forward, and Nadine, as she was displaced, gave a humorous little pout behind the authoress's shoulder.

"Well, I'll see you when I return," said Nadine. "Look after yourself."

"I will. Good hunting," he called.

Miss Fermoy-Jones waited a moment or two, and when Nadine had gone she asked:

"Did you read *Steep Hill*, by any chance?"

"No, I think I missed that one," replied John, striving to be polite against his inclination. Actually, he had missed every book Edyth Fermoy-Jones had ever written, and was none the poorer for it.

"It might have interested you," the authoress went on. "There was a character in it almost exactly like Mrs. Leveridge. She's an interesting type—don't you think so?"

"Type?" queried John, without enthusiasm.

"We're *all* types," she answered. "*You* are. *I* am. Oh, yes, certainly I am." She spoke as though she were making a handsome admission. "Learn to classify people, and that's half the battle. This type reacts this way, that type reacts that way. Get your situation, group your characters around it, and if you've got a good situation, and if you understand your types—that's essential—the book practically writes itself. I remember when I began *The Crack in the Floor*. That was the title of the *novel;* it came out serially under the name of *Lovely Lady*. It's an odd thing, Mr. Foss, but no two people ever agree about titles—"

While she rattled on, John focused his eyes beyond her and watched the moving picture in the hall, framed by the limits of the doorway. Nadine had met Zena Wilding in the hall, and after a moment or two had vanished with her. Lord and Lady Aveling had passed immediately afterwards. Lord Aveling was saying, rather querulously, "Where's Anne? Earnshaw's out there—you know, my dear, I wish she'd—" A few seconds later the Rowes came and went, hastening like a line of hens at feeding-time....And now, Anne and Harold Taverley—the former looking harder than ever, as though consciously tuning her mood to the callous necessities of the chase, the latter watching her with a kind of unassuming, almost secret, protectiveness. "I've forgotten something—my handkerchief!" exclaimed Anne, stopping suddenly. "Carry on, Harold. I'll follow."

"Of course, different writers have different methods," said Edyth Fermoy-Jones, with dreary zest. In subsequent retrospect, her voice became a fretful accompaniment to a dark melody. "Edgar Wallace used a dictaphone. He could write a novel in a week-end. Bret Harte spent a morning putting in a comma and then the afternoon taking it out again. I mean Oscar Wilde. Agatha Christie…"

Anne turned and vanished. Taverley turned also and looked after her.

"Now, my own method is *quite* different! Would you like to hear it? Before I start—before I even think of putting pen to paper—no typewriter for *me*!—I take long walks.…"

Chater entered the moving picture. His hand was just coming away from his hip pocket. "I thought I was going to be the last," he said, "till I passed Anne on the stairs."

"Anne?" murmured Taverley.

"Sorry, I forgot the Honourable," replied Chater. "Seen the wife anywhere?" He passed on.

"You see, as I was telling you before, Mr. Foss, I *must* get to know my characters first. I must know how they will *react*. And then—"

She paused abruptly. Taverley had strolled to the door, and as he came John had a queer sensation that a figure he had been watching on a screen was shedding its two-dimensional condition, and acquiring solidarity. It was a blessed solidarity, for it also entered the consciousness of Edyth Fermoy-Jones and ended her soliloquy.

"Ah, Mr. Taverley!" she cried. "Shouldn't we be going?"

"I believe the motor party's about to leave," replied Taverley, "so you had better hurry."

"No, really? Why didn't some one tell me? I must fly, Mr. Foss; but we'll continue our interesting talk later."

As she flew, John murmured:

"I hope you won't think me uncharitable, Taverley, but God bless you for your interruption!"

"Has she been telling you how to write a novel?" smiled Taverley. "It can be rather trying."

"And God bless you, also, for not asking how I'm feeling!"

"Yes, that can be equally trying. How are you?"

"Dippy, you rotter!" grinned John.

Taverley glanced at his watch.

"Nearly half-past," he muttered. "I ought to be going, too."

"Are you waiting for Anne?" asked John. "Or should I, like Mr. Chater, say 'Honourable'?"

Taverley raised his eyebrows, then laughed.

"You've got good eyes and ears! Well, the watcher sees most of the game." He turned suddenly. "And here comes Anne—without the Honourable."

For an instant John stared. This was not the Anne of a minute or two ago. Nor was it the Anne of the night before. It was a new Anne—nervously bright, boisterously merry, laughing at nothing.

"Come on, Harold, come on, Harold!" she cried. "What a day it's going to be! Huick-halloa!"

Taverley stared at her, too. But she seized his arm, and a moment later they had vanished.

John gazed after them. They had not thought to close the door. He felt horribly disturbed, and did not know why.

Some one passed through the hall as the clock struck the half-hour. He called, and Bessie appeared.

"Would you mind closing the door?" he asked.

He was not in a mood for Bultin or Pratt.

"Yes, sir," answered Bessie.

She had a small tray in one hand, and as she closed the door John caught another glimpse of blue glass on the tray. Only this time it was broken.

Chapter XIII

The Meet

"Hang on to me, Harold!" murmured Anne. "Won't you?"

"O.K." answered Taverley quietly, drawing his horse a few inches closer.

On Anne's other side was Sir James Earnshaw, portly and solid in his saddle. If his political party were dissolving, he gave no impression that he was dissolving with it. He had, in fact, no intention of dissolving. He was listening to Chater, but his eyes were on a distant wood, giving the impression that Chater was not really there. Chater looked less impressive on horseback. As he had ridden away from Bragley Court, Pratt had commented to Bultin, "If I were a horse with an inferiority complex, I'd get Chater on my back to regain my self-respect." Chater's horse certainly looked the superior animal.

"Yes, that was a very interesting chat we had in your bedroom last night, Sir James," said Chater. "What time did I leave? Two a.m., wasn't it?"

"Your memory is better than mine, Mr. Chater," replied Earnshaw, still gazing towards the wood, "for I do not recall the conversation at all."

"What, when it lasted a couple of hours?" said Chater, keeping his voice low. "And when you explained so fully your reasons for joining the Conservative Party? I understand them perfectly."

"You understand so many things before other people do," returned Earnshaw. "That I am going to join the Conservative Party, for instance."

"I think other people understand that! I am sure Bultin does. I'll bet his column next week will mention a new Conservative recruit—and that Lord Aveling's daughter will shortly figure as one of the party's most popular hostesses. But not even Bultin will mention that Lord Aveling's daughter has had anything to do with it, or that the new recruit she has just become engaged to…well, just brush up your memory about our little chat last night. From midnight to two a.m."

He turned his horse abruptly, and ambled towards another group.

"Odd crowd your father's collected this week, Anne," said Taverley, watching Chater go.

"Horrible," answered Anne. "I wonder how much longer we'll have to wait? I'm bursting to be off."

"I heard the harbourer had marked the stag."

"Yes, but they move sometimes, you know. The last one did from South Hill Wood. Poor Dick's face—I'll never forget it. If he lets the crowd down, I'm sure he goes on his knees and prays to God for forgiveness! Look! Is that anything?"

She also was staring towards the distant wood, where a stag would have prayed had it known how. Perfectly motionless among bracken and briar, it seemed to possess life only in its large round eyes, which were assuming a glassy alertness.

"Something stirring," answered Taverley.

The field waited on a great sweep of brown-green stubble. The stubble rolled away in every direction, purpling towards the horizon, and broken in many places by shallow undulations and deep dips, and woods that looked small till you came to them. Only one road was visible. It dissected the moor whitely and blatantly. It was the intruder in country to which it did not belong. But its usefulness was indicated by the number of cars stationed upon it, and the pedestrians who lined it or splayed from it on to the stubble.

Edyth Fermoy-Jones and the Rowes were in one of the cars, their destinies in the hands of the capable chauffeur, Arthur. When the stag broke cover and the pack, now waiting with uncanny obedience round a red-coated huntsman, began to move away, Arthur would read the signs, let in his clutch and make for the spot from where mere motorists would have their best chance of "seeing something."

"'Course, you can't count on it," he had told his party, to arm them against disappointment, "but I'm generally lucky."

"Bring us the luck, and you'll certainly be lucky this time!" winked Mr. Rowe, tapping his pocket, always the most important part of his clothing. "Don't forget that, my boy!"

"That Mrs. Leveridge looks very well on a horse, doesn't she?" said Mrs. Rowe.

"Damn smart," agreed Mr. Rowe. "And so does her ladyship. I shouldn't have thought it." His wife tried to tread on his foot, and missed. "Of course, the actress'd look well in anything. Or nothing. Ha, ha! What's the matter, dear? Mayn't one joke?"

"I wish I could ride," exclaimed Ruth suddenly. "Can I have lessons?"

"Can she have lessons!" repeated Mr. Rowe. "She can have anything she likes! Books aren't the only things that pay, you know, Miss Jones."

"I'm sure not," smiled the authoress, secretly wincing at the absence of the Fermoy.

"Only you'll have to look a bit better on a horse, Ruth, than that other one—what's her name?—Chater? I always want to chop off the C. Well, I suppose she's enjoying herself."

"I wish you wouldn't talk so much, Bob," fretted Mrs. Rowe. "One can't follow what's happening."

"Yes, but nothing's happening!" retorted her husband rather irritably. He turned to the chauffeur. "What happens when it does? Do they fire a gun, or something? And is there a chance the stag'll come in our direction? The wind's blowing this way."

"Only foxes take note of the wind, sir," replied Arthur, airing his knowledge.

Edyth Fermoy-Jones pricked up her ears. She never let a little bit of information go by. Her reputation for being knowledgeable was due to other people's conversation and her encyclopædia. Her next novel would probably contain a fox that took note of the wind and a stag that didn't.

"Well, what decides 'em?" inquired Mr. Rowe. "Besides what's behind 'em?"

"They've generally got another spot in their mind, sir, and make for it," answered the chauffeur. "Of course, hinds run all over the place."

"What's happening now?"

"The tufters are getting the stag away. Sometimes you can hear them giving tongue, even as far as this, when the wind's right like it is to-day.... There you are! Now!"

The field stirred. A red-coated huntsman spoke to the pack. The Master, bearing the touch of distinction that raised him to pre-eminence, galloped importantly from one spot to another.

"Well, why don't they start?" cried Mr. Rowe, as the field still seemed to hesitate. Yet, through the strange telegraphy of the hunt, even Mr. Rowe knew that the game had commenced, and that a stag in that distant patch of foliage towards which all eyes were directed was beginning its last race against Death.

"You have to give them a bit of law, sir," replied Arthur.

"What's that mean?"

"Well, a start."

"I see. Play cricket."

The soothing idea was knocked on the head the next moment.

"See, you can't attack it before it's tired, or you'd lose some dogs....Ah, there they go. We'll get round to Churleigh, and see what's happening."

The pack came to life. The well-ordered mass moved forward at a useful but, as yet, not rapid pace. Each hound became intent on its own little instinct, while remaining obedient to the more potent instinct of man. Behind them moved the field, tingling with permitted blood-lust, as the "view-halloa" came to them across the moor, and was taken up.

"Are you dead keen to be in at the death?" Anne's voice sounded softly in Taverley's ear as they began to trot.

"Not particularly," he answered.

"Good," said Anne. "When I go mad, see you do!"

For a little while parties stuck more or less together. They wound down a long gentle slope, through a miniature valley, and up to the next brow. When the pack, well in advance, veered suddenly to the left, the riders farthest ahead wheeled round also, but those behind saved the big curve and pre-served their breath and their horses'.

"Spinney Cross!" called Lord Aveling.

"Wonder if you're right?" Anne called back.

"For a certainty," replied Lord Aveling.

Soon the pace increased. The dogs, noses well down, looked more like business. An excited horseman galloped out of a thicket, yelled something nobody could interpret, turned round, and galloped back again. Some followed him. Most did not.

"What did that signify?" inquired Sir James Earnshaw.

"A lunatic or a practical joker," answered Lord Aveling. "Well, it's thinned the field out a little, so we won't complain. Are you enjoying it, Miss Wilding?"

"Too wonderful!" she cried.

"She won't last long!" murmured Anne. "I'll tell you who *will* be in at the death!"

"Who?" asked Taverley.

"Nadine....I say, Harold."

"What?"

"Is she going to make a fool of Mr. Foss? I hope not. I like him."

"Yes, it would be a pity," he answered. "I like her, too."

"So do I—only *she* can face things. That's one reason I admire her. She can give hell, and go through hell, and always emerge with her chin out! Well, don't let's talk about them. Oh, damn—'ware Chater!"

They had been riding a little apart. Now Earnshaw separated himself from Lord Aveling and veered his horse in their direction. Chater was at his heels.

"Get ready for the escape!" muttered Anne.

The others drew up. Private conversation ceased. After a few fragmentary remarks, the quartette travelled in silence, Anne slightly ahead and steering an almost imperceptibly curved course. The curve took them farther and farther away from the main body of followers.

All at once Chater noticed it.

"Are we going right?" he asked.

"My father wouldn't think so," called Anne. "He's making for Spinney Cross."

"So are the rest," Earnshaw pointed out.

"What's *your* hunch?" inquired Chater.

"A little place called Holm," replied Anne. "Short cut, but rough going. If you don't like jumping, follow in father's footsteps!"

She put her horse at the gallop and made for a low hedge. A few moments after she was sailing over. Taverley followed her. The other two, after a little hesitation, detoured round to an open gap.

"You there?" asked Anne, without looking round.

"Always, when wanted," replied Taverley, drawing up to her.

"You know, Harold, you're quite a brick," she said. "Come on! Top gear!"

They flew on. Behind them, steadily losing ground, lumbered Earnshaw and Chater. Neither was a good rider.

"That girl's a fool!" grunted Chater.

Earnshaw made no reply.

"If ever there was one!" continued Chater. "I'd like to teach her a lesson!"

"Perhaps you need one?" suggested Earnshaw.

"Perhaps you do," retorted Chater, with impudent rudeness. The nerves of both were frayed. "You'd think she was cock of the walk, but I'll bet she's got her vulnerable spot."

"If she has, you'll find it!" snapped Earnshaw, losing his usual diplomatic composure. "Can't you keep quiet?"

Chater laughed unpleasantly.

"*You* ought to know I can!" he exclaimed derisively.

"Well, don't forget how to do it, or this'll be the last invitation you receive through me! Look, they're going over another hedge. Follow them, and break your neck!"

"Yes, you'd like it if I did, wouldn't you?…What's their damned idea? They're making for a wood!"

In the wood, Taverley put the same question, though less indignantly.

"Is this the way to Holm, Anne?" he asked.

"One way," she laughed. "But we're not going to Holm!"

"I rather guessed that."

"Thought you might." A minute later, when the narrow tree-lined track through which they were threading their way divided, she pointed with her riding-crop to the right fork. "See that sign? It says 'To Holm.' So we take the left."

"Wasn't your uncle a general?"

"Yes. Why?"

"You inherit his strategy!"

"Let's pray that it works!"

By the time Earnshaw and Chater reached the spot, they had vanished. Chater swore.

"This is the last bloody hunt I'll ever attend!" he announced prophetically.

Chapter XIV

The Finding of Z

Shortly before tea-time, two cars drew up before Bragley Court. One contained the Rowes and Edyth Fermoy-Jones, the other, Lord and Lady Aveling, Zena Wilding and Mrs. Chater. The second car had been telephoned for from Churleigh, where the eight had met and lunched, and grooms were bringing back the four vacated horses.

It had, Lord Aveling considered, been a very disappointing affair. He had been vaguely conscious of the many little shadows that brooded inside Bragley Court, and he had hoped that the crisp autumn air and the atmosphere of what he designated as clean English sport would dissipate them. But the shadows had increased, and he felt them all around him now as he stepped into the hall, its brooding silence abruptly broken by the voices of the returned wanderers.

First there had been Anne. Why had she chosen this particular week-end to be so trying? Nothing definite, you know—just little things—and going off like that with Taverley hanging on to her heels! She should have stuck to the party. For a little longer, at any rate.

And then, Zena Wilding. It hadn't been her fault, naturally, that she had tired so soon and turned faint. As a matter of fact, he had been really concerned about her. But he had had to restrain his complete sympathy in public, with his wife watching him—how suspicious women were!—and when he had suggested giving her lunch and seeing her home, too many others had accepted the excuse to desert the hunt also and return. Mrs. Chater was a blight on any company!

As for the hunt itself, none of them had had even a glimpse of the stag.

But Mr. Rowe was enthusiastic as he entered the spacious hall and reacted to its pleasant warmth. Now it was all over, he could praise the memory; at the time he had struggled not to let his toes freeze. "Unlike you, Mrs. Jones," he had said, "I've a poor circulation!" Miss Fermoy-Jones had not enjoyed the joke, since he had deleted the hyphen and was now giving her a husband.

"Well, a thoroughly enjoyable day!" he exclaimed, racing for the fire and rubbing his hands. "After all, who wants to see the animal? You can see all you care to at the Zoo! But the ride—well, there you are! Don't you agree, my dear?"

"Very," replied his wife absently.

"Is Mr. Chater back yet?" Mrs. Chater asked a butler. Her flat, harsh voice grated.

"Not yet, madam," replied the butler.

"Any of the others?" inquired Lord Aveling.

"No, my Lord, you are the first."

Lord Aveling paused for an instant, then turned to Zena. He was in the position of many men of his age. He had never been unfaithful, and he was beginning to wonder why; and the wonder sometimes made conversation with pretty women difficult. He found it particularly difficult with Zena Wilding, because, by the lightest change in the balance of his mind, he knew it could become so dangerously simple.

"I hope you are feeling better, Miss Wilding?" he said.

"Oh, yes, much better!" she exclaimed.

"We shall all feel better when we've changed," remarked Lady Aveling. "I'm sure we're all longing to."

There was a movement towards the stairs. Lord Aveling did not join in it.

"Aren't you coming?" asked his wife.

"Yes, in a minute—I'll go and have a look at Foss. Oh, by the way," he added, turning again to the butler, "are Mr. Pratt and Mr. Bultin in?"

"They are both out, my Lord," answered the butler.

He moved towards the ante-room, and nearing the door he suddenly stopped short. Zena had not yet begun to ascend the stairs, and she was standing only a few feet away from him. With his eyes on the door, he was recalling that on the previous night she had stood in exactly the same spot when he had suggested taking her into the ante-room to see the Chinese vase. For the first time he wondered whether Foss had been asleep.

John looked up as Lord Aveling entered, gladly laying down his book. He had passed too quiet a day.

"Well, we have returned, Mr. Foss," announced Lord Aveling. "I hope you have not been very bored?"

"Not in the least bored, sir," answered John. "Much too comfortable! But Masefield would have saved me, in any case."

"Ah, Masefield," said Lord Aveling, glancing at the book. "A fine writer. But you've had some other company as well?"

"Mr. Bultin looked in to see me this morning."

"And Mr. Pratt?"

"No, only Mr. Bultin."

"Not Pratt? Well, I dare say we must blame the artistic temperament. He said he would be working on his pictures, and he has probably spent the day in the studio. I suppose Bultin interviewed you on the subject of your accident?"

John detected no real interest behind the question. His host's mind seemed to be elsewhere, and his eyes were roaming.

"Yes, he did mention the accident," answered John, "but perhaps I didn't encourage him." As Lord Aveling looked vaguely inquiring, he added in explanation: "He was only here a couple of minutes just after you left. Did you have a good day, sir?"

"A good day? Ah, the hunt. Yes, very enjoyable, though none of my own party saw much of it. I dare say some of the others saw more—they'll tell us later."

"You're not all back yet, then?"

"No."

"Is—?"

John stopped abruptly. He had been on the point of asking whether Mrs. Leveridge had returned, and he just saved himself in time from the foolishness. It occurred to him that possibly Lord Aveling would not have heard the question even if he had got a little further with it, for the roaming eyes had now come to rest at a cabinet and were regarding it contemplatively. On top of the cabinet was an oriental vase.

"That is one of my show pieces, Mr. Foss," said Lord Aveling, casually. "Are you a connoisseur, by any chance?"

"Completely ignorant," answered John.

"Then you can't guess where that vase comes from?"

The tone was still casual, but John was conscious that the question was deliberately put.

"The subtle devil!" he thought. "If I guess right, after having admitted ignorance, *he'll* guess that my knowledge came last night through a door!" Aloud he guessed, obligingly, "India?"

Lord Aveling was not subtle enough to hide his relief. He laughed, for the last time that day.

"No, China," he exclaimed. "Han Dynasty. Two thousand years old. Well, I must go and change."

He turned, then started slightly. The sight of Leicester Pratt in a doorway would not ordinarily have upset one, but as the artist stood there now, with mud on his trousers, a tear in his right sleeve, and untidy hair, he sent a chill through both men. It was the expression in his eye, however, rather than the condition of his clothes that caused the chill.

"Is anything the matter?" demanded Lord Aveling sharply.

"More than a dead dog," answered Pratt. "A dead man."

"Good God!" gasped Lord Aveling.

"Quite dead," said Pratt. "Still, I suppose one sends for a doctor to confirm the obvious. Shall I phone Dr. Pudrow?"

"Yes! No, I will! But wait a moment! Where is he? Who found him—?"

"He's in the little wood at the bottom of the quarry."

"Did you find him?" asked Lord Aveling, glancing at the artist's clothes.

"With Bultin's assistance."

"Fallen down there, eh?" Pratt did not reply. John looked at him suddenly. "Do you know who the man is?"

"He is not one of your guests," replied Pratt. "But—"

He paused, hesitating.

"Please go on, Pratt," insisted Lord Aveling.

"Bultin has an idea that three of your guests could identify him."

"Really? Who?"

"May I leave that to Bultin?"

"Where is Bultin?"

"In the quarry. He said he would wait there, while I returned to report."

Lord Aveling nodded and left the room. For a few moments Pratt and John remained silent. Then John said bluntly:

"Unpleasant business."

"Very," agreed Pratt.

"It seems to me I started a pack of trouble when I came here."

"You're not guilty. The pack of trouble was due."

"What's that mean?"

Pratt shrugged his shoulders. Vaguely, across the hall, Lord Aveling could be heard telephoning.

"If it means anything, which it may not, it means there will be more trouble," remarked Pratt, taking out his cigarette-case. "Have one?"

"Thanks."

As they lit up Pratt went on: "I am an artist, Mr. Foss, and the reason sensitive people do not like my work is because I see what is behind the skin—and what I see, I paint."

"We're more than just skeletons," said John.

"You have expressed an unfortunate truth," answered Pratt dryly. "Skeletons, left all alone with their bones, would be quite harmless. I did not cause the death of our friend in the quarry—I never saw him in a live state, to my knowledge—yet, because I am more than my skeleton, a turn of the wheel might hang me for it." John stared at him. "I should object, of course—but, do you know, I think I should also get some amusement out of it. As Bernard Shaw has pointed out, we are all born under the death sentence, so the time and the form may be mere details."

"Will you tell me something?" asked John.

"Probably not," smiled Pratt. "Still, there's no harm trying."

"How did you and Bultin come to find this man?"

"We did not wander in the wood to gather buttercups and daisies. We found him by looking for him."

"Good Lord!"

"So waste no more time, young man, but ring up the police."

John frowned.

"Do you think I'm pumping you?" he demanded.

"I'm sure you're not," replied Pratt. "*That's* not how I'd paint you. You've a special reason for asking questions."

"Have I?"

"Your window here looks across the lawn. And, if blinds are drawn, one still has ears."

Pratt did not underrate himself. He saw many things. But this was a chance shot, and he gathered from John's expression that he had scored a bull.

"I believe I may presently be pumping *you*," he said. "But finish your questions, if you have any more."

"The next one is fairly obvious."

"So obvious that I can guess it. Why were we looking for the corpse?"

"Exactly."

"Well, strictly speaking, we did not know it would be a corpse, but we had a special reason for being interested in this alleged poacher who killed Haig last night—"

"What's that?" cried John.

Pratt raised his eyebrows.

"Didn't you know that the dog had been killed?"

"No one told me!"

With Pratt's eyes upon him, John tried to readjust his mind to this fresh knowledge. He guessed the time Haig had been killed as he recalled his dream of broken glass and barking, and as he remembered that the barking had suddenly ceased. Round about one a.m. But other things had occurred round about one a.m., and he could not decide, since they involved many people, whether this was the moment to reveal those other things, or, even if it was, whether Pratt was the person to whom they should be revealed.

"It may help you to make up your mind," said Pratt with uncanny intuition, "if I tell you a little more. You know I am painting a picture of Lord Aveling's daughter?" John nodded. "Yesterday evening, at a quarter to seven, I went to the studio and found the picture ruined. This morning, at a quarter past seven, I went to the studio again and found a window broken. Without knowing it, I had locked somebody in on the night before, and he had escaped, and, apparently, killed a dog. Well, that broadly explains my interest."

"You mean, the person who was in the studio, and who killed Haig, spoilt your picture?"

"Not quite. I mean, that person *may* have spoilt my picture. There's no proof yet. But if the proof turns up, and if the dead man in the quarry is the same man, shall I have to stand my trial for a crime of revenge? Quite between ourselves, Mr. Foss," added Pratt, "I haven't killed anybody, and never saw our corpse in a live state. It would be bad luck to be hanged for a justifiable murder without having had the actual fun of committing it!"

The door was pushed open, and Aveling returned.

"I got on to Dr. Pudrow's house, after the usual delay," he said, "and found he was already on his way here to see Mrs. Morris. But we won't wait for him. Come along, Pratt. I must have a look at this fellow." He did not move immediately, however. Something was still on his mind. "I wonder whether we ought to get in touch with the police?"

"That perhaps *could* wait for Dr. Pudrow," suggested Pratt. "It will depend on the doctor's opinion, I should say, and also on whether the man remains unidentified."

"Yes, you're right," agreed Aveling, "especially as Bultin is going to give me the names of three of my guests who know him—"

"Who may know him," corrected Pratt. "I think I'll change my mind and anticipate Bultin. The guests are Mr. and Mrs. Chater and Miss Wilding."

Lord Aveling looked disturbed.

"Are they all back?" asked Pratt.

"All but Mr. Chater," answered Lord Aveling, "and the ladies are changing. We won't worry them just yet."

Something ran by the window. They turned their heads and stared in surprise. It was a riderless horse, making for its stable.

Chapter XV

In the Quarry

The horse galloped across the lawn. Its homing instinct had been diverted a few moments previously by a man who, in an attempt to catch it, had sprung at it ineffectively from the roadside, causing it to jump a hedge into a flower-bed; but it was not to be kept from home, hay, and comfort, and it was finding its way back to the stables by an unaccustomed route.

A gardener caught it finally near the stable door, and was soothing it when Lord Aveling and Pratt arrived.

"Chater's!" exclaimed Aveling, recognising it immediately.

"Then I suppose Chater will follow on Shanks's pony," remarked Pratt.

"If he hasn't had a bad fall," answered Aveling.

He gave an instruction to the gardener—the grooms were all on duty, and had not yet returned—and then made for the path leading to the wood in the rear of the grounds.

"This seems to be a day of misfortunes," he commented to Pratt, striding at his side.

"Yes, but I'm afraid the misfortunes began yesterday," replied Pratt. "This is the time to tell you of another."

As Lord Aveling heard for the first time of the ruined picture, his expression grew more and more unhappy. He had always prided himself on his expression. It signified that he kept on top of circumstances, no matter what those circumstances were, and recently they had been particularly trying. Ambitious enterprises had received a check. Money was tight, owing to unfortunate investments, but a baron with ambitions must not show any signs of poverty; he must go on spending. A few months previously Anne had refused to marry a man who would have brought new wealth and position, if no brain, to the family. Now she was threatening to adopt the same attitude towards another eligible candidate. True, Sir James Earnshaw was double her age, but he would become a force by joining the Conservative Party, while Aveling's own force would be augmented through his assistance towards the happy political event.

Tact, dignity, patience, courage, and the well-known expression of courteous solidarity had been used to fight these troubles, and Lord Aveling had even established a necessary but unpleasant association with a retired sausage merchant without, so far, too much embarrassment. It was mainly due to the Rowes that Edyth Fermoy-Jones owed her invitation this week-end. He had thought the Rowes would like to meet a well-known authoress (who had been promised an invitation to Bragley Court in an incautious moment), and that the well-known authoress would occupy most of her time impressing the Rowes.

But now, to his consternation and humiliation, Lord Aveling was oppressed with a hideous sensation that circumstances were getting the upper hand, and that this was the week-end selected by Fate to prove the point. Each new trouble attacked a nervous system that had previously refused to yield to the demands made upon it; each new trial became invested with exaggerated significance. He found he was battling against a nameless panic from which Zena Wilding seemed the only escape. Why Zena Wilding? He had asked himself that question. Would any pretty woman, not too young and not too old, have sufficed his mood, or had he really detected that she, like himself, was fighting difficulties behind a mask? He had also asked himself what he wanted of Zena Wilding. The usual thing—or just to be a little boy again, and lay his tired head in her lap?

He did not know. All he knew was that Zena Wilding, whose companionship he craved, was not dissipating his panic, but adding to it.

And now this dead fellow...and this ruined picture...

"But this is most shocking!" he exclaimed. "Yesterday evening, you say?"

"Between half-past four and a quarter to seven," answered Pratt.

"Why did you not mention it before?"

"I thought I might find the culprit more easily by not mentioning it."

"You had a suspicion?"

"Quite definite."

"May I ask who?"

"If you don't mind, I will keep that to myself. You see, if the man in the quarry did it, I shall be wrong."

"But you don't know the man?"

"Never seen him before in my life."

"Then why should he have done it?"

"I have no idea."

"Perhaps he ran amok after you locked him in the studio?"

"We have no proof yet that this is the person I locked in the studio."

"Quite so, but it seems obvious!" retorted Aveling. "It would be a coincidence if there were two men around. He got out of the studio, killed the dog, and then—ended down the quarry."

"You are forgetting one point," said Pratt. "The picture was ruined before I locked the studio, so, if he did it, he did it before being locked in."

They entered the wood.

"Perhaps he's a lunatic?" suggested Aveling.

"Anybody who spoils a picture by Leicester Pratt must be a lunatic," came the dry response.

Bultin rose from a tree-trunk and slipped his note-book away as they drew up.

"Are you writing the account already, Bultin?" inquired Aveling, with a frown.

"Provisionally," answered the journalist.

"Well, kindly keep it provisional till we know a little more," said Aveling.

"Publicity produces knowledge," observed Bultin.

"Also crowds," added Pratt. "Have sympathy, Lionel. If there are any plums, you won't have to work for them—they will drop right into your mouth."

They walked together to the edge of the great dip. The quarry was a relic of past activity. No longer in use, much of its bareness had been reclaimed by vegetation. Lord Aveling stared down into the tangled space.

"See him?" inquired Pratt.

Lord Aveling nodded.

"What brought *you* up?" went on Pratt, turning to Bultin.

"My feet," answered Bultin.

"Not really worthy. Try again?"

"Well, I like writing about corpses, but I don't like sitting by them. This one is a nasty sight. Even nastier than when I saw him alive—"

"What! Saw him alive?" exclaimed Aveling. "When? Where?"

Bultin produced his note-book again, turned to a page, and read:

"'Our train drew in at 5.56. We stepped out upon an ill-lit platform. The knowledge that we should shortly enjoy the greater cheer of Bragley Court—Lord Aveling's cordial welcome is almost famous—'" He paused for an instant, and noted how, during that instant, the world grew a trifle brighter for Lord Aveling. "'—modified to some extent the horror of a British platform in the British gloaming of a British October evening. But even so I had a strange sensation that unseen fingers were stretching through the dusk, and a curious incident accentuated the feeling. In reply to a famous actress's question, I informed her that she undoubtedly *was* keeping us all waiting, and that no press photographers were about. With the famous laugh rendered even more famous by her imitators, she ran towards the waiting Rolls. And now the incident occurred.'"

He paused again.

"No, not 'occurred'—'took place.'" He made the alteration. "No, after all, 'occurred.'" He altered it back again. "'And now the incident occurred. A man suddenly loomed before her. She stopped immediately. For a moment I thought she was going to faint. But she controlled herself with an effort, pushed by him, and entered the car. Of two other guests—a Mr. and Mrs. Chater, I being the fourth who completed the party—Mrs. Chater had already taken her seat, but Mr. Chater went up to the stranger and offered him a light. The offer was not accepted. "I'll see you presently," spat out the stranger. "I wouldn't," Mr. Chater spat back, and, in the words of Barrie, 'joined the ladies.' Delete, 'in the words of Barrie.' 'But I did not immediately join the ladies. My business is news. You want it. I supply it. So I thought I would have a few words myself with this interesting stranger.

"'I told him who I was. To my chagrin, he did not swoon with joy. He looked more as if he could have bitten me. I told him where I was going. This information softened him slightly. I felt that now I might touch him without being mauled. I offered him a light. His unlit cigarette hung uncared-for from his moist lower lip. This time he accepted. As I struck a match I mentioned my duty to the public. He stared at me. People say I have some gift of expression, but I could never express the look that suddenly leapt into his eyes. "*You'll* get something to write about!" he promised.

"'Did he mean to fulfil that promise? Shall we ever know? The next time I saw the man, between twenty-one and twenty-two hours later, he was lying at the bottom of a quarry, dead.'"

Bultin closed his note-book and returned it to his pocket. Then a voice hailed them, and they turned. It was Dr. Pudrow, followed by a gardener and two grooms. The gardener, with lugubrious forethought, was wheeling a barrow.

"Where is he?" cried the doctor.

The definite task before them came as a relief to Lord Aveling. Anxious thoughts, disturbing conjectures, policies to be pursued, all were necessarily shelved while the grim business of descending to the quarry was engaged in. They found the man lying, face upwards, in a crumpled heap, and the doctor did not have to examine him to confirm that life was extinct.

"No doubt about it?" murmured Aveling.

"After rigor mortis, my Lord?" replied the doctor. "He has been dead several hours."

"Can you say how many?"

Dr. Pudrow was now bending over the body. He did not answer for a minute. Then he remarked cautiously that he did not want to commit himself at the moment.

Pratt, who thought little of doctors, and particularly of this doctor, suggested the rigor mortis might give him some indication.

"It may occur half an hour or thirty hours after death," retorted the doctor, well aware of Pratt's opinion, and particularly sensitive when the opinion was implied before Lord Aveling, "and the condition may last for from twenty-four to thirty-six hours. The time varies according to the subject and the cause of the death."

"The cause we know," answered Pratt.

"Perhaps you will handle this case?" exclaimed Dr. Pudrow.

Lord Aveling interposed.

"You mean, of course, Pratt, that he died from his fall," he said. "Quite so. But I think we can safely leave these matters to Dr. Pudrow."

"If you want to know what time the man died," observed Bultin, in a voice that suggested he was stifling a yawn, "it was at nineteen minutes past one last night."

"How do you know that?" demanded the doctor, astonished, while Lord Aveling stared.

"By his wrist-watch. It is broken, and the hands mark the time it stopped. I am assuming," Bultin added, "that your 'several hours' meant more than three—otherwise he could have died at nineteen past one to-day."

Against his will, Dr. Pudrow was impressed. So was Pratt. "Bultin did not waste his time while I went to the house to report," he reflected. "I wonder what else he's discovered?"

"He has certainly been dead more than three hours," the doctor replied, "so you are probably right. Can you also tell us who he is?"

"No, I can't tell you who he is," answered Bultin. "There is nothing on him to suggest his identity. But there are three people up at the house who may be able to."

"Only two at the moment, I think," murmured Aveling, as Bultin glanced at him.

"Can you get them here?" requested the doctor. "Some one connected with him should be notified as soon as possible."

"Yes, yes, I agree—but both these guests are ladies," objected Aveling. "It would not be reasonable to ask them to make this descent, especially as it is getting dark, and they are tired. In fact, I doubt whether they could do it. Why not let my men carry him up?"

"To the house?" inquired the doctor.

Aveling's frown grew. The house was depressed enough, as it was.

"Or the studio," suggested Pratt.

The frown vanished. Lord Aveling was living, emotionally, from instant to instant. Bultin's account of the incident at the station had filled him with wretched forebodings, and he discovered that his main impulse, rightly or wrongly, was to protect Zena Wilding from unhappiness. His own happiness was being invaded from so many sides that it was almost a relief to have some one else's to concentrate on. "Besides," he argued with himself, with the self-deception of the would-be virtuous, "isn't it my duty to protect my guests from annoyance? If I happen to be particularly interested in one of them, I must not remove that protection through self-consciousness." His over-sensitive mind was once more developing situations in advance. "I have done nothing wrong!" He thanked God for that, though it was a sign of his anxiety that he had to produce the statement to himself.

"A good idea, Pratt," he said aloud. "Yes, the studio. But what about you? Your work?"

"My work?" Pratt smiled. "My work is obviously postponed."

Aveling made a sign to his waiting men. As they commenced their task, under the doctor's direction, Bultin looked on with vague disapproval. Pratt drew him aside.

"Your expression is not heavenly, Lionel," he said. "What's the matter?"

Bultin shrugged his shoulders.

"That's not good enough for me, you oyster!" insisted Pratt.

"Bodies are not usually moved till the police arrive," answered Bultin.

"Nor, perhaps, are their pockets searched," replied Pratt, "though I know journalists sometimes imagine they have special privileges."

"Did I search his pockets?" asked Bultin innocently.

"You knew there was nothing on him to indicate his identity. It would not surprise me to learn that you so searched for laundry marks. You can't have it both ways, my boy. If the police eventually arrive, the more you anticipate their work the bigger your scoop. At the moment, you can pretend you are helping. To the local inspector you may merely be a nuisance."

"If you were as clever as you thought you were, you'd be a gargantuan," said Bultin.

"If you were as clever as you thought you were, you'd be the size of a pea-nut. My picture of you will be called 'The Splendid Spoof,' and it will be of a drugged Inferiority Complex inside enormous bulges of inflated skin. We never really change, you know, but some of us are devils at make-up. Well, what else have you discovered?"

Bultin turned his eyes towards the workers.

"They've got him up," he said. "We'd better be moving."

"The knife, for instance?"

"What knife?"

"The knife that killed the dog?"

"Is that all the knife was intended to kill?" asked Bultin. "Come along."

But Pratt suddenly laid a detaining hand on Bultin's sleeve.

"Tell me something, Lionel," he said. "A different sort of a question this time."

"Well?"

"Are you interested in justice?"

"What's that?"

"Perhaps, after all, only a word of seven letters. I'm not asking the question ethically. I'm just curious. If a man commits a murder, are you glad when he is hanged? If a man hasn't committed a murder, do you rejoice when he's acquitted? Or, provided you get a good story, don't you care a damn?"

Bultin thought for a moment.

"Provided the public get a good story," he replied, "do *they* care a damn?"

"That's a devilish good answer," said Pratt. "Put it in your biography. By the way, have you heard about Chater's horse? It's come home without him."

Chapter XVI

The Second Victim

The yellow teacups were tinkling when Lord Aveling looked through the doorway of the pink-and-cream drawing-room. Six people were there, and the absence of the anticipated seventh caused him to withdraw quickly before he had been noticed. Retracing his way to the hall, he ascended the stairs and walked along a passage past his bedroom to another two doors beyond. Here he paused, hesitating.

He started almost guiltily as the door suddenly opened, but he regained his composure as the maid Bessie came out.

"Is Miss Wilding having her tea in her room?" he asked.

"Yes, my Lord," answered the maid. "I've just taken it in."

"Ask her if she could see me at the door for a moment," he said. "Tell her it is important." As the maid turned to obey, he added, to set himself right with her, "There's been an unfortunate accident. You'll hear about it presently."

The maid returned into the room, and was back almost at once.

"Miss Wilding will come immediately, my Lord," she said. Then, after a moment's hesitation, plucked up courage to ask, "Is—is he badly hurt, sir?"

Lord Aveling looked at her sharply.

"Do you know who he is?" he demanded.

Bessie turned red with confusion.

"I beg your pardon, my Lord, for asking—only I heard that his horse—"

"That was Mr. Chater's horse," he interrupted. He wanted to get rid of her. "This is not Mr. Chater."

The bedroom door opened again. The maid vanished. Zena Wilding, in a blue silk dressing-gown, stood before him. No longer fortified by her complete rejuvenating make-up, she looked pale and fragile, and a wave of intense sympathy swept over him.

"I am sorry to disturb you like this," he began gently.

"That's all right," she answered. "I've just got a slight headache, so I thought I wouldn't come down till dinner."

"The day has tired you."

"Isn't it stupid? But I haven't ridden for some time, so I expect—" She broke off abruptly. "I hope nothing has—happened?" As he hesitated, an expression of deep anxiety shot into her face. "Nothing about last night?" she whispered.

Her anxiety made him forget his own. His sympathy increased, and with it his desire to protect her, if protection were needed. Last night he had felt as though he were her contemporary; now, although she looked quite five years older than she had then, he felt almost paternal. It relieved as well as surprised him.

"No, nothing about last night," he reassured her quickly. "I would like to apologise to you about last night."

"Oh, please, don't!" she murmured, and glanced along the empty passage. "I—don't mind." He tried to be sorry she had said that. It made the paternal feeling harder to maintain. "What do you want to speak to me about?"

"Something not very happy, I am afraid," he answered. "But remember while I tell you that if this means any trouble for you—it probably will not, but if it does—you may count on all the assistance I can give you."

She stared at him.

"Please go on. You're very good to me."

"Well, Miss Wilding, there has been an accident. A man has fallen down a quarry in a wood near here. We've brought him up, and he is now lying in the studio."

"Do you mean—?"

He nodded. "Yes. He was dead when we found him. Unfortunately we do not know who he is, but Mr. Bultin—" Damn Bultin! Of course, that account of his was just stupid, journalistic exaggeration! "Mr. Bultin has some idea that two or three of my guests know him. He mentioned Mr. and Mrs. Chater and you. I shall not be surprised to find that Mr. Bultin is wrong. The man was at the station when you arrived yesterday evening, and apparently he—"

He caught her as she swayed. "My God!" he thought. "Bultin wasn't wrong!"

He held her for a few seconds that seemed like minutes; but the passage remained blessedly empty. During those seconds he struggled against many emotions, among which were concern for her, contempt for the hateful pleasure he was deriving from her dependence on him, and confusion as to the next step. He had no idea what to do. If she had fainted, of course he would have to carry her back to her room....

She gave a sudden shudder that was like a little breeze abruptly stirring stillness, and he loosened his grip as he felt her regaining control of herself.

"Don't hurry," he said.

"I really think—I'm not very well," she stammered weakly.

"I am quite sure you are not very well," he replied. "You had better lie down."

"Yes, I will—in a moment. Imagine—feeling faint like that, just hearing about an accident!"

He waited. In a second or two she went on, a little more steadily:

"You remember, I came over the same way at the hunt, didn't I? If I'd known this poor man it would have been different. No, I don't know him. I remember seeing some one at the station—he looked rather odd, I thought he was going to snatch my bag or something—but I didn't know him. Mr. Bultin was wrong. I'd never seen him before in my life." All at once a look of stark terror entered her eyes. She gasped, "Dead? My God! You believe me, don't you? You do believe me?"

He patted her arm.

"Of course I believe you," he answered. "Why shouldn't I? Mr. Bultin has identified him as the man at the station, but it will not now be necessary for you to come to the studio and identify him also, since you do not know him." He was speaking to her and thinking aloud. "There will be nothing for you to worry about. Go back and lie down. And if I were you, Miss Wilding, I should not trouble to come down to dinner, unless you feel very much stronger. Your meal can be sent up to you, and you have had a very tiring day. Every one will understand."

He had never seen such gratitude in any other woman's eyes. Nor, for many years, had his rather tired soul experienced such direct and moving emotion.

He waited till she had returned to her room and closed the door, and then descended to the hall.

On the bottom stair he paused. He was walking straight into a scene. Mrs. Chater was the centre of it, and she appeared to be having hysterics. It was as though the silent scream with which she lived had suddenly burst from the confines of her soul, to discover it had a voice.

Near her stood Bultin, his calmness contrasting impertinently with her shrill fury, and Sir James Earnshaw, watching with a heavy frown. Earnshaw had just returned alone, and the dust of riding was upon him. Between them and the half-open drawing-room door was Lady Aveling. She had tactfully requested the Rowes and Edyth Fermoy-Jones to continue with their tea, but their cups were motionless while their ears strained to hear what was going on in the hall.

"Where's my husband?" Mrs. Chater was shouting. "I knew there'd be trouble if we came here! Where is he?" Her eyes were accusingly on Earnshaw. "And why is everybody looking at me like this? I don't know anything! Nothing's to do with me!" Her voice rose almost to a shriek. "I tell you I don't know the man, and nor does my husband! Where is he? What's in offering a light? Do you think I came here to go and look at dead faces….?"

Her voice became incoherent. She started sobbing, while Lady Aveling advanced and took her arm firmly.

"Where's the doctor, Bultin?" asked Lord Aveling.

"He came in with me," replied Bultin. "He went up to see Mrs. Morris while I spoke to Mrs. Chater. Pratt's waiting in the studio."

"Bultin again!" thought Aveling. "Why can't he let things alone?"

Yet he was grateful for the concise information, and the calming monotone in which it was delivered.

Mrs. Chater wrenched her arm from Lady Aveling's grip.

"Don't touch me!" she cried, with physical repulsion. Then, abruptly—the change was startling—she stopped crying and became as calm as Bultin himself. "I'll go to my room," she said.

No one moved as she walked to the stairs saving Lord Aveling, who stepped aside to let her pass.

"And don't you send any doctor to *me*," she added. "I'm not seeing anybody till my husband returns. Not anybody."

Aveling glanced towards Earnshaw. Earnshaw shook his head.

"He'll return soon, Mrs. Chater," said Aveling.

She stopped for an instant, and also glanced at Earnshaw. "Try not to worry."

"*Worry!*"

It seemed as though the suppressed scream were about to escape again, but a laugh came instead. More than one who heard it woke up that night with its recollection bursting their ears. Then she continued up the stairs. Lady Aveling followed her.

"How did it happen?" inquired Lord Aveling, after a short silence.

Bultin shrugged. "That's how she took it."

"I seem to have started the trouble," added Earnshaw. "She was in the hall when I returned, and she apparently held me responsible for not bringing her husband home with me. Is it true his horse came back without him?"

"Unfortunately, it is," answered Aveling. "When did you last see him? You and he joined Anne and Taverley soon after we started. They are not back yet, either."

"Aren't they?" The news appeared to displease the Liberal member. "Yes, we were all four together for awhile. Anne said something about a short cut through a place called Holm. But Chater and I soon lost them, and though we went through Holm we never saw them again. Then I lost Chater, and then I lost myself, and that briefly is my story. Rather disturbing about Chater's horse. I hope he's not had an accident. And I understand there has been another?"

"Yes. Some one fell into a quarry near here, and we had an idea that Mrs. Chater might be able to identify him."

"I had just asked her when you came down," said Bultin to Aveling. "You heard the result. Were you more successful with Miss Wilding?"

"No—though Miss Wilding took the situation more reasonably," replied Aveling. "And, being tired, she had just as much excuse for a nervestorm. You were mistaken, Bultin. She recalls the man, but doesn't know him. His appearance rather frightened her, that's all. She thought he was a bagsnatcher." Pleased with himself, he turned to Earnshaw. "You'll want to go up and change. But don't take longer than you must. We need your parliamentary manner down here to steady the boat."

"And I need a good tea to steady my own," smiled Earnshaw. "I've had no lunch!"

As he moved, Lady Aveling came down the stairs.

"Well?" asked Aveling.

"She has locked herself in her room," answered Lady Aveling. The sudden recollection that the Chaters had been invited at Earnshaw's suggestion prevented her from adding, "Thank God!"

"Just as well, perhaps," murmured Aveling, putting her thought more tactfully. "It will all straighten out. We will join you, my dear, in a few moments."

His wife accepted the hint, and returned to the drawing-room. Aveling lingered, while Earnshaw went up the stairs.

"So, in common parlance, Bultin," he said suddenly, "that is that."

"Not much progress," answered Bultin.

"My own view is that it will be better to try and forget these things, if we can, and allow matters to take their natural course."

"What is the natural course, my Lord?"

"Eh?"

"Of three people who might have identified the man, two say they don't know him, and the third hasn't returned yet."

"Which reminds me of my next job!" exclaimed Lord Aveling.

"A search for the third?"

"Yes, of course!" He looked despairing. "Really, there has been so much to think about. I'll go up and see Earnshaw again—I must find out the exact spot where he and Chater separated."

"May I have the use of a car meanwhile?"

"What for?"

"Well, if Chater doesn't return, and if your search fails, I may find out something at the railway station. That's where we first saw the man whose identity we need."

Lord Aveling regarded Bultin thoughtfully.

"It is an excellent idea," he answered, "but you are taking a lot of trouble, Bultin."

"For copy."

"May I check the copy?"

"The facts will be correct."

"But the interpretation of facts?"

"That is for the public. If I don't make inquiries at the station, the police may later."

"The police?"

"Am I wrong?"

Lord Aveling knew that Bultin was not wrong. Dr. Pudrow had not yet pronounced the cause of the man's death, but whatever it was an inquest seemed inevitable, and identity would have to be established. Aveling's soul groaned at the thought of the publicity, and of the questions that would have to be asked and answered. The man had died, apparently, at 1.19 a.m. He and Zena had been up that night till nearly one. He had not noted the time exactly. He wished now that he had. And particularly the time when he believed he had heard Zena leaving her room again shortly after they had said good-night.

Out of nowhere came a sudden vision of Mrs. Chater giving evidence. What would the evidence of such a bitter, jealous woman be like? He recalled a trivial incident that had occurred in the ballroom. Sir James Earnshaw, inspired by a latent sense of duty, had relinquished Anne, and moved towards Mrs. Chater. A vague smile had flitted across the gloomy woman's features, but Zena had passed, and Earnshaw had turned abruptly to her instead. As the two had danced away, a spasm of hatred had shot into Mrs. Chater's eyes, though a moment afterwards the face had become once more expressionless....

"Well?" asked Bultin.

Lord Aveling wrenched his mind back to the present, and wondered whether he preferred Bultin to a policeman. Then the telephone rang.

He hastened to the receiver and picked it up. A moment later he exclaimed, "Anne!" Then, for a full minute, he listened in silence. "Yes, yes, of course, you've done quite right," he said at last. "Don't delay."

He glanced up the stairs as he replaced the receiver.

"They've found Chater?" asked Bultin quietly, watching his host's face.

"At Mile Bottom," answered Aveling. "With a broken neck."

Chapter XVII

Nadine's Story

"Well, Mr. John Foss," said Nadine, as she sat on the pouffe that had been waiting for her all day, "shall we pool our knowledge and see whether we can make anything out of it?"

"I'm afraid my own knowledge is very incomplete," answered John.

"So is mine. So, I believe, is everybody's. Just bits and pieces which they're trying hard not to give up. Even Mr. Taverley." She paused, and added suddenly, "I don't know whether you can feel it in here—this room is a sort of backwater—most reposeful—but the atmosphere in the rest of the house is positively—what?"

"Secretive?" he suggested.

"Gives one the creeps. Yes, even quite apart from the fact that two dead people are lying in the studio. We're all on guard against each other. Split up into small parties. That's why I want to form a party with you. I wasn't born for just my own company."

"I shouldn't have thought you ever had to endure loneliness."

"I don't often. Perhaps that explains why I object to it so strongly when it happens. We're all divided into groups of fours and twos and ones, and I refuse to be one of the ones!"

"Who are the other ones?" he asked, smiling. She considered for a moment, puckering her brow, then became conscious of his smile and responded to it.

"You've got a nice smile, John," she said. "Frank. I like it. But don't take that as too much of a compliment—these are meagre times. And I gathered this morning that *you* were worried, too. Who are the other ones? Well, Sir James. Do you like him? Mrs. Chater. I won't ask if you like her. And—all this is strictly private."

"Of course."

"At the moment I'm counting Lady Aveling. I hope it's only at the moment, because I like the Avelings immensely and have had some wonderful times here....Am I speaking too freely? Yes, I expect I am. But it's not gossip, it's—reaction. Perhaps also because I want to help. Though I'm not sure about that. I'm not usually a very helpful person."

"If you start pitching into yourself, we sha'n't make a good team."

"All right. I won't. We'll say, rightly or wrong, that part of my impulse in talking to you is because I have a wonderful nature and burn to do good in the world!" She made a grimace. "Nadine Leveridge, Good Samaritan! That's almost worthy of one of Bultin's posters!"

"Who are the twos?"

"At the risk of shocking you, I'll begin with Lord Aveling and Zena Wilding. That's why I've isolated Lady Aveling. I don't like your expression quite so much now, John."

"What's the matter with it?"

"It's almost disapproving."

"It's not meant to be."

"What is it meant to be? Are you going to become an oyster like the rest? I'm human, my dear man, and this is going to be a fifty-fifty business, or nothing."

"It's fifty-fifty, Nadine," he answered, after a moment's pause. "And that means I believe you really *do* want to help. So do I. I've nothing against gossip—"

"Liar!"

"Right. I loathe it. But I know this isn't gossip. My expression meant that—that I agreed with you. I'll explain more later. Please go on."

She nodded.

"Our collaboration continues. Mr. Taverley and Anne make another two. I sensed that when I rode back with them from Mile Bottom. I came upon them just after they had made their unpleasant discovery. Straight from one 'kill' to another! But luckily I wasn't in at the second death!"

"He was dead when you arrived, then?"

"Yes. You've heard all about that, haven't you?"

"No one's told me anything."

"Then how do you know anything?"

"That wasn't quite accurate," he corrected himself. "Lord Aveling and Pratt were in this room shortly before tea, and I heard from them about the man in the quarry, and then the maid who brought my tea said the doctor had arrived. But beyond that all I've heard has come through the door."

She listened.

"You've got good ears. I can't hear anything."

"The hall's probably empty at the moment. Still, I have got good ears. Not that one needed good ears to hear Mrs. Chater when she went off the reel. It was pretty horrible. Then I heard Lord Aveling at the telephone—that was when Anne phoned about Chater—and, later on, I heard you all return. That was an hour ago, wasn't it?"

"And nothing since?"

"Nothing and nobody. It's been as quiet out there as it is now."

"Yes—it's quiet," murmured Nadine. "We're talking in whispers. Even Mr. Rowe's voice is almost musically soft." She stared at the toe of her shoe, raising it slightly from the ground. Once she had done it consciously to attract attention to her shapely foot, but now it was a habit. Last night, John recalled, the shoes had been gold. Now they were red-bronze, matching her hair. "You haven't heard the latest, then?" she said, lowering her toe again as though to dismiss it.

"What?" he asked.

"Well—in a minute. I'll go back to Mile Bottom, and lead up to it. Or down to it. When I came upon Anne and Mr. Taverley, they were staring at Mr. Chater. They were off their horses. Mr. Chater's had already gone. It's a wild spot. It has always rather appealed to me—I like wild places—but I shan't think of Mile Bottom again without a shudder! He was lying on a patch of stubble a little way from some boulders. The stubble was quite soft. There was a stream close by, and the ground was wet." She paused. "Anything strike you?"

"I can't say that it does," he answered.

"It struck me at once. I've seen plenty of accidents. But I didn't say anything, and Anne and I went off to the nearest village to telephone while Mr. Taverley stayed by the body....I always think that transformation of terms is particularly callous. Alive we are people, but the moment we die we become bodies!

"Well, we telephoned, as you know. Did you hear the conversation?"

"Lord Aveling's end."

"Did you gather how Anne reported it?"

"Yes. You had found Chater with a broken neck." Nadine nodded.

"He certainly looked, from his position, as though his neck had been broken, but when we got back after telephoning, bringing assistance, we found that it wasn't."

"Do you mean he wasn't dead?" exclaimed John.

"Oh, yes, he was dead," she replied. "What I said was that his neck wasn't broken. He had just fallen off his horse into some wet earth, and died from shock."

"I see," murmured John, slowly.

"Do you?"

"I hope not. Well?"

"We got him in a car, and followed the car home. We didn't talk much. Of all the depressing rides! I'd been bursting before I met them to describe the end of the hunt—it was a wonderful run and I'd stuck it to the finish and seen the kill—but I expect my appetite for blood was gone, and I never said a word about it. Instead I found myself watching Anne and Mr. Taverley, and growing more and more depressed. I'll be frank with you," she went on, "and admit I didn't feel in the least depressed for Mr. Chater. Call that rotten, if you like, but it's the truth."

"I don't call it in the least rotten," answered John. "What did depress you, then?"

"I hardly knew. Something in their attitudes. Not Anne's, perhaps. Behind her horror she seemed puzzled, but that was natural. *I* was puzzled. No, it was Mr. Taverley who worried me. There was something very personal in his anxiety—and I'm quite sure he didn't love Mr. Chater any more than you and I did. Excepting, of course, in the sense that his idiotic philosophy tries to find an excuse for everybody!"

"Let me get one point clear before we go any further," said John. "You haven't got any idea, have you, that Taverley has had anything to do with the accident?"

Nadine laughed.

"That idea is as likely as the idea that Mussolini could turn into a pacifist," she answered. "No nothing of that sort." Then she quickly grew serious again. "When we got back, a second shock was waiting for us. We heard about the other accident. Dr. Pudrow has had a busy day."

"He has. What does he say? About Mr. Chater?"

"Do you know what he's said about the other man?"

"No."

"From something I overheard I believe there's a suggestion of strangulation."

"That sounds pretty bad."

"It does rather. And so does the way you're taking it. A few hours ago you'd have said, 'My God!' Now you're so numb that you merely think strangulation is pretty bad. Don't take that personally, of course. I am merely being symbolic! I'm afraid the next suggestion will give you a shock, though. It's that Mr. Chater was poisoned."

John stared at her in astonishment. The only reason he did not say "My God!" this time was because she had taken the words out of his mouth.

"Believe me, John, things are pretty grim," said Nadine. "My nerves are supposed to be a hundred per cent., but they've been severely tested these last two hours. Mr. Chater poisoned! Do you realise what that means, if it's true? Not many of us here had any reason to love him!"

John nodded. More had reason to fear him. Whose secrets had died with Chater?

But secrets can be resuscitated. John strove to steady his mind while the events of the previous night began to whirl round it in a chaotic circle.

"Now you know why the house is so silent, and why we are all talking in whispers," Nadine went on. "And why I have come in here for a little cheerful company! I feel—I believe we all do—that if I wanted to pack my bag and walk out of the house, I wouldn't be free to do it—that even if I took a stroll in the grounds, some one would follow me.... This means the police, John."

"Obviously," he replied.

"And questions."

"*You* needn't fear those."

"So that makes it all right?"

"I'm sorry. I didn't mean it like that—I know you're thinking of others."

"I can sometimes, if I strain very hard."

"But—look here—you said it was a suggestion. Dr. Pudrow isn't *sure* Chater was poisoned?"

"His conviction hasn't been officially made public. It probably won't be till he's had a heart-to-heart with the local police inspector."

"Then how did *you* hear of it?"

"By overhearing a scrap of conversation between the doctor and Lord Aveling," she answered. "They were in the room next to mine—'What! You think Chater's been poisoned?' It was Lord Aveling's voice. Then it dropped again."

"Still, Dr. Pudrow may be wrong. He can't have proved it yet."

"I'm certain he's not wrong."

"What makes you certain?"

"You remember I told you that something struck me when I first saw Mr. Chater lying on the ground?"

"I remember you mentioned the ground was soft—I suppose you meant it was unlikely he'd have been killed by the fall?"

"More unlikely than if he had fallen and struck one of the boulders."

"But it could happen."

"It could."

"Or the horse might have kicked him. Or what about a weak heart?"

"Yes—all those things. As a matter of fact I believe Mr. Chater's health was rotten—his wife wouldn't let him take his whisky neat yesterday—she reminded him he'd been ordered not to. But there's something I haven't told you yet—something that convinced me this wasn't an ordinary riding accident. It was his colour....I've seen that colour once before, and I've never forgotten it."

After a pause he asked:

"How is Mrs. Chater taking it?"

"I believe there was a ghastly scene. Thank God I escaped it."

"Have you seen her?"

Nadine shook her head.

"I was in a hot bath. Something's in your mind? What is it?"

He met her challenging gaze with a depressed smile.

"I don't quite know," he answered. "Perhaps just a feeling of impotence. One feels that one ought to be doing something, and one doesn't quite know what."

"Don't you mean, one doesn't quite know whether?" she returned shrewdly. "If you're referring to the unburdening of awkward knowledge?"

"Yes," he nodded. "I don't want to make matters worse."

"It won't make matters worse if you unburden it to me—and I think it's your turn. You'll be asked to unburden it to the police before long, anyway!"

"And the question is—do I? I mean, the lot? Some, of course."

"I can't help you to answer that question unless I know what the lot is."

"You're forgetting something."

"Am I?"

"If some of the knowledge isn't unburdened—I'm only saying 'if'—won't it be easier for you not to know it? When *you're* being cross-examined?"

"That's a point," she admitted. "I can't say. But—well, it would be rotten team-work, John! You see, I might advise you to get rid of that 'if.' I might advise that, with things in their present muddle, it may be better to take all the fences."

"You'd probably be right," he answered thoughtfully. "After all—if a murder *has* been committed....Queer how one seems to forget that this is really Mrs. Chater's tragedy—"

"I know. I keep on trying to remind myself. It's so difficult to feel sympathetic towards a woman of that sort—and I dare say Mr. Chater was a tragedy to her alive as well as dead, so—" She broke off. "Anyway, she's bent on spreading the tragedy."

"What do you mean?"

"I gather she's saying she's going to make some one swing for it. And, as you said, *if* a murder has been committed, it may be that somebody should. But, don't forget, I haven't definitely advised you *yet* to part with all your knowledge, and I'm not going to till I hear it. So—may I?"

He nodded. To have his knowledge shared would be a relief. As clearly as he could, he recounted the various disturbances of the night. When he had finished, she stared at the carpet for a long while without speaking.

"Well?" he asked.

"Personally, I shouldn't mention Anne," replied Nadine. "Anne's O.K."

The next instant she raised her head.

"Hear anything?" she inquired. "I don't believe the hall's empty now!"

She jumped up from the pouffe, ran to the door, and opened it.

"*Prenez garde!*" she whispered over her shoulder. "*Les gendarmes sont arrivés!*"

Chapter XVIII

Enter the Police

Detective-Inspector Kendall made no secret of the fact that he never did things by halves. He left nothing to chance—or so he boasted—and his methods, with which he permitted no interference from anybody, were almost blatantly complete. "If I'd been born with a kink in my brain," he said, "I'd have been one of the big criminals, but fortunately for law and order my brain is not pathological, so I catch 'em instead." That was why he was moved from place to place when a district needed gingering up, and how he happened to be in Churleigh when an agitated country doctor phoned to the station one grey October evening. He had been doing some gingering up just before the bell had tinkled.

He stretched out a large hand and picked up the receiver. He listened intently for a few seconds without any change of expression, then said, "Wait a moment," pulled a pencil and note-book towards him, and called, "Now begin all over again." The agitated doctor at the other end stifled his indignation and obeyed. Kendall could send his compelling personality even along a wire. As the doctor spoke, the detective wrote, interrupting occasionally to ask a question, but never an unnecessary one, and when the conversation was over, with every detail recorded in shorthand, Kendall had given his first practical demonstration of the completeness that was his official religion.

"Half a dozen men, yourself, and a car to take the lot of us to Flensham," he barked to a sergeant.

"Are we going to raid the Black Stag?" inquired the sergeant.

"No, we're going to call on Lord Aveling at Bragley Court," replied Kendall. "Look lively. Particulars on the way. And a bad mark to you for letting your police surgeon get ill when he's wanted."

Sergeant Price looked lively. He was already reacting to the gingering-up process. But when he had learned the particulars, while obeying instructions to "keep her at sixty," he could not quite understand the tearing hurry, and decided in his own mind that this new hustler was rather overdoing it.

"I thought it was a fire or civil war or something," he permitted himself to comment.

"No, only a couple of murders," replied Kendall.

"Alleged." Kendall nodded. "The last alleged murder I looked into turned out to be an accident," said the sergeant.

"After a month of pottering," answered Kendall scathingly. "Well, now we're reversing the process. The accidents are turning into murders. And we'll see whether we can do the clearing up in thirty hours instead of thirty days."

"Why not make it minutes?" murmured the sergeant.

Kendall smiled.

"Might even do that—you never know," he remarked. "But we're up against one handicap from the start, and mind we all see eye to eye about it. This is for you boys behind there, too," he called over his shoulder.

"What's the handicap?" asked the sergeant.

"Journalist."

"Ah."

"And Bultin, of all journalists! He's dropped in on the ground floor, and he's probably planted there now with both feet."

"Is that why you've brought along the army?"

"What's *your* opinion of journalists, Price?" inquired Kendall.

"There's journalists and journalists, sir," came the non-committal response. "Some help."

"Well, this one'll help when we want him to. Get that, everybody. And the same applies all round. We're going to a house choked with guests and each one probably thinks he's the world's amateur detective. Yes, and one or two may have to come back with us on the return journey in less attractive rôles! No amateurs this trip, understand. Don't encourage 'em or let 'em pump you. No 'too many cooks.' I'm the only cook, and I'll serve up the dish. And no leaving the premises, either, till I say so. Anybody who attempts to leave will be under increased suspicion."

"Begin by suspecting the lot, eh?"

"That's the idea. From Lord Aveling himself downwards. Now you know why I've brought along the army, Price."

The sergeant looked rather gloomy.

"There was a chap told me once—detective-inspector like yourself, sir—let's see, how did it go?" said Price. He stared ahead at the long beam of brilliant light sweeping up the gloaming. "I've got it. 'Never declare war,' he said, 'just wage it. Leave the declaration to the lawyers.'"

"Did you catch Threepenny Tim last July, or was it somebody else?" inquired Kendall with a snort. "I'm ready to learn, Sergeant, the same as anybody else—"

"Is he?" wondered the sergeant to himself.

"—and this time last year I was a mild-eyed deacon tripping up a bogus parson. I waged war then without declaring it—till the bracelets went on. But sometimes you've got to be a bull in a china shop, and it's no good wearing a beard and pretending you're a goat. A picture's been mutilated—probably served it right—a dog's been stabbed, a man's been strangled, and another's been poisoned, so we can hardly call at Bragley Court and say, 'How do you do, isn't it lovely weather?'"

"The four items are alleged," the sergeant reminded him softly.

"So is your brain," answered Kendall, "but unofficially I'm taking it for granted. What's Pudrow like? Reliable man?"

"His work for us has always been satisfactory, though there hasn't been much of it."

"Been in the district long?"

"Five or six years."

"Which?"

"Which what?"

"Five or six?"

"Why?"

"To see if you know."

"Five years, eight months, three weeks and five-sixths."

Kendall gave a short laugh.

"I think we'll get on together, Price," he said. "In fact, I'm sure we shall. But don't pull out too much of that stuff at Bragley Court. Keep it for the nuts and wine."

They fell into a silence as the car raced through the darkening lanes. They passed near a spot where, a few hours earlier, a stag had died unmourned; then stopped at another where a less noble creature had met his death, to cause greater trouble. Kendall jumped out here, and the sergeant followed him with a torch-light. They vanished into the shadows, and returned in a few minutes, their return heralded by a dim, shapeless glow that gradually contracted and became smaller and more distinct. "Probably come back to-morrow," said Kendall, as the sergeant switched out the torch.

Then they resumed their way, and did not stop again till their headlights picked out the gate of Bragley Court.

A figure was standing by the gate, smoking. He had stood there for fifteen minutes, watching the dark road. He had a key in his hand.

"I am Lord Aveling," he said, as they drew up. "You have been quick."

"Not too bad, my Lord," replied Kendall, and introduced himself and the sergeant. "This is a very unfortunate business."

"Most of your business is, Inspector," answered Lord Aveling, his eyes on the constables as they tumbled out of the car. "I thought I would meet you here so we could have a few words before going to the house. Some of my guests are very upset."

"That's quite natural, sir."

"I hope I may count on your co-operation?"

"Co-operation?"

"In this sense, Inspector. Any consideration you show, should you question any of my guests, will be greatly appreciated by me. I cannot help feeling terribly responsible for having brought them into this."

"I understand exactly, sir. I'll do my best. But I'm sure you want to get to the bottom of the trouble just as much as we do, and the sooner we do that, the sooner you'll be rid of us. Have I your permission to take possession, so to speak, for a little while? We don't want any more—accidents."

His tone, courteous but firm, implied that the request would have to be granted.

"By all means," responded Aveling, hoping a momentary hesitation had not been noticed. "As far as I am concerned, you are free to act as you decide."

"Thank you, my Lord. That will save a lot of bother." He turned to Price. "Take the men to the house, Sergeant, post them, and then join us at the studio. No, wait a moment. You had better leave one man here, by the gate."

"What is that for?" inquired Aveling, with a frown.

"I am taking you at your word, sir. My first order is that nobody leaves the house without my permission."

"Your permission?"

"If you don't mind."

"I gather it will make no difference if I do mind. Well, after all, I don't think any one is likely to leave the house."

"It would be very unwise if they did." Kendall's voice hardened for a moment, and Lord Aveling noted it, as he was intended to. "Oh, and the telephone, Price. Cover that, too."

Price nodded.

"Your methods are thorough," commented Aveling.

"They need to be with a peer watching them," the inspector answered. "I don't want any questions asked about me in the House of Lords!"

"This man is clever!" reflected Aveling, uncomfortably conscious of the shrewdness of Kendall's little thrust. "I wonder if he is going to be too clever?"

"Are all the guests at the house?" inquired Kendall.

"All, I think, but one."

"Oh! Which one?"

"Mr. Lionel Bultin, the journalist."

"It would be!" muttered Kendall. "Do you know where he is?"

"He went out some while ago, and has not come back yet. At least I haven't seen him."

"Do you know where he went?"

"To the station."

"Do you know why?"

"He was following some clue or other concerning the identity of the first man we found—the man in the quarry."

"What was the clue?"

Suddenly Aveling realised how close these questions were to Zena Wilding's name. He became cautious, while the inspector watched him quietly.

"Journalists prefer to speak for themselves," he smiled, "and I certainly don't intend to speak for them! You will probably find, Kendall, that Mr. Bultin is full of clues—and that your own are the best to follow. I understand that Dr. Pudrow has given you an account of what has occurred here?"

"Yes, but I should appreciate your own account as well," replied Kendall. "Perhaps you'll let me have it as we go along?"

"Certainly."

"The doctor is still here?"

"At the house, waiting. He was on his way here when I originally phoned him up. He comes daily to attend my wife's mother, Mrs. Morris. She is very ill."

"I'm sorry to hear that, sir."

"That is really another reason why I am hoping we can manage this quietly. We have, of course, not told her anything."

"Does she keep to her room?"

"She has not left it for two years."

"Price," called Kendall, as the sergeant was about to lead his five men on their grim march to the house. "Did you hear that?"

"Yes, sir," replied Price.

"Find out which is Mrs. Morris's room, and see that we do not disturb her. Also get a complete list of the guests and every one in the house. And let Dr. Pudrow know that Lord Aveling and I are at the studio. I suppose Lady Aveling will let the sergeant have the list?" he added to Lord Aveling.

"Of course," nodded Aveling. "You can tell her I have said so, Sergeant."

On their way to the studio Lord Aveling repeated the facts which Kendall had already learned from the doctor. Kendall listened silently, reserving questions till later. They found Dr. Pudrow already at the studio door when they reached it, and while Aveling inserted the key the doctor explained his promptness.

"I was in the hall when the sergeant arrived," he said, "so came along immediately. Mr. Pratt wished to accompany me, but the sergeant would not let him."

"My orders," replied the inspector.

"Yes, so I gathered," answered the doctor. "Mr. Pratt did not seem to appreciate them, but personally I thought them excellent."

Lord Aveling pushed the door open and switched on the light. "When all this is over," he reflected, managing to repress a shudder, "I'll have this wretched place pulled down!"

It was certainly a gloomy room into which they walked, exuding an atmosphere that would not be easy to eradicate. The picture with its sinister smear of crimson paint formed in itself a sufficient scar, to which the broken window added its contribution; but it was the two bodies lying on the ground that supplied the definite evidence of gruesome tragedy. They did not lie side by side. They had been placed some distance from each other, as though through a sense of delicacy. Twenty-four hours previously, one had offered the other a light.

The inspector walked to the unidentified body first. He regarded it fixedly, while the doctor behind him murmured, "A pity it had to be moved."

"A great pity," agreed Kendall.

"But with the darkness coming on," added the doctor

self-defensively, "and the belief that we could identify him if we brought him up—well, there was no alternative."

"There was an alternative," replied Kendall.

"What?"

"*Not* moving him."

He turned to the second body. For a moment his eyes regarded it vaguely, as if he were still thinking of the first. Then suddenly they narrowed. He moved swiftly to the body and stooped over it.

"Not a nice colour," said the doctor.

But Detective-Inspector Kendall was not thinking of the colour.

"Did you know Mr. Chater well, my Lord?" he inquired, still scanning the dead man's features.

"I never met him before yesterday," replied Aveling.

"Then he wasn't a personal friend of yours?"

"No."

"Of some other member of your family?"

"None of us knew him."

"But he was your guest?"

"That is so."

"Then may I ask how he came to receive his invitation?"

"He was a friend of another of my guests," explained Lord Aveling.

"I see," replied Kendall. "Who was the other guest?"

"Sir James Earnshaw?"

"Thank you, sir."

He stared at the late friend of Sir James Earnshaw for several more seconds. Then his eyes left Chater's face and roamed over his suit, and the hat lying by his side.

"Anything been taken out of his pockets?" he asked.

"Not as far as I know," answered Lord Aveling.

Kendall examined them.

"Empty," he said. "Odd? Or not?" He looked at the hip-pocket. "Something's been in that one."

"And it's not there now," added the sergeant.

"You amaze me," said Kendall.

He rose and walked slowly round the studio. He paused at the broken window, at the enormous canvas of the stag, and at the ruined picture of Anne. "Yes, and we've got to find out about this, too, haven't we?" he murmured. "Crimson." Sergeant Price, watching him, noticed that he was about to add something and changed his mind. "Well, let's go to the house," said Kendall instead. "I'll come back here presently. I want to see Mrs. Chater."

They left the studio. When Lord Aveling had locked it, the inspector asked for the key, and pocketed it.

"Is there another?" he inquired.

"Only the one you have," replied Lord Aveling.

Crossing the dark lawn, the inspector regarded the windows that loomed at him like watchful yellow eyes. He stopped in the middle of the lawn and studied them.

"What room is that?" he asked, pointing to one on the ground floor.

"An ante-room," replied Aveling.

He followed the wall to where it right-angled towards the lawn. At the end of the protrusion was a door.

"Can we go in that way?"

"Yes."

"It isn't the tradesmen's entrance?"

"No. Just a passage we use ourselves, leading to the grounds here at the back."

"Can anybody use it? You don't keep it locked?"

"Only at night."

They entered the house by the back door, and walked through the narrow passage to the great hall. Kendall glanced towards the right. A policeman stood near the door of the ante-room.

"I think we ought to have some one at the back door, Price," said Kendall.

"Is all this necessary?" wondered Price. "Or is he just showing off?"

Lord Aveling conducted him up the stairs. Two flights. He stopped at a door and knocked. There was no answer. He knocked again. There was still no answer.

"Mrs. Chater," he called.

"Not there, eh?"

Lord Aveling turned the handle. The door was locked.

"Mrs. Chater!" he called, more loudly.

Kendall looked grim, and lowered his eye to the keyhole.

"No key in the lock," he said. "Find another quickly, or we'll have to do some smashing."

Lord Aveling glanced anxiously along the passage towards another door. Beside it was a wall-table, with the flap down.

"What's the trouble?" demanded Kendall, sharply.

"That is Mrs. Morris's room," murmured Aveling, looking worried. "I hope we can avoid noise."

"We must avoid it, if we can," added the doctor. "She is very ill, inspector."

"Then of course we'll avoid it if we can," said Kendall quietly. "But we may find some one else—very ill—behind *this* door."

For a minute doors were robbed unceremoniously of their keys. Four keys proved useless, but the fifth slipped in and turned. Kendall threw open the door of the Chaters' bedroom. It was empty.

Chapter XIX

Short Interlude

"I can't find the piece that goes here, Anne," said old Mrs. Morris. "A straight edge. And brown."

She was lying in her bed, propped up by pillows. Her thin, worn hands lay listlessly on a jig-saw board, but her eyes were patient. Anne had watched the patience in those tired eyes for over two years—had seen it summoned by an iron will, till it had slipped into a heroic habit; and it had made her despise the fretting world outside that quiet bedroom where pain and relief from pain were the only incidents. Above all, it had made her despise herself. She moved quickly to the bed now, and began searching earnestly for the piece with the straight edge. Nothing in the world mattered at this moment but a small piece of three-ply wood.

"It must be brown, dear," said Mrs. Morris, "because it's a bit of the squirrel."

"We'll find it," answered Anne optimistically.

"Brown," said Mrs. Morris.

Suddenly Anne's hand shot towards a piece. It rested momentarily against her grandmother's, the one firm and strong, the other white and fragile almost to transparency. The cruel contrast sent a dart of pain through Anne's heart, and she withdrew her hand hastily, loathing its youth and beauty and the carefully manicured nails.

"No, not that one," said Mrs. Morris.

"I believe it is," replied Anne, more loudly than she intended. But she was trying not to cry. "Look! Oh—so it isn't!"

"It must have a straight edge," said Mrs. Morris, as Anne took the piece away again.

"You're always right," answered Anne. "Well, what about this one?"

She tested several pieces unsuccessfully. Presently, conscious that she was receiving no assistance, she glanced up. Mrs. Morris's eyes were closed. But Anne continued with her task. The interest must be maintained. There was nothing else.

"I was sorry the bottle was broken," said Mrs. Morris. Her eyes were still closed. "I liked that bottle."

Anne was motionless.

"Didn't some one give it to me?…Last Christmas. Your Uncle Harry."

Uncle Harry had been dead ten years.

Quiet feet moved past the bedroom door. They were very quiet indeed, and did not pause, but Anne heard them. They wove into the rhythm of her heart-beats.

"Did they get the stag?"

"Yes, Granny," answered Anne.

"That's a good thing," said Mrs. Morris. "It's over."

Anne knew that she was envying the stag. Mrs. Morris did not feel the trembling lips that touched the counterpane where her drawn knee made a tiny mound.

In a few seconds the old lady opened her eyes. The pain had gone again.

"Isn't that the bit over there?" she said.

Her thin fingers stretched forward, and fitted it.

Chapter XX

Bultin's Time-Sheet

The presence of Mrs. Chater in Bragley Court had added a definite contribution to the gloom of the atmosphere, but her absence, coupled with its baffling circumstances, introduced fresh discomfort. "Don't you feel," said Edyth Fermoy-Jones, in a dramatic whisper, "as if it had somehow brought things right *into* the house?"

"It seems to have brought Mrs. Chater out of the house," retorted Mr. Rowe.

"I don't think we ought to joke, dear," murmured Mrs. Rowe, glancing at Ruth as though fearing she might be influenced by this bad example. But Ruth had never made a joke in her life.

"Joke? Who's joking?" exclaimed Mr. Rowe indignantly. "I was merely making a statement! What's the matter with everybody?"

He was battling against a secret, irritating nervousness. Not that he was scared! Bless his soul, no! After all, this *was* England, wasn't it, and you couldn't go far wrong once you had a houseful of policemen! They'd probably find simple explanations for everything, and that nobody had really murdered anybody! All this jumping to conclusions—it was silly. But, well, one—two—three—four—five things had happened, starting with the damned dog, and you never knew when they were going to stop!

"What I meant," said Edyth Fermoy-Jones, who did not intend to have her meaning spoilt by family bickering, "was that everything else has happened outside. This happened inside. While we were all sitting here—in this very drawing-room—Mrs. Chater *went*!"

"And no one saw her go," added Mrs. Rowe.

"And no one knows where she's gone," nodded Miss Fermoy-Jones.

She closed her eyes and thought. She always closed her eyes in company when she thought, so that the company would know she was thinking. Sometimes she cheated, and opened her eyes again without having thought at all.

But this time she did think. She wondered where, if she created a similar situation in a novel—and she fully intended to—she would have the disappearing person found? She decided on a well.

"I hear that detective's going to cross-examine us all," said Mrs. Rowe.

"Oh, dear, how awful," murmured Ruth.

"Why? *We've* got nothing to worry about!" answered Mr. Rowe.

"Somebody has," declared Miss Fermoy-Jones. "I wonder who?"

All at once she rose from her chair. If she had not been so heavy she would have jumped. A brilliant idea had occurred to her.

"What is it?" asked Mrs. Rowe anxiously.

"I believe—yes, I believe I've *got* it!" she replied, sepulchrally.

"What—you mean?—who?"

But Edyth Fermoy-Jones shook her head, and set her lips firmly.

"No! It wouldn't be right! I must tell it to the inspector! Does anybody know where he is?"

"I should have thought he'd have consulted you first," said Mrs. Rowe. "I mean, writing mysteries yourself."

The authoress had had the same thought. But, after all, the police are apt to think as little of mystery writers as mystery writers are apt to think of the police. If Detective-Inspector Kendall had read her last novel, he was probably getting his own back.

"No, after all, I'll wait," she said, sitting down again.

She was not going to risk a snub. And she would have received a snub had she attempted to intrude on the inspector at that moment. A car had just stopped outside the house, and Kendall was on the doorstep, absorbed in the event.

Bultin stepped out of the car. He almost stepped into the arms of Kendall.

"Mr. Bultin?" inquired the inspector.

"I am Lionel Bultin," replied the journalist.

"You've been doing some of our work, I understand?"

"Journalists don't wait."

"Nor do the police, once they're called in. I'd like a chat with you."

"I am sure you would," said Bultin. "Here? Or in my room?"

"Your room, I think," answered Kendall, considering. "But one question here. Did you come across any one outside—apart from policemen?"

"You mean in the grounds?" Kendall nodded, and Bultin turned to the chauffeur. "Did you see any one?"

"No, sir," answered the chauffeur.

"Nor did I," said Bultin.

"What about outside the grounds?" inquired Kendall. "Did you meet any of the visitors?"

"No one."

"Ah—then Mrs. Chater was wrong. She told me a moment ago that one of the visitors had gone, and no one is supposed to leave the house."

"I thought Mrs. Chater herself had left the house?" said Bultin.

"What made you think that?"

"Your sergeant. He stopped us near the gate and said he was looking for her. No, I haven't kidnapped her, Inspector. I never thought of it. It would have made a good story."

Kendall was not in the least abashed.

"I'm not apologising," he smiled. "In spite of the good story, I didn't think you had kidnapped her; but I try everything once. Well, let's be moving."

"Before we move, I will return good for evil," said Bultin. "Don't look only for Mrs. Chater. Look for a black bag and an old Hercules bicycle with the front mudguard bent and the bottom screw missing from the makers' name-plate at the back. An old Hercules lady's bicycle with the front mudguard bent is really enough, but it's the missing screw that will please the public and make the headline."

"This sounds interesting," admitted Kendall. "But what's the idea?"

"That you look for them," replied Bultin.

Kendall frowned slightly, then beckoned to a constable.

"I wonder if you're going to be useful to me, Mr. Bultin?" he queried as the constable approached.

"Only if you're useful to me," answered Bultin. "Not out of affection."

Kendall gave the constable an instruction, then followed Bultin up to his room on the second floor. Leicester Pratt looked up from a book as they entered.

"If you two wish to talk, I'm not going," he warned.

"I don't want you to go, sir," replied Kendall. "I hope you'll talk, too. I require both your stories—for a book I'm writing myself," he added, producing his note-book from his pocket and sitting down. "Yours first, Mr. Bultin. And while you're telling it please don't be a journalist, but a sub-editor. A sub-editor cuts, and I've a lot to get through."

"I'm glad you're rude," said Bultin. "Now I can be."

Pratt smiled. His friend did not usually need a reason. But already he had noted a vague uneasiness behind Bultin's manner, and it intrigued him.

"As rude as you like, provided you make it snappy," returned the inspector. "Now, then. About this bag and this bicycle?"

Bultin glanced towards a drawer. Pratt, watching, recalled that Bultin had glanced at the drawer once before. "What's in it?" he wondered. "Bultin's skeleton?"

"We're working together?" asked Bultin, removing his eyes from the drawer.

"I don't make bargains," snapped Kendall. "Have you heard that two people have been killed?"

"I helped to find one of them," murmured Bultin.

"And have you heard that the wife of the one you didn't find has been making definite accusations?"

"Against whom?"

The inspector leaned forward with a cynical grin.

"I haven't got your infinite tact, Mr. Bultin," he said, "but I am not a fool. I see you didn't know that Mrs. Chater has been making definite accusations. Never mind to whom, or against whom, but accept the fact that I arrived here with that information—to find the lady's door locked and the room empty. Now perhaps we can get on? By the way, before I leave this room, you won't mind if I look in that drawer?"

Bultin's expression did not change. He had trained it into a dog's obedience. But a sudden memory disconcerted him. He recalled how, years ago, people used to get on top of him. He recalled the exact sensation, and it leapt close to him through the vista of time. "No, you're not the reason," he told Kendall in his thoughts, denying him the credit. "It's that one silly slip I made. Well, I won't make another."

"You can look in the drawer now, if you like—it's not locked," said Bultin. "But you may like to hear about the bag and the bicycle first."

"Go on," nodded Kendall.

"You know that Mr. Pratt and I found Body Number One. That's not a bad title. Body Number One. Mr. Pratt went back to the house while I waited—"

"And poked around?"

"I should not have been a journalist if I had not poked around. I should not even have been human. I tried to find some clue to the man's identity. I examined his pockets."

"Oh, you did?"

"Why not? There was no question then of foul play. A man had fallen down a quarry. Or, if there was any question, his pockets might have indicated the answer. Lord Aveling was still at the hunt—"

"I understand he had just returned?"

"As a matter of fact, he had, but I did not know that."

"Did you find anything?"

"I found the time the man died. Nineteen minutes past one."

"The broken wrist-watch?"

"Count up my good deeds."

"You can reckon the broken wrist-watch with your missing screw, Mr. Bultin," said Kendall. "It sounds well in print, but to the police it's just A B C."

"Perhaps, but I said my alphabet before the doctor did. And I found something else, besides the time the man died. A key."

He took it from his pocket and handed it to the inspector.

"Bultin's a devil," reflected Pratt, "but I believe rather a tired devil."

"It will probably fit the black bag," commented Bultin.

"Yes? And then?" said Kendall, pocketing the key.

"Lord Aveling arrived, and later the doctor. When the question of identity arose, I told them of the little scene at the railway station. You've heard about that?" Kendall nodded. "So when both Miss Wilding and Mrs. Chater denied any knowledge of Body Number One, even refusing to go to the studio to see it, and when Miss Aveling telephoned through to her father the news about Body Number Two, I asked Lord Aveling for a car and went, with his approval, to the railway station. Mrs. Chater, of course, had not left the house at that time. The last I heard of her was that she returned to her room, refusing to see anybody."

"But she saw somebody when she learned of her husband's death," interposed Pratt. "She saw the doctor."

"Yes, I understand he told her," answered Kendall, "and there was a bad scene."

Pratt glanced towards the wall. The Chaters' room was the next one.

"A very bad scene. I heard Mrs. Chater shouting that somebody would swing for it, but I didn't hear who was going to swing. The doctor may have given her something to quieten her—but, after all, he will have described all that to you."

"But you heard the doctor leave?"

"Yes. I left my room at the same time. He said he was going to phone the police."

"And then you went back to your room?"

"Not at once."

"You did not follow the doctor to the phone?"

"He wouldn't let any one follow him to the phone."

"He was quite right. What did you do?"

"What did I do? Let me think, Inspector. What *did* I do? Does it matter?"

"I wouldn't ask otherwise."

"True. I keep on forgetting you are intelligent. I think it must be the influence of my friend Mr. Bultin. Ah, I know what I did. I went to a bathroom to wash my hands. They weren't dirty. I don't know why I did it. Restlessness, very likely. Then I began to come back to my room. Then I changed my mind—more restlessness—and went down to the hall."

"Wasn't the doctor telephoning from there?"

"He had finished. I washed for a long while. Vinolia soap." He raised a hand to his nose. "The evidence is still there. I really went down to find out if Mr. Bultin had returned, but he hadn't. Then I came back, and tried to drown reality in the imagination of Edyth Fermoy-Jones." His hand now touched the book in his lap. "I fear it was a case of out of the frying-pan."

Kendall turned back to Bultin.

"Well?"

"I thought you'd forgotten me," answered Bultin.

"I don't forget anything," said Kendall. "I haven't even forgotten that drawer. What happened at the station?"

Now Bultin drew out his own note-book and read from it.

"'Body Number One. Arrived Flensham 12.10 p.m., Friday. Single third from London. Seemed restless. Watched other passengers depart. Stayed on platform a few minutes. Asked porter when next London train was due. Told 3.28. Left station. Next seen at Black Stag, inn adjoining station, twenty minutes later. Asked for lunch. Put bag on chair and sat by window overlooking platform. Black bag. Shiny leather, about fourteen inches. "Seemed to bulge like," said Mrs. Blore, proprietress of inn. She also bulged like. Lunch served 12.50. Cold beef and pickles. Ate little. "Well, how can you eat when you smoke at the same time?"—Mrs. Blore. Smoked continually. Also kept looking at his wrist-watch. Note: Must have been going all right then. Left inn at 1.25, circa. Took bag with him. Seen by farm-boy at 1.40 and 2.15 passing gate to field. Same direction both times. Bob Smith, Brook Farm, quarter-mile from station. Note: Does not seem to have walked far. Round and round in a circle? Returned to inn at three. Sat in window as before. Bag on chair as before. Watching platform so intently, did not notice Mrs. Blore come in and look at him and then go out again. Was at window when 3.28 train came in. Did not move (assumedly) till train had gone out again—'"

"Half a moment!" interrupted Kendall. He turned to the cover of his own book, to the inside of which he had fastened a loose sheet. "3.28. That was the train Mrs. Leveridge and Mr. Foss arrived on."

"Correct," answered Bultin, looking up. "Have you questioned them, then?"

"Not yet," said Kendall. The particulars were down on his list of guests, and he was adding to them. "Carry on."

Bultin continued:

"'Left room at about 3.40. Met Mrs. Blore in passage. Asked her time of next London train. Was told 5.56. Returned to room for bag. Left again. Said he was coming back, and confirmed time of next train. Getting dark. Not seen by anybody till he was back, and not then till Mrs. Blore went in with the lamp and found him at window. Must have slipped in quietly. Bag on chair, as before. Note: Never let bag out of his sight. Query: What's in bag? Asked third time when train arrived. Still smoking and consulting watch. "If ever a man seemed dippy."—Mrs. Blore. Had tea at 5.10. Bread-and-butter and seed cake. Ate very little, and returned afterwards to window. Was asked if staying the night. Didn't know yet. Was asked if bag should be taken to his room. Shouted, "Don't touch my bag!" "You'd have thought some one had trod on his toe."—Mrs. Blore. Mrs. Blore wheezed before speaking. Compare telephone bell. Later Mrs. Blore heard him laughing. Gave her the jellies. Left room with bag at 5.35. Paced road outside station till 5.56. See A3 for continuation.'"

Bultin paused. "Do you want it?"

"Of course," replied Kendall.

"It's less concise."

"I want every word."

The inspector's tone was more friendly than it had been. Bultin felt better, then became annoyed with himself for feeling better. It reminded him that he had felt worse. He liked the complete upper hand, not this sense that he was a small boy regaining favour with his master.

He turned back several pages of his note-book, and read out his account of the station episode. The last time he had read this aloud had been by the quarry. When he had finished, he returned to the pages he had left, and resumed, in concise style again:

"'Man did not go back to inn. Did not pay his bill. I paid it for him. Henceforth, Mrs. Blore mine for ever. Even told me sardines gave her wind. Searched for somebody who had seen man. No luck. Tried Brook Farm. Found Bob Smith in trouble. Left bicycle against gate while working, forgot it, went back for it, found it gone. Distressed because it was his sister's bicycle, and had borrowed it without permission. Got description of bicycle. Old Hercules, front mudguard bent, bottom screw of makers' name-plate on back missing. Gave Bob half a crown and promised to find bicycle. Query: Did man follow our cab on foot, see bicycle, and use it for rest of journey? Worked out distance. Our car reached Bragley Court about a quarter-past six. Minute after Earnshaw's car. Man in a hurry on bicycle could arrive soon after half-past—'"

"I was in the studio about twenty minutes later," interrupted Pratt, who was following these details as intently as the inspector. "The time I found my picture ruined."

"I've got that," said Bultin. "Here's your complete time-sheet. 'Pratt left studio unlocked after showing picture to Rowe, 4.35. Left bedroom to return to studio, meeting Taverley in passage, 6.43. Talked to Mrs. Leveridge at back door to lawn, 6.45. Entered studio, 6.50. Found picture ruined. Left studio, locking it, 6.55. Picture was ruined, therefore, between 4.35 and 6.50. If ruined by man from inn, time narrowed to from 6.30 to 6.50. But after locking some one in studio at 6.55, Pratt had tussle with unknown man outside studio at 6.56. Query: Which was the man from the inn, i.e. Body Number One? Query: Which ruined the picture? Query: Must it have been the man locked in the studio? Query: Who was the other man, whether he ruined the picture or not? Probability that the man from the inn—i.e. Body Number One—*was* the person locked in the studio. But why should he ruin the picture?'"

He paused, and glanced towards Pratt.

"Yes, have you any theory?" asked Kendall.

"None at all," replied Pratt. "I have never seen the gentleman described as Body Number One. By the way, we used to call him Z, and the other unknown man X. Shall we revert to these less lugubrious titles?"

"Have you any theory why *anybody* should have ruined your picture?" inquired Kendall. "I notice that Taverley and Mrs. Leveridge are mentioned in Mr. Bultin's time-sheet."

"At first I thought it might be Taverley," answered Pratt.

"Why?"

"He does not think the picture does the subject justice. In fact, he loathes it."

"Has he said so?"

"Some things do not need to be said."

"Have you quarrelled?"

"No one has ever quarrelled with Taverley. He is one of those irritating individuals who present the other cheek."

"You have no other reason for suspecting him, then?"

"I found a cigarette-end outside the studio. A brand he smokes. He had given Mrs. Leveridge a similar cigarette just before I spoke to her at—your list, please, Bultin?—6.45."

"I have a note about Taverley," interposed Bultin. "'Taverley clear. Have spoken to him. Said he was going to studio to look at picture, but heard some one there and changed his mind. Thought it might be Pratt. Dropped cigarette-end when turning away from studio—saw Mrs. Leveridge at back door—gave her cigarette—and went up to his room to shave. Story fits, and Taverley an oddity who cannot lie. Plays life with a straight bat, God help him!'"

"Wait a bit—that gives us another item for your time-sheet," exclaimed Kendall. "Did Taverley stop and talk to Mrs. Leveridge?"

"No. Just long enough to give her the cigarette."

"Then he heard some one in the studio, say, three minutes before Mr. Pratt met him outside this room at 6.43. Agree to that?"

"Indubitably."

"Which means, Mr. Bultin, that somebody was in the studio at 6.40. He might even have dived in when he heard Taverley coming. We've no proof yet, however, whether this was the person who spoilt the picture—or whether it was Z or X. It's a puzzle."

"I trust, for Art's sake, you will solve the puzzle," observed Pratt.

"With no disrespect to Art, your picture is a secondary consideration," retorted the inspector, rather sharply. "I am merely hoping it will give me a line on graver matters. Is there anything you can add to Mr. Bultin's notes?"

"Nothing," answered Pratt. "Otherwise I would be charmed to oblige after your pretty compliment."

"Would it be too much, Mr. Bultin, to ask for a copy of your notes?"

"It would be asking a lot," replied Bultin, "but perhaps not too much."

"Thank you. And now, please—the drawer?"

Bultin got up from his chair. He paused for a moment. It was a nasty moment. He considered his tactics.

"Have I been of any service to you, Inspector?" he asked.

"Indubitably," smiled Kendall.

"If I continue the service—duplicate the notes, for instance—you will interpret a small irregularity committed before you came upon the scene—to zeal?"

"I've already told you that I don't make bargains," answered Kendall, his smile changing to a frown.

"Then I must trust in your wisdom—and your knowledge of the power as well as the necessities of the press. Before going to the station I found something. I found it in a little pond between the studio and the wood. I thought it might be useful to withhold my discovery for a short while."

"Useful to your newspaper?"

"Certainly. Like the notes I made and am going to copy out for you. I work for my newspaper. My editor pays me for it, and millions of people read and enjoy what I write. But my work can incidentally benefit the police, and any work I should have done regarding my find in the pond would have benefited the police. But now the police can do the work themselves."

He walked to the drawer.

"Well, what did you find?" asked Kendall.

"A knife," replied Bultin. "I put it in here till I had time to examine it."

He opened the drawer, and then stood motionless. For once, Lionel Bultin was beaten by a situation. The inspector sprang to his feet.

"Not there?" he cried sharply.

Bultin blinked and slowly shook his head. Then he turned to Pratt. But Pratt, looking very solemn, also shook his head.

"No—not there," said Bultin.

Chapter XXI

A Woman With a Knife

"Stay here—don't leave the room!" ordered Kendall. "And don't touch that drawer. Let it remain just as it is!"

As the inspector darted out into the passage Pratt regarded the open drawer with its ominous lack of content, and then his eyes sought Bultin's quizzically.

"Have you been quite wise, Lionel?" he inquired.

"Yesterday you left a studio door unlocked," answered Bultin.

"And paid the price."

"I see—and my price will be to swing for two murders? I'm not worrying."

Pratt's eyes returned to the open drawer.

"I suppose two is the right number?" he queried.

"I've thought of that," said Bultin.

"So has our detective."

"Obviously he has. And the reason we are not to touch that drawer is because it may have finger-prints. I wonder what time we shall get dinner to-night?"

Pratt glanced at the clock.

"Fifty-eight minutes to go," he commented. "It looks like being a busy fifty-eight minutes. What about the finger-prints on the knife? They'd have been useful."

"You surprise me," murmured Bultin. After a little pause he added: "But of course flowing water does not preserve them."

"Where did you find the knife exactly?"

"The little pond near the top of the drop. At the spot where it narrows just before spilling over."

"And when?"

"Are you carrying on for the inspector?"

"Was it while I returned to the house to report?"

"To be precise, at 5.11 p.m."

Pratt smiled rather dryly.

"You're a sleuth on time," he admitted. "You ought to edit the A.B.C."

"I have written a detective novel," replied Bultin. "Also, the notice of it."

They fell into a silence. Presently the inspector returned, looking warm. He made straight for the drawer.

"We've been good boys," said Pratt.

"I'm taking that for granted," answered Kendall. "One of you has got to be particularly good for having been particularly bad."

He drew the drawer out carefully—there was nothing in it saving lining-paper—and left the room again. They heard him turn into the Chaters' room. But he did not stay, returning almost at once.

"Drawer being examined for finger-prints?" asked Bultin.

"Sometimes detectives get good ideas," replied Kendall. "Hallo! That's almost ironic!" He stared suddenly at a ward-robe. The empty drawer had been extracted from a small chest. "I ought to have begun here, and I've left it to the last! Like to open that wardrobe for me?"

Pratt turned towards the wardrobe, with its long door.

"Speaking for myself, I should positively hate it," he said. "Are you looking for the third body?"

"Perhaps I think two's enough, and am trying to prevent a third," retorted Kendall, and crossed to the wardrobe himself.

He pulled the door open. Two dress-suits hung innocently from hooks. He closed the door and looked under the beds and behind a screen.

"This is most unpleasant," commented Pratt, "but I suppose it is necessary. You are searching for the Woman with the Knife?"

"Good title," murmured Bultin.

"Just his habit," explained Pratt. "It has nothing whatever to do with his inside emotion. Nor have my own words much to do with mine. I am beginning to feel thoroughly uncomfortable."

"So is everybody else," said Kendall, "and particularly the individual who killed Chater—if Chater was killed. Or if his wife has any logical reason for thinking he was killed," he added. "It's her mind we've got to think about, rather than its accuracy." He returned to Pratt and Bultin. "Look here, do either of you know anything at all about Chater?"

"Nothing," answered Pratt, while Bultin shook his head.

"Well, I do," went on Kendall. "Years ago—his name was Green then—he was imprisoned for blackmail. He probably hasn't lost the habit."

"I am sure he hasn't," replied Pratt.

"Oh! Then you do know something?"

"Only that I had already sized him up, during our happily brief acquaintance, as World Snooper Number One."

"Perhaps you agree there may be more than one person here who—to put it bluntly—may be quite relieved that Chater is out of the way?"

"Yes, if you'll take that as a general agreement, Inspector. I am not naming anybody."

"But could you?"

"I might try a few conjectures, and set you on some wrong tracks. I think you had better follow your own conjectures, if you have any. Don't forget a journalist is present."

"I'm not forgetting it. I've had a lot of assistance from journalists in my time. And also a lot of bother with them. One found a knife once, and was a bit too long in admitting the fact. I expect he forgot what might have happened if the knife had been found on *him*? Where exactly, and when, did you find the knife, Mr. Bultin?"

Bultin told him.

"Never thought of finger-prints?" barked the inspector.

"Constantly," replied Bultin. "That's why it seemed such a pity the handle was immersed in water. Still, I treated it gently."

"Well? Go on. When did you put it in the drawer?"

"Before my journey to the station. It was about five when Aveling and I were in the hall, and he heard over the phone about Chater. I came up immediately afterwards. We can say I put it in the drawer at 5.5."

"And Mrs. Chater was back in her room by then."

"So I understood from Lady Aveling, who had followed her up. But that was a few minutes before I went up, and I thought I heard her going into her room myself."

"Perhaps she went in and left it again, and you heard her going back. Did you close your door while putting the knife away?"

Bultin thought. "No. I left it ajar."

"You did? Then if Mrs. Chater, in her highly-hysterical mood—anxious—suspicious—frightened—heard you in the passage, she could have crept from her room for a moment, peeped in, and seen you put the knife away?"

Bultin thought again, and turned his eyes towards the chest. "Let's test that!" exclaimed Kendall. He ran out of the room, leaving the door ajar. Bultin walked to the chest. Kendall turned and looked in.

"Yes, that's when she could have seen the knife," he said, re-entering.

"And taken it?" asked Pratt.

"Possibly. Possibly. But why should she take it *then*?" mused Kendall. "Why *then*? She hadn't been told that her husband was dead. She only knew—at 5.5—that his horse had returned without him." Suddenly he snapped his fingers. "Bathroom! Here are some more times for you! Chater's body was brought back at about half-past five. The doctor phoned to me about ten minutes later. He'd seen Chater. He'd seen Mrs. Chater—in her room. It was these two facts that largely influenced him to phone me so urgently. You see, gentlemen—Mrs. Chater *did* mention some names. And—so the doctor told me—she wasn't only suspicious and revengeful—she was *frightened*! Do you get that?"

"Certainly I get it," answered Pratt. "Sharing her husband's knowledge, she thought she might be the next victim, I suppose that's why you rushed here with so many men."

Kendall nodded and continued.

"And when you went to the bathroom, at the same time that the doctor left her room and went down into the hall to phone, she could have remembered the knife and stolen it. For revenge—or protection."

"The logic seems sound," agreed Pratt. "So what's the next step?"

"To continue my questions elsewhere," replied Kendall. "I've already had the house searched from top to bottom, and we can't find any trace of her."

"May I make a suggestion?"

"Always ready to receive them."

"I suggest that you interview that young fellow who's laid up in the ante-room. Though I don't suppose she named him?"

"She didn't. But why do you suppose he'll have anything to say?"

"His window has an excellent view."

"I've already noted that," nodded Kendall, walking to the door. "I'll see him in his turn."

"Whose is the next turn?" inquired Pratt.

"You needn't follow me to find out," retorted Kendall. "I've advised every one to stay in their rooms till the dinner-gong."

"The advice seems excellent," murmured Pratt. "I shall certainly take it. We *are* having a happy week-end."

Chapter XXII

Earnshaw Answers Some Questions

Sir James Earnshaw looked through his mirror as he called, "Come in." The door opened, and the inspector's face loomed over the white shoulder of his evening-shirt.

"Ah, Inspector, I was wondering when I should have the pleasure," he greeted the reflection. "You will forgive my shirt-sleeves."

"No ceremony on an occasion like this," replied Kendall, as Earnshaw turned.

"And a shocking occasion it is," answered Earnshaw. "Have you any news of Mrs. Chater?"

"Not yet, sir."

"I had your sergeant in here a few minutes ago, examining cupboards. What was the idea?"

"He didn't tell you?"

"He was much too well trained! As a matter of fact, I have heard very little. Please sit down. Do you mind if I shave while we talk? I am filling in the time by dressing early, since social activities are temporarily at a standstill. You have some questions to ask me?"

"A few, sir," responded the inspector, as he took a chair. "You won't object if I jot down your answers?"

Earnshaw eyed the official note-book with a slight smile.

"No—not in the least," he said. "I realise my position."

Kendall looked at him sharply.

"As far as you know, I was the last person to see Chater alive," explained Earnshaw. "I have already given Lord Aveling the particulars, but you will naturally want them, also."

"I shall be obliged," nodded Kendall. "Mr. Chater was a friend of yours?"

"Well, perhaps hardly that."

"But he received his invitation through you?"

"That is true. Mr. Chater assisted me at the last election—he was quite useful—and as his work was entirely voluntary, I said I hoped I would be able to return the service some time."

"He was a keen Liberal?"

"One would think so. But I have wondered since—"

He paused and regarded the chin he was lathering.

"What did you wonder?" pressed Kendall.

"Well—he never struck me as politically minded. When he asked whether I could return his service by giving him an insight into how the rich live—that was how he put it—I did wonder whether perhaps his assistance had had an ulterior motive. Whether, in fact, he had been less interested in the Liberal Cause than his own smaller cause—and wanted to use me as a stepping-stone for the satisfaction of social ambitions. And his wife's. Not an uncommon type, Inspector."

"One comes across them," agreed Kendall. "So you decided to satisfy the ambition?"

"I did not see why not. At the time. Perhaps I see more reason why not now."

"Would you explain that?"

"Well—this is in confidence?"

"I can't make any promise, sir."

"No? Even if the lack of the promise bars my tongue?" Kendall smiled rather grimly.

"I shall learn what I need, sir—whether now or later."

Sir James Earnshaw smiled back through a layer of white soap.

"You are quite right. I withdraw my hesitation, and shall rely on your discretion....I had not seen Mrs. Chater when I gave the invitation. I hope nothing has happened to her, and I am sincerely sorry for the poor lady, but—well, she has not assisted the week-end gaiety. Glum. Moody. To be candid, I doubt whether she is very well."

"What about Mr. Chater?" asked Kendall. "Did he work out better?"

"Mr. Chater is dead," murmured Earnshaw, stropping his razor.

"Yes, that's why we're talking about him," answered Kendall.

"True. Well, then—Mr. Chater was not more helpful than his wife. I did not like the man."

"Just his general manner? Or did he do anything special to worry you?"

"His general manner worried me."

"In what way?"

"He was rather too curious, for my taste."

"Poking his nose into other people's business?"

"That is my meaning exactly. He himself did not seem to have any other business. I felt like apologising to Lord Aveling for having introduced him—and I very nearly did."

"Did you quarrel with Mr. Chater?"

"What makes you ask that?" demanded Earnshaw, pausing in his stropping.

"A natural question, sir. You might have spoken to him about his behaviour. Anyway, whether it's a natural question or not, I have my reason for asking it."

Earnshaw touched the edge of his razor with his finger and began shaving. The inspector watched his hand, and noticed it was quite steady.

"I can guess your reason," replied Earnshaw. "Yes, I did speak to him about his behaviour, and we did have a quarrel."

"When?"

"To-day."

"Can I hear what happened?"

"Certainly. Chater and I got separated from the rest of the party soon after we started—"

"What time was that?"

"I'm afraid I cannot tell you exactly. Round about midday, I should say. We got lost, and eventually struck a small inn at a place called Holm. We decided to have lunch, and it was while we were waiting for our lunch that we had our little argument. Chater had been in a very surly mood. Over breakfast he had been almost rude. I considered this a good moment to—well, give him a little instruction. He didn't appreciate the lesson."

"What did you say to him?"

"You mean, my exact words?"

"If you can remember any of them."

"I can remember how I, so to speak, opened fire. I was quite blunt. 'Look here, Chater,' I said. 'What's the matter with you?' 'What do you mean?' he replied. 'Your attitude,' I said. 'Do you know, you are putting me in a very difficult position?' 'What the hell are you talking about?' he answered."

"He spoke like that to you?"

Earnshaw paused in his shaving to nod.

"That shows you his humour. Once he had got the invitation, he lost all sense of social responsibility. 'I am talking to you about your behaviour,' I said. 'Take a word of advice from me, and don't ask so many questions about other people's affairs. Even Mr. Bultin, who is a journalist and who deals professionally in other people's affairs, shows less curiosity than you do.' The debate did *not* continue. He flew into an atrocious temper. It was so atrocious that I left him—to consume both lunches. Yes, and now I come to think of it," he added, "also to pay for them."

"What did you do then?" inquired Kendall.

"Well, I felt pretty warm myself," answered Earnshaw, "and I rode my horse hard. Lost myself again—not that this mattered, for I was in no hurry to return to the rather uncomfortable atmosphere here—and eventually got back just before five. I walked into the middle of a painful scene with Mrs. Chater in the hall—I expect Lord Aveling has told you of this?" Kendall nodded. "She went up to her room. I went to mine. And just after I left the hall, I understand, the phone message came through about Chater. I think that's about all I can tell you—unless you have any questions you want to ask?"

Kendall did not answer for a few moments. He studied his notes, and then made one or two additions while Earnshaw continued with his shaving.

"Yes, I have a few questions I would like to ask, if you've no objection," said Kendall, looking up from his book.

"My only object is to help you," responded Earnshaw.

"What was the name of the inn where you left Chater?"

"Oh, yes, I should have told you. The Rising Sun."

"Had you stopped previously at any other inn?"

"No."

"Then, as far as you know, Chater had not eaten or drunk anything during the ride? Up to lunch?"

"As far as I know."

"Did he carry a flask?"

"I should think it highly probable, but I did not see it."

"No flask was found on him."

"Then apparently he did not."

"Well, sir, I am inclined to think, from the condition of his hip pocket, that he did. However, I shall find that out later. Had the lunch been served before you left the inn?"

"Fortunately, no."

"Why fortunately?"

"If it had been served, I might have sprayed poison over it, in revenge for being called a something fool."

"You know the doctor's theory, then?"

"I imagine everybody knows it."

"And you know where Chater was found?"

"At a spot called Mile Bottom. By the way, the innkeeper at the Rising Sun will be able to corroborate the fact that I left before the meal was served. I expect you have already made a note of that."

"Did you pass Mile Bottom on your way home?"

"I did."

"About what time? Can you say?"

"I can say approximately. Between a quarter and half-past four."

"Did you look at your watch?"

"No. I judge by the time it took me to ride from there to here. Half an hour, it should be, or a little over."

Kendall stared at his pencil rather intently. Earnshaw watched him through the mirror.

"Mrs. Chater was with the main party, wasn't she?" asked Kendall abruptly.

"I believe so," replied Earnshaw.

"Did she see you ride away with her husband?"

"She may have done so. I can't say."

"Who were the last people you saw before you rode away?"

"Miss Aveling and Mr. Taverley. As a matter of fact, they broke away from the main party with us, and a little later they took another direction by themselves."

"It was Miss Aveling and Mr. Taverley who found Chater's body."

"Yes."

"On their way home."

"I believe so. Yes, of course."

"They must have reached Mile Bottom after you."

"That is obvious."

"Yes. The phone message came through at about five, so we may guess they were fifteen or twenty minutes behind you."

"And in that fifteen or twenty minutes Chater reached Mile Bottom and fell from his horse?"

"Oh, no," corrected Kendall. "Chater's horse returned without him soon after four, just as Lord Aveling was on his way to see the other dead man in the quarry."

Earnshaw frowned.

"Then I suppose your next question is, why did I not see Chater's body?"

"I'll give you your answer, sir," smiled Kendall. "Chater's body was well off the road."

"Quite true. I was told that. And now I recall that the others only turned off the road because they saw his hat—as *I* should have done, had *I* seen the hat. Does that cover the point? Really, Inspector, this is worse than question time in the House—but carry on!"

"I shall only keep you a moment or two longer, Sir James. You got lost on two separate occasions, did you not? Once with Chater, before lunch, once alone, afterwards?"

"I must have got lost twenty times."

"You do not know this district very well?"

"Not particularly."

"Is there a signpost at Mile Bottom?"

"Signpost?"

"Or anything else to identify the spot?"

"Inspector," remarked Earnshaw, "I am very glad I have a clear conscience. Lord Aveling came to my room after the phone, and he described the spot to me. It is a wild spot, and there is a brook and a stone bridge. I recognised it at once."

Kendall nodded and closed his book.

"Thank you, Sir James," he said. "You have answered my questions very patiently, clearly and helpfully. Now I will go and torture somebody else."

"Give them my sympathy," replied Earnshaw. "But, before you go, I would like you to answer one question for me."

"What is it?"

"Unless Chater was poisoned at the Rising Sun by a total stranger—we only went to this inn by the merest chance—how could the alleged poison have been administered?"

"That is what I am here to find out," answered Kendall. "Of course, I shall make inquiries at the Rising Sun, but I don't imagine I shall find that he was poisoned there."

Outside Earnshaw's door, Inspector Kendall paused to reflect that Sir James Earnshaw had taken very considerable pains to clear himself. On the other side of the door, Sir James Earnshaw wiped his razor, and then his brow.

Chapter XXIII

Theories of an Authoress

A figure darted towards Kendall, like a ghost that had suddenly materialised out of a shadow and had urgent business to do before dissolving back into ethereal form.

"Ah, Inspector! Can I have a word with you?"

He found Edyth Fermoy-Jones's large tense eyes goggling at him.

"Certainly," he answered. "Have you discovered anything?"

"We mustn't talk here!" she whispered. "You never know who may be listening!"

She seized his sleeve and drew him towards the door of her room. It was at the end of the passage. When he had entered, and she had closed the door behind him, she glanced suspiciously at the walls, then asked:

"Is an authoress privileged to suggest a theory?"

"I'll listen to any theory," he replied. "I've listened to thousands."

"Yes, I expect you have," she nodded. "Everybody has a theory. At least, they have in my own mystery novels. Though, of course, I write about sport, too—that's why it seems so—so ordained, almost—that I should have struck both here. In *A Fool Surprises*, it was the fool's theory that proved correct."

"I should very much like to hear yours," said Kendall.

She looked at him with a slight frown. Had he meant anything? She decided not to dwell on the possibility.

"It's about Mrs. Chater," she answered. "But, first, have you found her yet?"

"Not yet."

"You know, your sergeant came here to my room and asked me to look in all the cupboards?"

"He was acting under my instructions."

"Then you think she is in the house?"

"You'll forgive me, I'm sure, but at the moment I am listening to theories, not giving them."

"Yes, of course. That's wise." Miss Fermoy-Jones recalled, with a sense of satisfaction, that she had once made a detective say almost the same thing—though, of course, it had not been to a well-known authoress. "Well, *one* of my own theories is that Mrs. Chater is *not* in the house."

"And the reason?"

"That brings me to my other theory. Of course, if she is not in the house, she may be wandering about anywhere, and a description of her should be circulated as soon as possible."

"Thank you."

"One is only too glad to help, if one can."

"The description has already been circulated."

"Oh!"

"We phoned through to the local station the moment the necessity arose."

"I see." Miss Fermoy-Jones managed to conceal her disappointment. "Well, the theory. Naturally, I am speaking in absolute confidence." Kendall maintained a non-committal silence. It was a pity he was not a little more chatty. "Has it occurred to you, inspector—of course, perhaps it has—that Mrs. Chater may have *run away?*"

"I should very much like to know why it has occurred to you?" Kendall answered.

"No, no, I won't say any more about it!" Miss Fermoy-Jones recanted. "After all, if we assume the fact, you can probably find a reason just as well as I can!"

"Probably," agreed Kendall. "But you may have more information to go upon." Now it was Miss Fermoy-Jones who maintained the non-committal silence. "Would you answer a question or two?"

"Certainly."

It was a humiliating fact, but the authoress had never spoken to a detective before, although she had written about dozens. She found them easier to deal with on her typewriter. Not that the reality before her was rude or discourteous. Nothing of that sort. But—well, there was something behind his manner that failed to augment an authoress's superiority complex.

"When did you last see Mrs. Chater?" asked Kendall.

"At tea. In the drawing-room."

"Who were with you?"

"Just ourselves and the Rowes—Mr. and Mrs., and their daughter. Oh, and Lady Aveling."

"Did anything strike you about her manner?"

"Something always struck everybody about Mrs. Chater's manner. She was one of those—I mean, she is one of those neurotic people. Belonging to what I call the Emotionally Suppressed Type. I dare say you have your own technical term for this class of person."

"Your own could not be improved on."

Miss Fermoy-Jones felt better.

"Well, we have to study and classify types, just as you do," she ran on. "I had some one very like Mrs. Chater in my first book, *Forty-Nine Stairs*. Mr. Buchan rather copied my title a year later, but of course I didn't do anything about it. These things happen. Everybody thought she had committed the murder, but she hadn't, that was the red herring. Still, you won't want me to talk about my work. Mrs. Chater. Well, she hardly said a word. She'd been like that during lunch, and all the way home. Really—since we *are* speaking in confidence—really a most uncomfortable person to be with. No, I don't think she said six words before Mr. Bultin came into the drawing-room. But when she heard about her husband's horse returning without him, and when Mr. Bultin asked whether she could identify the man who was found in the quarry—well, she said enough then, though she got so excited no one could hear exactly what it was she *did* say! She stormed out of the room into the hall, and—so I heard; I wasn't actually there—no, perhaps after all I'd better not mention it." She paused dramatically. "Or shall I?"

"You know best whether it is important," answered Kendall.

"Very well, then, since you put it like that," she responded. "Sir James Earnshaw had just got home, and she practically accused him of having something to do with her husband's accident."

"Is that true?" demanded Kendall sharply.

"It wasn't in words—it was in looks," replied Miss Fermoy-Jones quickly. "Quite definite looks, though. So I understand."

"Who told you?"

"Lady Aveling. Well, no, I didn't say anybody told me!" The authoress developed a sudden internal panic as she recalled how often she had brought her own characters low by a trip of the tongue. "What I said was that I *heard*. I happened to hear Lady Aveling mentioning it to Lord Aveling."

Kendall's expression was not complimentary. It was unfortunate for his opinion of the literary profession—never very high—that he had struck a member who could only be effective in her own study, where she had everything her own way, and where people did and said exactly what she wanted them to.

"Tell me if I have interpreted you correctly," said Kendall. "I understand you overheard Lady Aveling telling Lord Aveling that Mrs. Chater had given a look that accused Sir James Earnshaw of causing Mr. Chater's accident—before the accident had been reported?"

Miss Fermoy-Jones grew warm.

"The riderless horse had been reported," she exclaimed, an indignant note in her voice. "She could have guessed about the accident! But, even if she couldn't, that would make it all the more ominous that she should act as she did—implying some private knowledge!"

"Ominous?"

"Well, don't guilty people ever try to throw suspicion on other people—and give themselves away by doing so?"

They frequently did in Miss Fermoy-Jones's novels.

"Thank you—I will make a note of your theory," said Kendall; "but I suggest that, for the time being, we keep it strictly to ourselves."

"Of course! I've made a special point of not mentioning it to any one else," retorted Miss Fermoy-Jones. "And now, if you don't mind, I really must get on with my dressing."

Kendall did not mind in the least. He did not even mind the reflection, as he left the room and mounted to the second floor, that in her next book Edyth Fermoy-Jones would probably give him a thorough trouncing.

Sergeant Price met him in the doorway of the Chaters' room.

"Well?" asked Kendall.

"Settled the point," answered Price. "The fingerprints on the drawer are Mrs. Chater's. She took that knife all right."

"What did you compare them with?"

"Hairbrush." He turned and pointed to a silver-backed hairbrush on the dressing-table. "Same prints on both."

Kendall nodded, then asked:

"Anything else?"

"Mr. Bultin came out of the next room and popped his head in."

"What happened?"

"I sent him back again. And Taverley went into his room. Door opposite."

"I thought Taverley *was* in his room?"

"So did I. The Rowes are on the other side here. They've nothing to do with it."

"How do you know that?"

"I can listen through a wall when I want to. Conversation quite innocent. Guessing right and left like new-born babes."

"Two tips about that, Price. New-born babes don't guess, and they're not always innocent."

"That's right, sir," agreed Price, with a grin; "but I'm not a new-born babe myself. You can learn more from hearing people talk than from asking them questions, and if the Rowes have ever murdered more than sausages, I'm an Italian!"

"And one point about that. How do you know the Rowes weren't aware that you were on the other side of the wall and talking for your special benefit?"

"Because one of the things she said to him was, 'And do be sure to-night, dear, not to make a noise over your soup.'"

"You're improving, Price," smiled Kendall.

The sergeant concealed his pleasure at the compliment.

"Have *you* got anywhere, sir?" he asked.

"All sorts of places, but that's not saying I've got to the right one. It's Mrs. Chater who's worrying me at the moment—especially as it's clear now that she took that knife."

"She's not in the house."

"You feel sure of that?"

"Not a spot we haven't looked in."

"Bold assertion, Price. Still, you're probably right. She got out of the house before we came, and relocked the door to gain more time."

"I suppose you've got your ideas why she went?"

"And plenty of other people's. If she went. What's yours?"

"Wind up."

"Does that explain the knife?"

"It might, sir," said Price solemnly.

"Yes—it might. This is a worrying business. I wish we'd hear something from outside."

"I'm banking we'll hear from the railway."

"That's a possibility, though I'm not banking on anything. Well, there's enough people searching and watching for her now, anyway—good thing, Price, we phoned through so quickly—so I'll go along and see Taverley. No news, of course, about the bicycle and the bag?"

"Not yet, sir. They've orders to report the moment they have any luck."

"Doctor gone?"

"To make tests."

"Right. Ring up the Rising Sun, Holm; speak to the innkeeper and find out all you can about a lunch that was served there soon after two o'clock. According to Earnshaw, he and Chater arrived at the inn at about two, ordered lunch for both of them, quarrelled, and then Earnshaw left. So two lunches will have been ordered, but only one eaten. See if the innkeeper's story fits Earnshaw's. Check the items. Find out exactly what Chater ate, if you can, and what happened to the remains. If they are still available—they're probably not—have them set aside and kept under lock and key. Then send a man over to cart the stuff to Pudrow for analysis. I don't think we're going to find the trouble there, but I want you to take care of all that for me."

"Right, sir," answered Price. "By the way, there's one bit of conversation I heard through the wall I might mention."

"What?"

"About the Chaters. They had a quarrel last night."

"Oh! Did they?"

"The Rowes heard the fuss—though not, I gathered, what it was about. Rowe said, 'If they'd gone on much longer I'd have banged on the wall!'"

"Any idea of the time?"

"Got that, too. At least, approximately. 'Getting on for two, it was,' he said. 'Damned inconsiderate, I call it, damned inconsiderate.'"

"Well, that's interesting," replied Kendall. "When you die, your ears ought to be framed."

He turned towards the two single beds. Their heads were against the wall next to the Rowes' room. He moved to the wall and listened.

"Anything?" asked Price.

"Yes," answered Kendall. "Soap in his eye!" He glanced towards the opposite wall.

"Nothing from there," said Price. "They're just thinking hard!"

"So am I," returned Kendall, and left the room.

Chapter XXIV

Taverley's Version

"Have you had time to copy out those notes for me yet?" asked Kendall, popping his head in at the door.

"Here they are," answered Bultin. "I'm only giving you the police rights."

"All I want—I don't intend to publish them," replied Kendall, as he took the sheets. "Oh, by the way, I don't suppose either of you gentlemen heard any conversation through the wall last night?"

"There's a chance missed, Lionel!" exclaimed Pratt. "You never thought of listening!"

"Our beds are on the wrong side of the room," remarked Bultin. "Otherwise I should have been delighted."

"Then I take it you heard nothing?"

"You take it right."

"Thanks."

He closed the door, crossed the corridor, and knocked on the door opposite. Harold Taverley, reading in an arm-chair, raised his head, and a look of anxiety shot into his eyes; but he quickly dismissed it as he called, "Come in!"

Kendall had already sized Taverley up as a useful type of man from a police point of view. Simple, direct, truthful— you could see it at a glance. Wasn't diseased with the bug of egotism. Wasn't always trying to say clever things. Looked you straight in the eyes. Exactly what a county cricketer who played the game should be. But as soon as the inspector entered the room his sensitive perception became vaguely uneasy. He couldn't have explained why. There it was. The secretive atmosphere of the house appeared to have worked into the systems of many of its inmates, and just as Kendall had been worried by Lord Aveling's semi-frank attitude at the gate, so he wondered now whether Taverley was going to give him the complete assistance he had a right to expect.

"Maybe I'm getting over-suspicious," he pondered, as he sat down. "It's an easy mood to fall into."

This possible explanation did not satisfy him.

"Well, I suppose you want me to tell you my story?" asked Taverley.

"That's the idea, sir," answered Kendall. "And you can make it as brief as you like, so long as you don't miss out anything. By the way, sir, may I first congratulate you on your 103 not out last week at Leeds?"

"If Tunnicliffe had held a catch in the first over, it would have been the three without the hundred," smiled Taverley. "Where shall I begin?"

"Where it matters."

"I suppose that's where we find Chater?"

"You and Miss Aveling, wasn't it?"

"That's right. We were returning—"

"No, wait a moment," interrupted the inspector.

"Can we start a little further back? When did you get separated from your party? And how did it happen?"

"That's inevitable at a meet."

"Quite so. Only you weren't following the stag then, were you?"

"Yes, in a sense. It was in the morning, soon after the thing had begun, and Miss Aveling suggested a short cut to somewhere or other."

"Remember where?"

"Yes. Holm."

"Ah! Did you get there?"

"To Holm? No—we changed our minds again, and tried another route."

"I see. But you passed through Holm later?"

"No," replied Taverley. "Should we have?"

Kendall smiled.

"No necessity, sir," he answered, "but I've got the habit of maps and time-tables. I like to visualise as much as I can, with one eye on the clock. Now I needn't visualise you in Holm. You missed a beauty spot."

"I've heard it's charming."

"Picturesque inn called the Setting Sun."

"Inspector," said Taverley, "are you trying to catch me?"

"What makes you think that?" inquired Kendall.

"Just your manner."

"Then I must change my manner. I'm trying to catch everybody, but I shouldn't show it. No good as a bowler, eh? Action not deceptive enough? Still, I bowl 'em sometimes. After I've caught 'em. There's no inn at Holm called the Setting Sun. It's the Rising Sun. Now be equally honest and let me know who *did* visit Holm?"

"I can only make a guess at it," replied Taverley.

"The guess being?"

"Chater and Sir James Earnshaw."

"That's such a good guess, I'd like to know how you made it?"

"Earnshaw might have told me."

"Then it wouldn't have been a guess."

"That evens the score," laughed Taverley. "I guessed because Chater and Earnshaw were with us when we began making for Holm. They had fallen behind when we changed our route. The assumption was that they did not change theirs."

"Nothing wrong with that, sir," answered Kendall. "Will you carry on from there?"

"You mean, where did Miss Aveling and I go?"

"Yes."

"We gave up the Hunt, and rode to a place called West Melling."

"May I know why you gave up the Hunt?"

"Certainly. Our original plan didn't seem to be working out, so we thought we'd stop swotting and just enjoy the ride."

"That's where the amateur hunter has a pull over us," commented Kendall. "I'm on the hunt, too, but I'm not allowed to give it up. Well, sir?"

"We got to West Melling at about one o'clock—mention that for your time-table—and stayed for lunch. The Valley Inn. And I mention that because it's about the last definite fact I *can* mention till we got to Mile Bottom on our way back. After lunch we rode all over the place—anywhere and everywhere. We got to Mile Bottom at about a quarter to five—"

"Can you fix that?"

"Approximately. I looked at my watch a little later, so know it can't be far out. It was the merest chance that we found Chater. I happened to see his hat lying on the stubble some way off the road. Of course, I didn't know whose hat it was, but we thought it would be a joke to return it if we could identify the owner. As you know, we found the owner a little way off."

"Beyond the need of his hat," nodded Kendall.

"Yes, there was no doubt about that. While we were examining him, Mrs. Leveridge came along—also on her way back. She and Miss Aveling went off to phone, and it was while I was waiting that I looked at my watch. Seven minutes to five."

"Where did they phone from?"

"An inn about half a mile away. I don't know its name, but they can tell you."

"They weren't away very long, then?"

"From fifteen to twenty minutes, I should say. They brought help back with them—a car from the inn and a couple of men—and I think that's the end of my story."

He paused. Kendall closed his invaluable note-book and replaced it in his pocket. This procedure, implying the termination of an interview, often preceded the inspector's most important questions.

"Thank you, Mr. Taverley," he said. "I'm much obliged. By the way, what did you do while you waited at Mile Bottom?"

Kendall had risen from his chair, and he made the inquiry casually, seeming barely interested in the reply.

"Do?" repeated Taverley. "Nothing particular."

"Just waited?"

"Yes."

The inspector's eyes wandered vaguely about the room.

"I see. You didn't search around?"

"What for?"

"Or find anything?"

The inspector's eyes ceased wandering and rested on Taverley's face, as though they had lost their way and were consulting a signpost.

"All I found was the hat," answered Taverley.

Suppressing his disappointment, Kendall inquired:

"Tell me, Mr. Taverley. You had plenty of time to examine the dead man. Were you satisfied that he had been thrown by his horse?"

"If you mean did I like the look of him, I certainly didn't," replied Taverley. "He had a very unhealthy colour. But I don't think I was worrying over the way he died—I was worrying over the fact that he was dead."

"Quite so," said Kendall.

Below, a gong sounded. The butler, Thomas, was breaking the brooding silence, and the metallic music floated up the stairs incongruously.

"We still seem to be carrying on," smiled Taverley.

"Yes, one must eat," answered Kendall. "Do you have two gongs here?"

"Yes. That's the first."

Outside in the passage the inspector sat upon an impulse to swear.

"Why won't anybody tell me the things I really want to know?" he asked himself. "Or have I got a bee in my bonnet?"

He moved thoughtfully towards the staircase, then paused as an idea occurred to him. "I'll give him thirty seconds," he thought, and filled in the time by listening unashamedly at doors. Through one came Bultin's languid voice: "What do you think of Kendall?"

"Everything that is complimentary," came Pratt's. "He may be listening."

Kendall smiled, and passed by the Chaters' door, behind which was grim silence, to the Rowes'. "It's no good—*you* tie it! Why you object to the ready-made bows, I'm damned if I know!"

The thirty seconds were up. He swung round and went back to Taverley's room, turning the handle without knocking. But the door was locked. Had it not been, he would have seen Taverley taking a flask out of a drawer.

"Who's there?" called Taverley, quickly replacing the flask and quietly closing the drawer.

"Kendall—can I come in?" replied the inspector.

The door opened a moment later.

"Do you know what I'm back for?" asked Kendall. "A drink."

Taverley smiled and went to a decanter.

"Ah, you're not a victim of the flask habit," commented Kendall.

"Only sometimes," answered Taverley. "Say when."

"Wonder if Chater was? When!"

"I don't know, but I should say very probably."

"What makes you think that?"

"You want my opinion?"

"I'm asking for it."

"Well," said Taverley, passing the drink, "Chater struck me as a man with a load of trouble on his mind—and as one who would sometimes try to drown it."

"Thanks," replied Kendall. "Here's drowning mine."

He drained the glass and laid it down.

"Do you make a habit of locking your door?" he inquired.

"When a detective's around?" responded Taverley. "Invariably!"

Some one appeared in the passage. It was the sergeant.

"Word with you at once, sir," he said through the open doorway.

Kendall turned and left the room. The sergeant whispered something. The next moment they were hurrying together down the stairs.

Chapter XXV

Dinner Under Difficulties

Whatever their secret thoughts or fears, it was a brave gathering that sat down at the long dining-table that evening. No one was absent saving those whose absence was inevitable; even Zena ignored the necessities of a splitting headache and descended, camouflaged with make-up, to play her part; and the conversation was almost studiously gay while the first half of the meal was being served. No observer, ignorant of the situation, would have guessed that death lurked nearby, and that only a little distance from the glitter of silver and glass and the hum of voices two victims lay silent on a studio floor.

Perhaps one explanation of this apparent callousness was that the horror surrounding the diners was not a personal horror. The victims inspired no private grief, for one was a stranger, the other unloved. But another reason was the definite determination of certain members to fight the horror lest it should shatter the company's morale, and to utilise the forces of reaction.

It was Nadine Leveridge who led the cheerful conversation. At the first threat of silence she launched into an account of her experiences at the hunt, and gave a vivid description of the final stages and the kill. Lord Aveling watched her with grateful admiration, noting how one by one other guests responded to her mood; and once, under cover of an unexpected laugh, he glanced at Zena in the hope that she would join it. He found her staring at her plate, but she looked up quickly, as though conscious of his gaze, and threw him a nervous smile.

Then, encouraged by what he subsequently described as "the damn good sense of the woman," Mr. Rowe told a funny story. It nearly killed Nadine's good work, but Edyth Fermoy-Jones saved the situation by following with another story not intended to be funny. This produced so much merriment that she decided she had meant it to be funny, after all.

"Do you think they'd like to hear about that little experience I had in Belgium a couple of years ago?" said Mr. Rowe to his wife. "You know—the one at the horse show, where I got on the horse and it ran away with me and I won the race!"

That one went better.

But dinner at Bragley Court was a long occasion, and it outlived heroism. The dreaded silence came at last. A butler dropped a plate. Pratt made a humorous comment which fell flat. In the resumed silence, self-consciousness returned, and dark thoughts came winging back.

Suddenly Lord Aveling cleared his throat. A humiliated as well as an anxious host, he could stand it no longer.

"I want—I want to apologise to you all," he said. "I have no words to express my grief that you should have been subjected under my roof to this tragic situation."

"I am sure I am speaking for everybody," replied Earnshaw, through a little murmur of sympathy, "when I say that no one can possibly attach any blame to you."

"Hear, hear!" cried Mr. Rowe emphatically. "It's your funeral, my Lord, as well as ours."

It was not the happiest way to put it.

"Thank you," answered Aveling. "It is true I cannot help what has happened. But I also cannot help feeling responsible, and I wish you all to know that, if I were free, none of you would be under any obligation to stay here."

"What, leave a sinking ship?" exclaimed Mr. Rowe.

"Are we quite sinking?" murmured Pratt, as he received a kick under the table from Mrs. Rowe intended for her husband.

"Well, you know what one means!" retorted Mr. Rowe, frowning. "I'm sure nobody would think of leaving. Why, even if we did, we'd soon have the police after us!"

This time he received the kick.

"Unfortunately, I am afraid that is true," said Aveling. "We seem to be virtually prisoners—I, of course, included. I made myself personally responsible to Inspector Kendall for your remaining here when he left so suddenly, just before dinner."

"Yes, that was certainly mysterious," observed Miss Fermoy-Jones. "I wonder why he went? Does anybody know if he's come back yet?"

"He has not returned, to my knowledge."

"We may not know when he does," murmured Pratt. "He will probably creep back and then pounce upon us. By the way, I hope no one has left any incriminating evidence upstairs? I expect our drawers are being searched while we eat."

"Hardly a joking matter," grunted Mr. Rowe, in an endeavour to get his own back.

"I wasn't joking," replied Pratt. "I happened to mean it. And the locked drawers will be opened first."

"Dear me!" muttered Mrs. Rowe. "They'd hardly do that, would they?"

Nadine found herself glancing at Taverley. He caught her eye, held it for a moment, then turned to Anne.

"You're not being a good advertisement for your father's cellar, Anne," he said, and raised his glass.

Her own glass had not been touched. She smiled and drained it.

"If *I* did that," exclaimed Ruth unexpectedly, "I'd go all wuzzy!"

"I've gone all wuzzy," replied Anne. "Fill it up again, Thomas!" As he did so, she added: "Is your hand wobbling, or is it me?"

It was Thomas who had dropped the plate.

"And yet it seems to me," Mrs. Rowe continued her train of thought, "those police think they can do anything. Do you know, they came into our bedroom and made us open all the cupboards!"

"The sergeant looked under my bed," remarked Nadine. "His reward was a pencil."

"Did he ask you questions?" asked Anne.

"Yes, and I told him all I knew in a single breath to get rid of him. As I knew nothing, it was easy. I suppose he put you through it, too?"

Anne nodded.

"They'd question everybody," said Miss Fermoy-Jones informatively; "and if you told them anything really useful they'd ignore it."

"Did you tell them anything really useful?" inquired Pratt incredulously.

"What I told them—well, I mustn't say anything about it here, because it was told in confidence."

"Well, nobody's asked *us* anything," observed Mr. Rowe in a voice rather aggrieved, "so they've missed some out!"

"I expect they have missed a great many out," Lady Aveling soothed him. "There are over thirty in the house."

"Over thirty?"

"Including the staff."

Mr. Rowe was impressed as well as soothed.

"Over thirty!" he repeated, making a rapid calculation. His arithmetic was irreproachable. "By jove, you must have a tidy wages bill!"

Suddenly conversation ceased. A car was heard in the drive. It was a sound for which many ears were instinctively waiting. The inspector's abrupt departure, unaccompanied by any explanation, had not eased frayed nerves.

"Is this the return of Sherlock?" queried Pratt.

"I'll go and see," replied Anne, jumping up. She stood unsteadily for a moment. "Do you know, people, I believe I *do* feel squiffy!"

"Then I'd better go with you?" suggested Taverley.

But she shook her head, pushed her chair aside, and ran out of the room.

"What did she do that for?" frowned Aveling.

"Well, there's no need for us all to go," answered Lady Aveling, for he looked on the point of following. "She'll be back in a moment."

No one was in the hall when Anne reached it. She stopped abruptly, wondering why she was there. She could not think of any definite reason, saving that the forced gaiety with which the meal had started, and the uneasy, half-irritable conversation which had developed afterwards, had given her an intense desire to escape from the room. Yet the inspector was not likely to prove a comforting alternative. She stood watching the front door, while the sergeant materialised from the back passage and hastened towards it.

The sergeant opened the door. The glow of the car's light illuminated the aperture for a moment before it was blotted out by the portly form of the inspector. He made a dark smudge against the radiance for an instant, then closed the door.

"Well?" asked the sergeant.

Kendall looked at him, and beyond him to Anne. She felt she would have given anything to see a smile dawn on those stern features. The longing was not satisfied. He made a sign to the sergeant, and the two men vanished along the back passage.

Still Anne did not move. She listened to their retreating footsteps, and to the sound of the back door closing. Now they would be walking across the dark lawn to the studio, with its silent occupants, and the picture of Anne with its crimson smear. "Something bad's happened," she thought. "Haven't we had enough?"

Rousing herself, she began to return to the dining-room. Again she stopped. The idea of returning oppressed her. She glanced up the staircase. Should she go and see her grandmother, and help with the jig-saw? But her grandmother had been drowsy when she had left, and suddenly the idea of seeking personal comfort from a tortured body filled her with self-loathing. "Idiot, idiot, idiot!" she rounded on herself. She found she was walking towards the ante-room.

"Hallo!" exclaimed John as she entered. "How terribly nice!"

"Yes, you must be having a lonely time of it," she answered. "I came to see how you were getting on."

"Ai, thanks," he answered. "Will you sit down? Or haven't you finished your dinner yet?"

"I've had all I want—barring coffee. I see they've brought yours. Shall I pour it out?"

"If you'll drink it."

"What about you?"

"I'll have the next cup."

She laughed. But he had a sense that the laugh was caged and hit the bars. He watched her hand as she poured the coffee out. It was not very steady.

"I'm afraid you're having a rotten time, really," she said.

"I've an idea I am really having the best time," he replied.

"Perhaps, after all, you are," she nodded. "It's rather pleasant having you here—you're so absolutely nothing-to-do-with-anything. This room is a sort of refreshing backwater."

"I wish I could help."

"I don't think any one can. We're just sitting around and—waiting. Have they been pestering you?"

"Who? The police?"

"Yes."

"No, I've been left severely alone." He paused. "After all, could I tell 'em anything?"

"No—I suppose not," she answered slowly.

He watched her covertly while she drained her cup.

"Mrs. Leveridge paid me a call just before the police arrived," he went on, "and a constable poked his head in once to ask if I'd seen Mrs. Chater. He seemed to think she might be under the couch! Apart from that—oh, and a short visit from your mother—I've not seen any one till the maid brought me my dinner."

There was a little silence. She sat perfectly still. All at once she exclaimed, "Oh—now yours!" and refilled the cup. Passing it to him, she asked casually, "Did you get to sleep quickly last night? After I left you?"

"Almost at once," he replied.

"Then you didn't hear me come down the second time?"

"No! Did you?"

"Yes. For the book. You probably didn't notice, but I forgot it the first time. *Typhoon*, by Conrad. I believe you'd adore it….A penny for your thoughts!"

"Eh? I was wondering whether I'd read it," he lied.

Actually he had been wondering why she had told him this.

The door opened and Taverley looked in.

"Oh, there you are, Anne," he said. "Are you coming back? I was sent to look for you."

She jumped up immediately.

"Neglecting my duties," she murmured. "Expect I must go and crack nuts."

"Not if you don't want to," answered Taverley. "I'll make your excuses."

"What would the excuses be?"

"Well, isn't Mr. Foss one of your duties?"

"No, I don't look upon him as one," she replied. "I'll come."

"I told you she liked you, Foss," smiled Taverley.

"I told you I liked her," John returned.

"Oh, for God's sake don't let's get mushy!" exclaimed Anne. "That'd finish it!"

She hurried to the door. Taverley's smile faded as he turned and followed her.

Chapter XXVI

Shocks for Earnshaw

Sir James Earnshaw did not join the ladies. The inspector was standing in the hall when the men left the dining-room, and he stepped forward quietly and barred the baronet's way.

"A word with you, sir," he said.

"Certainly," replied Earnshaw.

While the others continued on their way, he stepped back into the dining-room. Kendall followed him and closed the door.

"Now, then," said Kendall. "What did Chater have on you?"

"I beg your pardon?" answered Earnshaw.

"I am afraid there can be no more beating about the bush, sir. We're getting down to hard facts. I know Chater was a blackmailer. He's been jugged for it. I know he came here by your invitation—"

"I have explained that—"

"And I know there's another explanation. I know that Mrs. Chater had some special reason to suspect or fear you—as a matter of fact, I gathered this a little while ago, but now I know it. And I know why she took that knife. Was your door locked at about a quarter to six?"

Earnshaw looked astonished.

"It was," he admitted.

"Any special reason?"

"No. Just a habit when I want to rest."

"Well, if you'd broken the habit that time, I should probably be investigating your murder at this moment, along with the rest. She went to your door."

Earnshaw sat down rather abruptly.

"But—why—?" he began.

"We're coming to that," answered Kendall. "When you went up to your room to change—about five o'clock—?"

"It would have been about that time."

"Mrs. Chater went up just before you. After the bad scene."

"That is correct."

"You know that?"

"I saw her go. Lady Aveling followed her, and returned to say she had locked herself in her room."

"Her room is on the second floor, and yours on the first?"

"That, also, is correct."

"Did she come down again from her room?" As Earnshaw did not answer immediately, he added sharply: "Was she waiting on the first landing when you got there? And did she speak to you? It is only fair to tell you, Sir James, that I know considerably more than I knew an hour and a half ago, so what you tell me will be largely corroboration."

"Thank you—I appreciate the warning," replied Earnshaw. "But there is something *I* should like to know. Is it an official warning? If so, you have not used the right words. Am I under arrest?"

"Certainly not, sir."

"But suspicion?"

"Mrs. Chater's suspicion."

"And yours?"

"That will depend entirely on the result of this interview and your attitude, sir. Any unfounded suspicion can always be disarmed by absolute frankness—even if that frankness is sometimes painful. If it will ease the situation for you, I may add that you are not the only person who may find the world a happier place without Mr. Chater in it."

"That, I confess, is a relief," murmured Earnshaw. "But how are you so sure, now, of Mrs. Chater's suspicions?"

"I have found Mrs. Chater," answered Kendall quietly. "I have seen her."

"Ah."

"But I want your version of certain matters, sir, and that is why I am asking you to tell me exactly what happened when Mrs. Chater stopped and spoke to you on the first landing—if, in fact, you admit that she did?"

Earnshaw stretched out his hand and poured himself out a glass of port.

"Will you have one?" he asked.

The inspector shook his head. Earnshaw raised the glass to his nostrils, drew comfort from the aroma, and then said:

"Mrs. Chater did speak to me, but I take leave to question whether that statement of fact forms an admission on my part. She was, as you doubtless know, in a highly excitable condition. She was on the border of hysteria. An almost chronic condition with her, but at this moment definitely acute. Her husband's death had not been reported at that time—to her, at any rate—and she merely knew that his horse had returned without him. But—yes—she *did* accuse me of having caused an accident. Naturally, I was angry."

"Did you express your anger?"

"In no parliamentary language."

"Could you be a little more explicit?"

"I cannot give you my exact words. I was tired, and the thing came upon me as a surprise. And naturally I did not want any one to come along and find us quarrelling." He paused. "I think I told her to go to her room at once, or I'd—" He paused again.

"What?"

"Send for the police."

"Would that worry her? Would she interpret it as a threat?"

"I don't know how she would interpret it! Yes, perhaps. You see—all this is very distasteful, Inspector—I make no excuses for my anger; but if you had seen the woman—if you knew her as I do—"

"I thought you had never seen her before she came here," interposed Kendall. "Only her husband?" Earnshaw frowned. "But perhaps you meant that you had sized her up even in a few hours?"

"It would not take longer than that to size her up," replied Earnshaw uncomfortably.

"Well, we will leave that for the moment. You were telling me why she might interpret your remark as a threat?"

"Yes. This is where perhaps I was not wise. When she continued to accuse me, I told her that, if any accident did happen to her husband, she might have as good a reason to have caused it as myself."

"Why?"

"They were always quarrelling. I'm sure she hated him."

Kendall nodded.

"So, when she eventually heard that the police had been sent for, she went to your room with a knife. That, on the face of it, might imply either of two things. First, that she wished to be revenged on you for sending for the police—"

"I did not send for the police."

"No. But she might have thought that. Second, that she wished to be revenged on you for causing the death of her husband. Again, I am merely implying her possible motives through what she may have thought, not through necessary facts. But why should she have been so quick to accuse you in her mind? Let us get back to that."

Earnshaw shrugged his shoulders, and suddenly remembered his port. He sipped it.

"Watch me, Inspector," he said with a sudden smile. "See that I do not slip a tablet into my glass to end the business."

"Why should you do that?"

"I haven't the slightest intention of doing that!" retorted Earnshaw. "But if I had murdered Chater, this might be the moment! Mrs. Chater saw me ride off with her husband."

"She also saw Mr. Taverley ride off with her husband, and Miss Aveling. They were all in the party."

"That is true."

"So she must have had another reason. And now, Sir James, we will get back to the very start of this interview, and I will repeat my original question. What did Chater have on you? What was the real reason why you were forced to get him this invitation—so he could look round for fresh victims? Your best protection is the truth, especially when it is liable to be exposed by some one else if you do not expose it yourself?"

"After which, *you* expose it?"

"If necessary. Not otherwise."

A look of angry despair suddenly shot into Earnshaw's eyes. "Hell!" he said. "I expect I've no alternative!" He glanced towards the door. "Well, I'll get it over. Of course, I have no idea what Mrs. Chater has told you—probably she has embellished the facts—but here *are* the facts. Chater's original name was Rawlings."

"And after that became Green," answered Kendall. "When his father turned him out of his business."

"Oh! You know that?"

"It was shortly afterwards that we nabbed him on the blackmailing game."

"That would explain his disappearance for a while. Do you know who took his place in the business?"

"Well, sir, you're supposed to be telling the story."

"Quite so. I took his place. And when he came back after his father died—there was no will, so he got everything—he continued the blackmailing game."

"By blackmailing you?"

"Yes, though not till he'd got through all the money. He'd found—and preserved—a letter and a forged cheque among his father's papers. Of course, I had left then, and was starting my political career—so it was awkward."

"It must have been."

"He only worried me periodically," continued Earnshaw. "He had other irons in the fire. But once the wretched business had begun there was no end to it. There was one break of three or four years. I thought I'd finished with him, but back he came, with a new name and a wife—and a story that matrimony was expensive!"

"Had his father known of your forgery?" asked Kendall.

"Oh, yes," replied Earnshaw. "He had found out. The letter was a confession he made me write, and he was keeping the letter and the cheque till I paid him back in full. His alternative to prosecution. But he died too soon—and his son has had ten times the original amount."

"And has asked for favours, as well as cash?"

"Favours? Oh, I see what you mean. This invitation was the first. If I had refused, my political prospects—and also certain private ones—would have been ruined." He shrugged his shoulders. "Well, now the power passes from him to you. That is, if I find some way of silencing Mrs. Chater."

He regretted the remark as soon as he had made it. In

the circumstances it had an unintentionally sinister ring. He found the inspector looking at him rather hard.

"But I did not silence her husband," said Earnshaw.

"And you won't be able to silence Mrs. Chater," answered Kendall. "I found her at the bottom of a hill, by a smashed bicycle."

Earnshaw looked astounded, then flushed angrily.

"You—you don't mean—?" he began.

"I'm afraid I do," replied Kendall. "She's dead. Sorry, sir, but my job's to get information, and if it isn't given to me the first time, I'm not particular about the method." He turned his head suddenly as a knock came on the door. "Yes? Come in!"

It was Sergeant Price.

"You're wanted, sir," he said. "We've found something."

Chapter XXVII

Contents of a Bag

"Well, what have you found?" asked Kendall, when he had left Earnshaw to his thoughts and joined the sergeant in the hall.

"The black bag, sir," answered the sergeant, with a touch of pride.

"Well done, Price! Where is it?"

"I took it to the studio—thought you might prefer to open it there, with no one around."

"Right. Come along! But where did you find it?"

"In an old shed, under a pile of straw," replied Price, as they made for the back door to the lawn. "I don't suppose you saw any odd bits of straw sticking to that bicycle? In the mudguards or anywhere?"

"Why?"

"There's some oil on the straw. Looks like lamp-oil."

"You mean the bicycle might have been stowed in the shed, as well as the bag?" queried Kendall. "That's very probable. Are you any good at making maps?"

"What sort?"

"I want a map showing certain spots and distances—the studio, the place where the dog was found, the quarry where the man was found, the pool where the knife was found, and the shed where the bag was found."

"You shall have it, sir, though it won't be a work of art. Did you get anything out of Earnshaw?"

"I got a motive."

"Ah!"

"But a motive isn't proof. Earnshaw isn't very fond of me at this moment. I got him to talk through a dirty trick. I was right about that button, Price."

"The one I found outside his door?"

"Have you found any other?"

"Sorry, sir," grinned Price.

"Yes, the one you found outside his door, and that *I* found was missing from Mrs. Chater's dress. Possibly it got loose because nervy people are apt to twiddle with their fingers. Earnshaw's door was locked when Mrs. Chater took the knife, and they had previously had a fuss—just before she saw Bultin put the knife in the drawer—which had given her cause to fear Earnshaw. That woman must have been in a ghastly state. On the verge of breakdown. Terror and revenge chasing each other. Very unpleasant. By the way, I dropped in on the doctor before returning here, and there's no doubt Chater was poisoned, though the Rising Sun proved a wash-out. When are you going to find that flask for me, Price?…Here we are."

They entered the studio, which was now guarded by a rather mournful constable. He did not care much for his company, and welcomed the arrival of living matter.

"They ain't moved," he reported, driving away depression with a callous jest.

"I'll hold you responsible if they do," answered Kendall.

The black bag was on the ground by the ruined portrait. Kendall took the key from his pocket and suddenly smiled.

"Funny if we've been wrong about this key all along," he said.

But the key fitted. In a moment the bag was open, its contents revealed. They were a revolver, a black wig, a small make-up box, and an old plus-four suit.

Kendall took each item out carefully, then broke the revolver.

"Meant for business," he commented, closing it.

He took up the wig and turned towards the man who had been found in the quarry.

"Try the fit, sir?" inquired the sergeant.

"Would you like to?" replied Kendall. "For the moment we'll take that for granted. And the same with the suit."

He opened the small make-up box and regarded the untidy conglomeration of grease-paint, powder, and crêpe-hair in the tray. He lifted the tray. His eyes brightened.

"Hallo, here's something!" he exclaimed.

He took out an envelope. On it was written, "Mark Turner, Esq., Theatre Royal, Stranford, E." He drew a sheet from the envelope and read. Then he passed the letter to the sergeant and turned to the two silent figures. "There are some rats in the world, Price," he said.

The sergeant read the letter, and nodded as he handed it back.

"Who is the lady?" he queried.

"We have five to choose from," answered Kendall. "But it may not be hard to guess the right one. Have *you* got a skeleton, Sergeant?"

"Don't go in for 'em, sir."

"Well, if ever you do, don't pay anybody to keep them locked up—have them out of the cupboard and finish with them."

He walked to the picture and stared at it.

"But where do *you* come in?" he demanded.

"P'r'aps it doesn't come in," the sergeant suggested.

"You may be right there, Price. This may be quite a separate matter. And yet I've a hunch it'll connect up somewhere.…Well, now for the next step."

"The lady?"

"No, there's some one else I think I'll have a few words with first." He had moved to the studio door and was looking along the bush-bordered path towards the lawn and the house. On the previous evening the lights of the ballroom had invaded the shadows, but to-night the ballroom was in darkness, and the lawn received its only glow from a single window. It was towards this window that Kendall's eyes were directed. "Some one I've not seen yet."

"Who's that?"

"The unexpected guest."

"Oh, you mean Foss. He's nothing to do with it, sir," declared the sergeant.

"If you're right, that may make him all the more useful," answered Kendall. "The spectator sees most of the game, and this one has a good view." He added: "And the spectator isn't vitally affected by the result."

"Unless it's on a race-course," murmured the sergeant. "Well, sir, while you're at the house I'll get on with that little map you want. Dinner's over, so if we go on pulling out drawers we may be interrupted."

"I hope you left nothing to show Taverley you've pulled out his?"

"No, sir. That was a neat bit of work, though I sez it as shouldn't. Yes, and precious small change from it! I thought I was going to find a live bomb in it, the way you spoke, and nothing but a score-card of M.C.C. *v.* Somerset."

"And perhaps you'll tell me, Price, why Mr. Harold Taverley, who must have had hundreds of score-cards in his time, should trouble to keep one locked in a drawer?"

"There you are, sir," answered the sergeant.

"Most helpful," said Kendall. "Hallo—somebody on the lawn!"

He darted out of the studio.

Bultin stood his ground and was perfectly composed when the inspector reached him. He was not wearing an overcoat, his badly-tied white tie made an almost impudent spot in the darkness, and his large squash felt hat was tilted at an independent angle.

"Hallo, what are you doing here?" asked Kendall.

"Out of bounds?" inquired Bultin. "Have a cigarette."

"He's trying to get back on his high horse," decided Kendall. "I've given his pride a jolt." Aloud he said, "Yes, to the first. No, to the second."

"Yes, you *are* almost as rude as I am," answered Bultin admiringly.

"Occasionally I try to be. You haven't answered my question."

"Oh, what am I doing here? Enjoying the peaceful atmosphere of an English ancestral home. If that is illegal, arrest me. My prison experiences would bring me a very big cheque."

"Is that all your journalists think about?"

"Of course."

"Then what about an article on 'Thoughts Before Hanging'?"

"That would bring an even bigger cheque, but it would be the last, and I have no progeny. I'd like a signed article, though. Can you tell me who to apply to?"

Kendall shook his head.

"I help you, and you will not help me," observed Bultin. "Very well. Good-night."

He turned away, but felt a hand on his sleeve.

"I'll risk a snub," said Kendall. "Have you found out anything more?"

"You get it," answered Bultin.

"I can stand it," replied Kendall. "You see, Bultin, I don't work for cheques, or for publicity, or for notoriety. Of course, I need my bread and butter, like you, and I'm always ready for a bit of cake if it drops in my mouth. But would it surprise you to learn that I'm keen on my job? Oh, yes. Just an inspector. Nothing special about me. There are thousands just like myself. But I like to see a thing through, and to do that I'm willing to be hurt or to hurt others. Am I saying things you understand, or is this double-Dutch?"

Bultin did not answer for a few moments. He understood perfectly. The question was whether he should admit it. Altruism, humanity, the common good, ideals beyond Self—these were his early companions, when his feet had stumbled over shifting sand. He had scrapped them years ago so that he could plant himself on hard ground.

"I can make up my mind about most things," said Bultin. "But I can't make up my mind whether I like you, Kendall."

"I'm quite ready to like you," responded Kendall. "You've helped me a lot."

"I can only repeat, you are not helping me."

"My job's to help justice, not journalism."

"A good alliteration? Do they conflict?"

"Not necessarily. Otherwise I wouldn't be talking to you. I'm not doing it to supply you with titbits for your column."

"Are there any titbits?"

"Maybe. Is your word to be trusted?"

"That is why I so rarely give it."

"Would you give it to me, in exchange for the first rights of a story, blue-pencilled by me? I wouldn't blue-pencil the fact that Lionel Bultin made me look for a black bag I've found."

"Ah!"

"It has given me the identity of, to use your phrase, Body Number One."

"Really?"

"And I've found the bicycle—also first mentioned by Lionel Bultin. And I've found Mrs. Chater beside it—stone dead."

Bultin stared. Kendall deduced that Sir James Earnshaw had not passed any news on.

"But I haven't found how, when or where Mr. Chater was poisoned, or by whom."

"You know there is a Chinese cook?" said Bultin.

"Who had no possible reason to poison Chater," answered Kendall. "The sergeant has been into the food question, and has put a few questions to him, and is quite satisfied on that point. We are a bit too quick to suspect the Orient! Any more suggestions?"

"No, not at the moment," replied Bultin slowly. "But I might have later, if I were free to roam again."

"That's what I wanted!" exclaimed Kendall. "You've got the type of mind I need. If I give you your freedom—even to go in the studio, if you like—will you give me my blue pencil?"

Bultin nodded. The inspector promptly took one from his pocket.

"Then here's for a start," he said, and wrote on a card. "Show that if any of my men challenge you—and don't boast to the other guests about your special privileges. You can boast when it's all over and you've shown the police how to do their own work!"

"I shall make a point of it," replied Bultin, pocketing the card.

Chapter XXVIII

John's Turn

"I hoped I was going to be let off," said John, as the inspector entered the ante-room.

"I don't let anybody off, sir, if I think they can tell me anything," answered Kendall.

"What makes you think I can tell you anything?" asked John.

"Well, for one thing, you haven't denied it," replied Kendall. "For another, a good deal has happened yesterday and to-day not far from your door and window. For another, some one has suggested I won't waste my time with you."

"Who?"

"I'll keep that to myself, if you don't mind."

But John guessed rightly that it was Pratt.

"I can understand your hesitation," continued Kendall, as John did not respond immediately. "You feel in a difficult position. You've been shown hospitality, and you don't like the idea of casting any reflections on anybody. That's a natural and a right sentiment. I'd feel the same in your place. But—well, we've got beyond that stage. If you've anything to tell, you may help to prevent me from arresting the wrong person."

"Do you suspect any one particular, then?" asked John.

"I know at least two people who had strong motives for murder."

"Guests?"

"I'm asking the questions, sir."

"Sorry," said John, "but I'm not used to this sort of thing."

He would have given much to be out of the business. He had decided that he would say nothing unless circumstances forced him to. The circumstances were now all too evident. If the inspector was already forming suspicions, how could he withhold what he knew? "Well, I'll start the ball rolling," he thought, "and see where it leads."

"There was a fuss outside this room late last night," he began. "Quite a bad one."

"What time?"

"I can't say exactly. Soon after one."

"It woke you up?"

"Yes. No, it was the dog that woke me up. That time."

"Oh, then there was another time? Well, we'll have that later. Please go on."

"I also heard glass breaking. Then the barking stopped—"

"For good?"

"I believe so. I was a bit muzzy. I don't remember hearing it any more. Then, shortly after that, the row in the hall started. It was between two men. One was Chater, the other was a butler named Thomas." Kendall's eye lighted. "They seemed to have bumped into each other by accident and were trying to find out why the other was there. I gathered in the middle that Chater had some sort of a hold over the butler—"

"Yes, but wait a moment!" interrupted Kendall. "This won't do! Can't you remember the actual conversation?"

John repeated it as far as he could recall, and the inspector listened intently. When he had finished, Kendall went into the hall and returned immediately. Then he walked to the window, raised the blind, looked out, and lowered it.

"And the butler, you believe, went back to his room?" he asked.

"Yes," replied John.

"And Chater went out?"

"Yes."

"When did he return?"

"Just after half-past one."

"You heard a clock strike?"

"There's one in the hall. Strikes the half-hours."

"Then this might have been one, and not half-past?"

"I looked at my watch immediately after Chater had come back and gone upstairs. It was twenty-five minutes to two."

"Let me see your watch now."

John showed it to him. Kendall went into the hall again, and again returned at once.

"You're half a minute fast by the hall clock," he said. "Have you altered it to-day?"

"No."

"Good time-keeper?"

"It gains a minute a week."

"What time did Chater go out after the row? Any idea?"

"Only a rough one. About ten past one. Don't take that as accurate, though—just a guess. Might be a minute or two earlier."

"You think he was outside twenty minutes?"

"That was my idea."

"But he took four or five minutes to go upstairs, after returning?"

"Yes, and I don't know where he went then, or what he did."

"Can you remember this, Mr. Foss? Get your mind back to the last time you heard the dog bark. Was it before or after you heard the breaking of the glass?"

"After," answered John. "As a matter of fact, the breaking of the glass came into a dream, and I only realised the sound was actual just after I woke up."

"I see. And it was about one. How do you know that?"

"Only another guess. Working backwards."

"Well, if it's a good guess, we may say that the glass broke at about one a.m., the dog's last bark was at—a minute past—?"

"Say two minutes past, if you want to be particular," interrupted John. "It barked three or four times."

"Then we'll put the last bark at two minutes past one. And the row at four or five past, till ten past."

"That won't be far out."

"Of course, the barking came from across the lawn?"

"Yes."

"What was the last bark like?"

"I've an impression it wasn't particularly nice, but that may just be retrospective exaggeration. You see, I know now what happened."

"Quite so. Do you remember whether the final bark was as close as the previous barking?"

"No, it was farther away."

"As though the dog was barking while it ran?"

"Definitely."

"That fits. Well, now, let's get to the other time you woke up. No, wait a moment, though. Was there anything else you can recall between one and one-thirty? Even if it seems trivial, it may be important."

"I believe I heard a gasp," answered John, with hesitation.

"When?"

"Just before the row."

"That might have been Thomas when he heard Chater coming down the stairs?"

"It might."

"Only you know it wasn't!" commented Kendall, with a smile. "How do you know it wasn't? Wrong gender?"

"You can't always tell the gender of a gasp," fenced John.

"Not always, but you could this one," replied Kendall, "and you are now ready to lie to save a lady's honour. But we know, from the conversation between Chater and Thomas, that Thomas is rather fond of Bessie?"

"I never thought of that," murmured John.

"And we know that Chater had some hold over Thomas. Was he threatening to expose a love affair? Well, I'll find that out when I interview Thomas. Meanwhile, let's talk about the other time you woke up, and what woke you."

John wrenched his mind to the occasion. He was growing a little dizzy. He was convinced it was not Bessie who had gasped, yet he had no desire to express his doubt....

"You know, I'm getting muddled," he confessed. "It was the dog that woke me both times."

"Was this other time before or after one o'clock?"

"Before."

"Do you know how long before?"

"Half an hour."

"You heard the hall clock strike?"

"Yes, and thought it was one or half-past. But my watch corrected me."

"Anything happen?"

"Nothing of importance. I just heard Lord Aveling going upstairs."

"Was he talking to himself?" inquired Kendall.

"No," answered John. "Why?"

"Did his boots have a particular squeak?"

"Yes, I see what you mean," said John, trying not to flush. "How did I know it was Lord Aveling? I didn't say he was alone!"

"But your chivalry was quite ready to imply it. I'm sorry I'm so annoying. Am I right in thinking that Lord Aveling did not go upstairs last night at 12.30 with Lady Aveling?"

"Of course, that sounds perfectly horrible, and I agree you are annoying!" retorted John. "I heard him saying good-night to Miss Wilding, who had been reading a play to him. You know she is an actress?"

"I have seen her act."

"Well, so that's in order. Lady Aveling knew she was reading the play to him."

"If that is true, her knowledge must have been a matter of regret to Mr. Chater," remarked Kendall dryly. "But you are making a mountain of this, not I. Did anything else occur?"

"Nothing else."

Kendall removed his eyes from John and fixed them on the opposite wall.

"I am sure you are keeping nothing you think vital from me," he said. "But unless, like nearly everybody else here, you have some personal axe to grind, there is no need to. Outside my job, I'm not interested in scandal. I have even mentioned this fact to our friend Mr. Bultin. Now, is it your private opinion that Lord Aveling and Miss Wilding are having an affair?"

"Is my private opinion of any value?" demanded John.

"On this point it is."

"I can't see it."

"You shouldn't have to. You should trust my sight. But I'll tell you, Mr. Foss. Do you know the sort of man Chater was?"

"He didn't appeal to me."

"Do you know he was a professional blackmailer?"

"That doesn't surprise me."

"And that if Lord Aveling and Miss Wilding were having an affair, and he got to know of it, they would both have motives for wanting him to be out of the way?"

"Look here!" exclaimed John. "You're surely not suggesting—?"

"I am not suggesting anything. I am just giving you some elementary reasoning."

"Very well, then. Here's my private opinion. Lord Aveling may or may not be interested in Miss Wilding, but I am convinced she is not having an affair with him. Will that do?"

"I expect it will have to, unless I bring the question up again," replied Kendall, "which I shall do if necessary. Did you hear anybody else in the hall between twelve-thirty and one?"

"Nobody. I went to sleep very soon afterwards."

"And woke up at one."

"Yes, as I've told you."

"And kept awake till one-thirty-five. And then?"

"I slept."

"At once?"

"Pretty well."

"And didn't wake any more?"

"There was no dog to wake me."

"That's hardly an answer."

"No, I didn't wake any more." To himself he thought, "There, now I've done it! Perjury! Well, if I'm hauled up for it, I'll take what's coming!"

Kendall looked thoughtful, then suddenly rose.

"Well, that's that," he said. "And now for our friend Thomas."

Chapter XXIX

The Troubles of Thomas

When Thomas heard that the inspector wanted him, he did a very foolish thing. He ran. All that trying day his nerves had been getting worse and worse. He dropped plates, jumped at shadows, and endured spasms of violent heart-beating. Even Bessie's attempts to sooth him had been unavailing, and now he was crowning his chaotic condition by flight.

But the inspector ran faster and caught him up by the stables. For a few moments he hung limply in Kendall's grip. Then Kendall's words sent his limp form rigid.

"Now, then, let's have it," barked the inspector. "Where did you get that poison?"

"Poison?" gasped Thomas.

"Never heard the word?" asked Kendall.

"I didn't take it—I swear I didn't—I was going to, but I didn't."

Kendall rejoiced secretly, while his stern features gave no sign of the rejoicing. He was getting somewhere at last. The truth was emerging out of panic.

"Well, tell your story," he ordered, "and remember while you're telling it that I know most of it already. You didn't know that some one was awake in the ante-room last night at one o'clock, did you, and heard your little business with Mr. Chater?"

Thomas's heart beat wildly. What had been said during those wretched minutes? He could hardly remember. It had all been too quick, and too confusing, and too painful. In his hopeless bewilderment he was driven now to the right course, and decided to tell the facts.

"It—it was only an idea, sir—I swear it was," he blurted out. "I meant to get it because—because I was off my head, sir, that's a fact! But I didn't mean it for anybody—at least—no, I meant it for myself. And then I changed my mind—well, you can prove that!"

"We'll do the proving in a minute, my man," retorted Kendall, "but first I want to know who you *did* mean that poison for?"

"I told you, myself—"

"And you told me a lie." Kendall had not missed those self-condemning words, "at least." "Perhaps you did change your mind. Perhaps you did think that, if matters went too wrong, you'd end them with a dose. But you had some one else in your thoughts first, and as I know already who it is, you'd better not try to hide it. There's only one thing that can save you, and that's the truth—every little letter of it. One slip may hang you."

"Oh, my God!" muttered Thomas, and nearly crumpled again.

"Take your time, if you need it," said Kendall.

But Thomas merely swallowed, and then his words came with a rush. He wanted to get it over.

"It was about one of the maids," he gulped. "She and I, we're engaged, and—well, you know how certain people look at a pretty girl. And when Mr. Pratt wanted her to be a model—she told me once, and I heard it myself the next time—well, you know what happens—"

His voice trailed off, and he suddenly took out his handkerchief and wiped his streaming forehead.

"Jealousy-phobia," reflected Kendall, while he asked, "Did Bessie agree?"

"Bessie? Oh, of course, you know who it is. No, not then. But he was pestering her—she said he wasn't, but one's got eyes—and—well—"

"And so you thought you'd get a bit of your own back by ruining Mr. Pratt's picture?"

Thomas was silent.

"Go on!" ordered Kendall sharply. "Everything. What happened after you ruined the picture?"

"I was sorry I'd done it afterwards," mumbled Thomas. "I'd happened to find the door unlocked. The key was in it. And then, a bit later, I went back to see if I could do anything about the picture—make it a bit better—and it was then that—"

He stopped dead.

"Yes?" said Kendall.

"Somebody caught me," muttered Thomas.

"Well, go on! Who?"

"The—the man that was found in the quarry, sir," answered Thomas tremulously. "I don't know who he is. I'd never seen him before. But he came running into the studio—I didn't know if he was running after me, or to get away from anybody else—anyhow, he got in, and, well, saw what I'd done."

"Half a moment," interrupted Kendall. "What time was that?"

"Time, sir?"

"Yes. Pull yourself together. Let's have all this clear. When did you go into the studio first and spoil the picture?"

"It was during tea, sir. I'd seen Mr. Pratt leave the studio with Mr. Rowe, and on his way to his room he asked Bessie again about being a model. You may think there's nothing in it, but I know what happens—"

"Yes, so you said before. Don't get excited. And the second time in the studio? The time you were caught?"

Thomas pressed his hand to his forehead and thought.

"I should say about an hour later. No, more. An hour and a half."

"Get your mind on it, my man! Five? Half-past five? Six? Half-past six? Seven—?"

"Half-past six," interposed Thomas. "Yes, it must have been. A bit after."

"That'll do. The first time, round about five, eh?"

"Yes, sir. It struck five almost as soon as I got back."

"Then we can say a bit before five for the first visit, and a bit after half-past six for the second. Right. Go on. How did the man find out that you had ruined the picture?"

"Well, you see, sir, at first I thought it was Mr. Pratt, and I said quickly that I hadn't done it. I'm telling you everything—"

"You'll be a fool if you don't!"

"And when I turned and found it was this man, I'd given myself away. I expect he saw I was upset. Anyhow, he said he'd tell on me if I didn't do something for him."

"What was that?"

"Take a note."

"Who to?" As Thomas hesitated, he repeated sharply: "Who to? Don't hide anything!"

"Miss Wilding, sir," answered the butler miserably. "He wrote it there, in the studio, while I waited. Then I left, but he stayed inside, because people were about. I hid behind a bush. One of the people was Mr. Pratt. That was the time he went in and—and found what I'd done."

"Why did you wait?"

"Well, sir, I wanted to see what would happen. You see, this man was inside…and then I thought there was somebody by the back door, but I might have been wrong about that. It was dark."

"Was Mr. Pratt inside the studio long?"

"No, sir. Only a few minutes. I listened for a row, but there was nothing. The man must have hidden somewhere, because Mr. Pratt came out again alone and locked the studio, and then he nearly caught me. I just managed to get away in the dark."

"Without his seeing who you were?"

"He couldn't have, sir, or I'd have heard of it."

"Nobody saw you?"

"I—I think Mr. Chater did."

"He'd have a shot," commented Kendall grimly. "What makes you think he did?"

"He came to the stairs when I was giving the note to Miss Wilding. I thought there was nobody about—I'd been told to give it only when there wasn't anybody looking—but Mr. Chater suddenly came, out of nowhere, like, and made her drop the envelope. He picked it up for her, and then she went off with it."

"I suppose Chater had a good look at the writing on the envelope before he gave it back?"

"I expect so, sir."

"Well? Did you have any trouble with Mr. Chater?"

"Not then, sir. But—it was funny—he seemed to be everywhere. Even when—"

He stopped again, and terror re-entered his eye.

"Even when—?" prompted Kendall. "If you're innocent, you won't hang."

"I am innocent, sir," replied Thomas earnestly. "I mean, about everything but the picture. I did that. I'm admitting it. It'll get me the sack. But what's the good? Only I didn't do anything else. Except—well—think about it."

"You're talking now about the poison?"

"Yes, sir." Thomas's voice was very low.

"Where was the poison?"

"Where it still is, sir—in the cook's bedroom."

"In the cook's bedroom," repeated Kendall slowly, as though he were checking the information and not receiving it. "Go on."

"That's where I was going to get it from."

"When?"

"In the night. The time I had the fuss with Mr. Chater."

"How did you know it was there?"

"Like this, sir: The chef is Chinese. He's all right, though, only you never know what's going on in his head. I got talking to him. I was nearly off my *own* head—that's a fact. I'm not making excuses. I'm just telling you. I wondered whether to finish it—not only about the picture, but Bessie—thinking I might lose her; we'd had a quarrel, you see—and so I said to the cook, 'How would *you* finish yourself if you decided to?' We talk about things."

"That's all right. Go on."

"He said, 'This way,' and he made as if he was putting something into his mouth. 'Velly quick,' he said—that's how they talk—'velly quick, no pain, all over.' 'Yes, but where would you get it?' I asked him, and told him you couldn't get it, not in this country, without signing things. So then he said—these were the words—'I no need to get it; I got it, in little cupboard over my bed, all ready,' he said, 'if I ever get big pain I can't stand.' 'Aren't you afraid some one'll steal it?' I said. 'Oh, no,' he said. 'Keep cupboard locked and key always in pocket.'"

"Well?"

"It was then, sir," went on the butler, twisting his head round as though searching for ghosts, "that I wondered if—if Mr. Chater had been listening."

"Why did you wonder that?"

"I thought I heard somebody, but when I looked round they'd gone."

"Only thought?"

"No, sir, I'm sure."

"What made you think it was Chater?"

"I'd felt he was watching me, ever since he saw me give that letter to Miss Wilding."

"Where was this? Where did you have your talk with the chef?"

"In a passage."

"What passage?"

"Near his bedroom. It's between the hall and the servants' quarters."

"Then his bedroom is near the hall?"

"Yes, sir."

"Let's go to that passage. No, wait a moment. What time did this conversation occur?"

"It was soon after dinner started, sir. As a matter of fact, I was bringing away a tray."

"Why wasn't the cook in the kitchen?"

"I don't know, sir. He pops about."

"Yes, perhaps that's not important. But this is: If the conversation occurred during dinner, how could Mr. Chater have heard it?"

"Well, sir," answered Thomas, "I found out something that made me all the more sure it was him. I found out he was late for dinner."

"Oh!" exclaimed Kendall. "You're certain of that?"

"Yes, sir."

"How are you certain?"

"Bessie told me, sir. You see, thinking it had been him, I asked her, and she'd seen him snooping about—I mean, she'd seen him—"

"Snooping was right. Yes?"

"Eh? It was on the first floor, outside Miss Wilding's bedroom."

"And Miss Wilding was down in the dining-room?"

"Yes, sir. All the guests were seated, I found out when the meal started. All but Mr. Chater, I mean."

"But didn't you notice his empty chair yourself?" demanded Kendall. "Why did you have to ask Bessie?"

"I wasn't in the dining-room till after the soup—the time I came away with the tray."

"I see. And had your chat with the cook in the passage. I suppose it was then you decided to get the poison?"

"Yes, sir," muttered Thomas.

"When did you change your mind?"

"Well, I don't know that I'd ever made up my mind, really. When I met Mr. Chater in the night—well, even then I was only thinking about it, as you might say, but of course that ended it. I guessed then that he'd heard—"

"But he made other suggestions, according to what I have been told about your conversation."

"What's that, sir?"

"About you and Bessie. Was Bessie there? In the night?"

"No, sir!" replied Thomas, with sudden emphasis.

"Is that the truth or gallantry?"

"The truth, sir. It was when Mr. Chater spoke about that—about me and Bessie, who's a good girl—that I tried to hit him. I don't know if you heard about that?"

"I did. And, though one isn't supposed to speak ill of the dead, it's a pity you missed him. But some one was there before you and Chater. Some one was in the hall, Thomas. Didn't you know that?"

"Well, sir, I did think I heard a sound, but I couldn't be sure."

"What sound?"

"A sort of gasp, sir."

"Male or female?"

"More like a woman, sir. No, I don't know. I wasn't in a condition."

Kendall looked at the butler hard.

"There's something in your mind, Thomas," he said, "and I want it. If a woman gasped, and if that woman wasn't Bessie—"

"It wasn't, I've told you!" interrupted the butler.

Kendall's method was to ride over everything that interfered with justice, but he always sympathised with men who defended womenfolk, truthfully or otherwise. His attitude to the butler had softened since the beginning of the interview, and he spoke now quite kindly.

"I am accepting your word that it wasn't Bessie. I'm sure you are telling me the truth. But I want you to go on telling me the truth. Who do you think that person was?"

Thomas hesitated, despite the inspector's encouraging tone.

"I may be wrong, sir," he muttered after a silence.

"Let me judge that," replied Kendall.

"Well, sir, I thought it might be Miss Wilding—you see, I'd given her that letter. And, then, the back door being open. But, of course, that's only what I thought."

"It may be quite a useful thought," answered Kendall. "Now, then, we'll go back to the house and you'll show me that passage, and the cook's room. If the poison is still in his little cupboard—well, we'll see."

Chapter XXX

Origins of Evil

The Chinese cook was interested, but showed no emotion when he received an order to meet the inspector in his bedroom. He entered blandly, glanced at Thomas, and waited. Kendall did not keep him waiting long.

"I understand you keep some poison in that cupboard over your bed," said Kendall, driving straight to the point.

"You tell him that?" asked the cook, glancing again at Thomas.

"Yes, he told me," replied Kendall. "I made him. Is it true?"

The Chinaman gave a little shrug, then nodded.

"You know it is wrong?"

"To you, not to me," answered the Chinaman.

"Are you ill?"

"Once I had velly bad pain."

"I'm sorry. But I'm afraid I must see that poison."

"You take it away?" inquired the Chinaman.

"I'm asking to see it."

For a few moments the Chinaman did not move. Perhaps he was summoning philosophy to combat a grief his placid features did not reveal. Then, with another little shrug, he moved quietly to the head of the bed and took a key from his pocket.

"Don't touch the front of the cupboard!" exclaimed Kendall suddenly.

The Chinaman obeyed, carefully inserted the key, turned it, and opened the small door.

After that, something did happen to his face. Kendall was watching it in preference to the cupboard. Amazement shot momentarily into the usually inscrutable eyes. But the moment passed. The smooth features became quiet again.

"Do you sleep heavily?" inquired Kendall.

There was an alarm clock by the bed.

The Chinaman did not reply; he turned towards Thomas, whose mouth was gaping.

"Well?" said Kendall.

"I never took it—I swear I didn't!" muttered the butler, his forehead wet.

"Some one did," answered Kendall. He addressed the Chinaman again. "Have you any idea who?"

The Chinaman remained silent, his eyes still on Thomas.

"Was he the only one you told?" Kendall demanded sharply.

"Nobody else," replied the Chinaman.

"Do you read in bed?"

"Velly bad habit."

"What time did you go to bed last night?"

"Eleven."

"And went to sleep at once?"

"Yes."

"Were you disturbed in the night?"

"No."

"Did you wake up at all?"

"Not till the clock sound."

"And that was?"

"Six."

"This poison. What was it?"

"I bring it from China. You do not know it. Velly quick. No pain. Velly sensible to stop pain."

"What was it in? Box? Bottle?"

"Little glass tube."

"Fluid?"

"Yes."

"Easily poured into something?"

"Velly easy."

"Such as a flask."

"Yes."

"Or you could drink it straight from the tube?"

"Velly easy."

"Thank you. That will do. Leave the cupboard open and the key where it is. You may have to find a bed somewhere else to-night. I want this room, and it will be locked. Out of it, the pair of you—and no talking!"

He followed them out and locked the door. The China-man faded away into the shadows, but in response to a word Thomas followed the inspector along the passage.

"I didn't take it," repeated Thomas dully.

"I haven't said you did," answered Kendall. "Have you anything more to tell me?"

"I don't think so, sir."

"Think again. About Miss Wilding?"

"No, sir."

"About Chater?"

"No, sir. At least—"

"Go on!"

"It's not important, but I don't want to keep anything back. This morning there was another little scene. He had me in his room and told me I'd got to be ready to do anything he wanted. It was shortly before they all went to the Meet. Then Bessie happened to come along the passage with a tray, and after he'd sent me out he called her in. She didn't want to go, and she was only there for a few moments. I took it that he did it to spite me, knowing how I felt."

"Very likely. Of course, it didn't make you love him any more?"

"No, sir."

"But that was *after* the poison had been stolen, so it wouldn't affect what happened last night."

"Of course—that's right, sir!" exclaimed Thomas, brightening. "I'd forgotten that."

His relief was almost pathetic.

"Then here's something to remember, Thomas," replied Kendall, as he beckoned to the approaching sergeant. "Many people who never dreamed they could commit murder have done so through jealousy. Watch yours. It's no good. Not to anybody."

He moved away from the butler and went to meet the sergeant.

"More fingerprint work for you, Price," he said. "Cook's room this time. See if you can find anything on the cupboard over the bed. Also on the key to it. But I'm afraid I'm going to be disappointed—people are too wise nowadays to leave obvious clues about, and I was too late with the key anyway. Bad slip, that. Anyway, have a shot. Here's the key to the bedroom door, and see nobody else gets hold of it."

"What was in the cupboard?" asked the sergeant.

"A child could guess," answered Kendall. "Poison. Details later. I've got to see Miss Wilding."

But as he reached the top of the stairs to the first floor he heard footsteps behind him. He turned and found Bultin's face looming at him languidly.

"Would a small glass tube, empty, be of any interest to you?" inquired Bultin in a bored voice.

"Where the devil did you find that?" exclaimed Kendall.

"It's in the studio," answered Bultin, "inside the leather turn-up of Chater's hat. Oh, and you needn't trouble to interview Miss Wilding. I've had a little heart-to-heart with her, and Body No. One was her husband."

"Oh, *was* he?" retorted Kendall. "Well, you can go and have another little heart-to-heart with her, and tell her that he wasn't! He had one wife already!"

Chapter XXXI

Almost the Truth

"Before reconstructing the events at Bragley Court which I was called upon to investigate," wrote Detective-Inspector Kendall in the final pages of his packed note-book, "I will briefly set down certain salient facts connected with the principal dramatis personae, as revealed by the various interviews and conversations already described, or as deduced from other information or discoveries.

"Henry Chater. Professional blackmailer. (Already known.) Original name, Rawlings. Dismissed from his father's business. Served term of imprisonment under name of Green. Swore would never repeat experience. (Refer current records.) But repeated the offences. Married under name of Chater. Situation at time of visit to Bragley Court: Had Sir James Earnshaw (q.v.) under his thumb, and received invitation through him. Object of visit, to keep his eye on Zena Wilding (q.v.) in order to increase pressure on Mark Turner (q.v.). Also to find fresh possible victims. Affairs getting in a tangle. Short of cash. (Refer letter to Mark Turner.) Probably feared Turner behind cool demeanour. Probably feared Earnshaw also. May have feared others. Previous observations indicate that fear was dominant, though usually well hidden, in his character, and that his criminal habits were developed through original weakness—that 'first slip' that leads to others—rather than through a natural bold callousness. Health not good. Fond of drink, but had been warned against strong drink. Safe deduction—unhappy with his wife.

"Mrs. Chater. No information about her. Depressed, neurotic woman, probably suffering from acute repression. Probably, or possibly, one of Chater's victims.

"Sir James Earnshaw, M.P. Public character in terror of his past. Succeeded Chater in his father's business, forged his employer's signature on cheque, was not prosecuted, but Chater in due course discovered this, using the knowledge for blackmailing purposes. Arranged Chater's invitation to Bragley Court, under pressure, but in a mood to rebel.

"Zena Wilding. Actress. Believed herself to be Mrs. Mark Turner. Met Turner three years ago on tour, had affair with him, and as result went through form of marriage. Hated him, and left him immediately, never acknowledging marriage publicly, and trying to shake him off.

"Mark Turner. Actor. Unsuccessful. Failure due to wine, women, and natural lack of talent. Never told Zena Wilding he was married, and after his affair with her, he married her in the hope that his real wife would never turn up. She did not, but Chater did, Turner's real wife being Chater's sister. This explains Chater's knowledge. Mrs. Turner died soon afterwards, but this did not make the marriage with Zena Wilding valid. Chater threatened Turner that he would expose true position to Zena Wilding, and bled Turner, who in his turn sponged on Zena Wilding. She gave him money to keep him out of the way. This was one reason why Turner wanted the truth kept from her—she would never have married him a second time, and he would have lost his hold over her. Another reason was that he continued to desire her, and retained his hope that one day she would return to him. Chater increased pressure and threatened to expose him to Zena Wilding at Bragley Court. Turner made counter-threat of following Chater to Bragley Court. Chater wrote again, explaining Turner's delicate position to him, conveying further threats, making further demands, and telling him not to be a fool. (See correspondence found in Turner's bag.)

"Leicester Pratt. Artist. Painting picture of Lord Aveling's daughter, Anne. Made suggestions to a maid, Bessie (q.v.), that she would make a good artist's model.

"Bessie Hill. Maid at Bragley Court. Definitely attractive, and engaged to Thomas Newson (q.v.).

"Thomas Newson. Butler. Mad with jealousy. No brains. Weak, impulsive, acting on the moment, and regretting afterwards. Angry with Pratt for suggesting Bessie should be a model. Angry with anybody who looks at Bessie.

"Leng. Chinese cook. Kept poison in cupboard over his bed, to put himself to permanent sleep should he ever desire it."

Kendall paused in his writing. He had come across trouble of most kinds; had watched men suffer mentally and physically; had seen their edifices crumble to the ground. "Do any of us know what lies ahead of us?" he reflected. "Even the most confident? Shall I mark this Chinaman down a wise fellow?"

He resisted the temptation, stretched, and resumed:

"In the following reconstruction, I shall confine myself as far as possible to matter bearing directly or indirectly on the five mysteries which succeeded each other in this order: (1) the ruining of Pratt's picture; (2) the death of the dog, Haig; (3) the death of Mark Turner; (4) the death of Henry

Chater; and (5) the disappearance of Mrs. Chater. Where times are mentioned, it will be understood that in most cases these are approximate.

"It is interesting to note that the particular form assumed by the tragedies moving towards Bragley Court were largely dictated by nothing more than a spasm of jealousy that had nothing whatever to do with them, but we must begin the reconstruction at just over four and a half hours before this spasm occurred, when the 12.10 train from London drew in at Flensham station. Four guests were on this train—the Rowes and Harold Taverley—but our attention concentrates on a fifth passenger who alighted. Mark Turner.

"He was not concerned with the four guests. He may have seen them leave by car for Bragley Court, but the guests he was interested in, and who he knew were due to arrive that day, were not on this particular train.

"So he waited for the next, filling in the time by taking strolls (never without the black bag he had brought with him), and having lunch at the inn by the station—the Black Stag. When at the inn he sat by the window overlooking the platform. He was in a highly-strung condition.

"But the next train, arriving at 3.28, gave him another disappointment. It brought two more guests—Mrs. Leveridge and John Foss, the latter an accidental one—but not the guests he was watching for.

"Turner did not give up. Nothing would have induced him to. He was a man with a fixed purpose from which it would have been impossible to divert him. He found that the next train would not arrive till 5.56, took another stroll (still keeping his bag with him), returned to the inn at five, and had tea. He left the inn just before the 5.56 drew in, and he saw Zena Wilding, the Chaters and Bultin alight.

"He was standing near the car that was waiting to take them to Bragley Court. He intruded himself in front of the woman who believed she was his wife—Zena Wilding. Confused and terrified (not only because she hated the man, but because his presence might interfere with her plans and Lord Aveling's interest in her), she pretended not to know him and entered the car. Chater, with sang-froid, pretended similar ignorance, and coolly offered a light to the fellow he was blackmailing. But he uttered a quiet warning and then entered the car himself. The car drove off.

"What Turner's exact intention was at the station is not quite clear. He may merely have wished, at this point, to ascertain the arrival of the Chaters and his alleged wife, or some scheme may have gone awry through accidental circumstances or the momentary loss of nerve. I am inclined to think, however, that up till now Turner's purpose was more fixed than his plan, and that he followed blind impulse when he started running after the car.

"But he did not have to run far, and it is possible that he had already noted the woman's bicycle against the gate in his previous strolls. In any case, he stole it, and probably rode it faster than it had ever been ridden before.

"He reached Bragley Court about twenty minutes after the car. Avoiding the front entrance, he found his way round to the back, and hid the cycle in a shed. The cycle was placed on a pile of straw in a dark corner, and the bag was concealed beneath the straw. Later he would need both, but for the moment he wanted to be free to reconnoitre.

"He began to approach the house from the back, passing near the studio.

"Physical passion and physical desire are at the root of countless tragedies. Nearly two hours previously it had driven another man to commit a crime (though not so great a crime as Turner contemplated), and this other man was already repenting his action. Let us at this point consider the case of Thomas, the butler.

"Pratt had twice suggested to Bessie, Thomas's fiancée, that she would make a good artist's model. Pratt may not have meant it seriously, but Thomas, the inflamed, jealous lover, took it seriously. His jealousy and possessiveness swept over his judgment, drowning it. He followed Bessie, quarrelled with her, and acting upon a sudden, uncontrollable impulse when accident gave him the opportunity, he entered Pratt's studio at a time when it was inadvertently unlocked, and ruined the picture Pratt was painting.

"He had committed this act at about ten minutes to five, while Turner was returning to the Black Stag for his tea, but the act had not yet been discovered. And now Thomas was back in the studio, wondering whether he could find any means of remedying his vandalism.

"It so happened that, also at about this time, Harold Taverley was returning from a stroll.

"Time now becomes an important element in the sequence of events, and the following time-table will explain how the clock now played its part in joining separate stories and weaving them into a tangled whole. While the exact times given below could not be sworn to in a court of law, they may be taken as sufficiently accurate to cover present purposes:

"6.33 p.m.—Turner leaves cycle in shed, concealing his bag in the straw.

"6.35 p.m.—Thomas enters the studio, and wonders whether he can get rid of the blemish he has made on the picture.

"6.38 p.m.—Turner, making his way towards the back of the house, finds himself by the studio. He hears some one behind him. This is Harold Taverley, returning from a short stroll in the wood. He dives into the studio. Thomas, terrified, imagines it is Pratt, and exclaims (with characteristic lack of intelligence), "I didn't do it!" Turner claps his hand over Thomas's mouth. Taverley moves towards studio, to look at the picture of Anne (which he dislikes), but hearing sounds assumes that Pratt is there, so changes his mind and enters the house by the back door. Either then or earlier, he has dropped a cigarette-end near the studio door.

"6.40 p.m.—Taverley meets Mrs. Leveridge by back door and gives her a cigarette.

"6.43 p.m.—Taverley enters his bedroom just as Pratt is leaving his own bedroom to go to the studio.

"6.45 p.m.—Pratt, having seen Taverley enter his room, reaches back door, and finds Mrs. Leveridge still there, smoking the cigarette given to her by Taverley. They chat for about five minutes—otherwise events would have taken a different course, and Pratt would have reached the studio before Turner had completed his business with Thomas. Mrs. Leveridge mentions that Taverley gave her the cigarette, and Pratt notices, later, the cigarette-end, of the same brand, outside the studio door. This makes Pratt at first suspect Taverley of having ruined his picture.

"6.50 p.m.—Pratt leaves Mrs. Leveridge, crosses the back lawn, and approaches the studio. By these times it will be seen that twelve minutes have elapsed since Turner and Thomas met, and during these twelve minutes Turner has taken advantage of the position to make use of Thomas. He threatens to expose Thomas unless Thomas consents to deliver a note secretly to

Zena Wilding. He scribbles the note, which says, 'Open the back door to-night at 1 a.m., or there will be murder. I mean it. I'm desperate. I must see you.' He puts the letter in an envelope, addresses it to Zena Wilding, and seals it. Thomas leaves just before Pratt arrives. Turner has no time to escape, and hides behind a big canvas. Pratt enters studio. Discovers the outrage on his picture. Does not discover Turner.

"6.55 p.m.—Pratt leaves studio, locking it and pocketing key. Finds Taverley's cigarette-end.

"6.56 p.m.—Thomas has been hovering nearby, wondering what will happen if Pratt finds Turner. Pratt now sees Thomas, and makes a grab at him, but Thomas hits him and runs. It is too dark where the encounter takes place for Pratt to identify Thomas.

"6.58 p.m.—Mrs. Leveridge has left the back door and gone inside, but Pratt now finds Chater there, talks to him, and leaves him. Chater, scenting trouble, spots Thomas, and watches him.

"7.15 p.m.—Thomas gives Zena Wilding the note as she is about to go up to change for dinner. Chater, who has spied on Thomas, suddenly appears, and contrives to see the writing on the envelope before Miss Wilding can escape with it. He recognises the writing.

"This incident had far-reaching results. Chater was designedly late for dinner, because he wanted an opportunity to search Miss Wilding's room for the note. He did not find it, for Miss Wilding burnt it. He may have found the ashes. But before taking his place at the dinner-table, he heard voices while passing through the hall, and listened to a conversation between Thomas and the Chinese cook, Leng. Thomas, in his morbid mood, was asking Leng how he would commit suicide if he ever decided to, and Leng replied that he had some painless, quick-working poison in a locked wall-cupboard over his bed.

"Whether the idea of securing the poison occurred to Chater then or afterwards is a moot point, but he did not act upon it at once. He went to the dining-room, and I incline to the theory that it was not until his encounter with Thomas at 1 a.m. that the idea came to him, or at any rate crystallised. His motive in securing the poison is also a matter for conjecture. He may have wanted it for a particular person. He may have considered that some particular person, such as Thomas, might want it for him. Or he may have considered that it would be useful to possess the poison, in case the need for it should ever arise.

"One thing we do know. When he stole the poison he left his visiting-card behind him in the form of a fingerprint.

"Before reconstructing the events of that night, let us ask why Turner, who all this while had been a prisoner in the studio, apparently made no effort to escape. He remained in the studio from the time Pratt locked him in till 1 a.m.

"The answer to this, I think, is simple. He may have contemplated the idea of an immediate escape. He may have attempted it. But the only method of escape was by the small window, and to break the glass while people were about was to take a big risk; and, even if he effected his escape, he had to find somewhere else to hide till 1 a.m. The minutes went by, and no one came. Gradually the sense of security gained on him—or, at least, of the best security he could obtain. He may have spent some time crouching by the door, to deal quickly with anybody who came. His revolver was in his bag under the straw in the shed, but he had his knife on him.

Or he may have kept close to the large canvas which had concealed him once, and which might conceal him again.

"But no one came, and, as we know, he did not break the window and escape till 1 a.m. His misfortune then was the dog, Haig.

"Now let us revert to our time-table and note how events followed and dovetailed into each other, culminating in the second and third tragedies. The death of a dog may not by some be regarded as a tragedy, but some dogs are more worthy than some men, and can be more justly mourned.

"The first of these events occurred at:

"12.55 a.m.—Miss Wilding slips down to the hall and opens the back door for Turner. She had not undressed, only having gone into her room some twenty minutes earlier, after concluding her interview (about her play) with Lord Aveling. She nearly decided not to open the door, but feared the threats in Turner's note, and thought it would be best to see him and have it out with him.

"1 a.m.—While she is waiting inside the door, Turner breaks the glass of the window and escapes from the studio. Probably he escaped later than intended because of the dog's growling or barking, which held him back. The dog is not chained. It is in a wire enclosure. Turner opens the door to the enclosure, to stop the barking, but the dog leaps out at him, and he runs. A running fight ensues, away from the house. Turner's hand is bitten, and the mark of this remains, but he succeeds at last in stabbing the dog with his knife.

"1.1 a.m.—Thomas, on his way to Leng's room to steal the poison, hears noises, and goes into the hall.

Miss Wilding gasps and attempts to return to the stairs, but is too late, and dives behind a big arm-chair as Thomas enters the hall.

"1.2 a.m.—Chater comes down the stairs. He has heard some one moving, and has descended to investigate. Or, alternatively, he has descended to steal the poison; but this is less likely, for it would imply a time coincidence. Thomas's time coincided with Miss Wilding's because he was waiting till every one had gone up to bed, and allowed twenty minutes' grace after Lord Aveling and Miss Wilding went up. Chater and Thomas meet, but neither sees Miss Wilding. Chater assumes he has caught Thomas in an affair with Bessie, finds back door unlocked, threatens Thomas, and cows him. Thomas, demoralised, returns to bed. He has no nerve now to steal the poison.

"1.8 a.m.—Chater goes out through the back door. Miss Wilding seizes the opportunity and flies back to her bedroom, too upset to leave it again. Probably Chater connects the unlocked door and the sounds outside with Turner, for, although he has not read the note, he knows that Turner is somewhere around. He crosses to the studio, sees broken glass, probably the open door to the dog-run also. He continues beyond, and comes upon Turner just as Turner is about to enter the shed for his bag, containing the revolver. (The revolver was a silent one, the knife merely being a second weapon. Turner may have hoped that some turn of events, such as a yielding on Miss Wilding's part, would avert the necessity for the murder of Chater. His thwarted passion for Miss Wilding was the mainspring of all he did. But he had made every preparation for the murder, even to bringing a second suit to change to—a wig and make-up—to assist his get-away after the crime and reduce the chances of being identified.) Too late now to get the revolver, Turner flies. His encounter with the dog, and the bite he has received, have reduced his morale. Chater also is the stronger man. The chase takes them towards the quarry. Chater gains on Turner. Turner swings round and hurls his knife at Chater. The knife misses, and drops into a small pool. Almost on the edge of the quarry the race ends. Chater seizes Turner, the men close, and Chater gets his hands round Turner's throat. He chokes Turner. Turner drops to the ground.

"1.19 a.m.—To create the appearance of an accident, Chater tips Turner over the edge. What Chater felt like, and what he did, immediately after this act can only be guessed. But we know he returned to the shed, and we know this for a curious reason. Next day Mrs. Chater left Bragley Court on the bicycle, and she could only have known where it was if Chater had seen it in the shed himself and had informed her. We may assume Chater went to the shed on his way back to find out what Turner was doing there, and that he discovered the bicycle, but not the bag beneath the straw. He might believe, on seeing the bicycle, that Turner was about to run away when they met.

"1.30 a.m.—Chater returns to the house, locking back door. He has committed murder. Suppose he is caught? Or suppose, if Turner's death is traced to him, he escapes the rope but has to pay the penalty of manslaughter? He has had one term of imprisonment. He has sworn never to endure the experience again. His desire to possess the poison 'that acts quickly and painlessly' is now complete. Swiftly—in four minutes—he goes to Leng's room (which, we may assume, he has already located), finds the key to the small wall cupboard in the pocket of Leng's trousers (Leng mentioned he always kept the key on him), finds a little glass tube containing the poison, steals it, and makes the one mistake, in his hurry, of leaving a fingerprint behind.

"1.34 a.m.—He is back in the hall, and going up the stairs to his bedroom.

"The concluding episode that concerns us on this night occurred when Chater reached his room. All we know for certain is that he and his wife quarrelled. Their voices were heard through the wall by the Rowes, and also, as I subsequently discovered, by Taverley, who had been disturbed by various sounds, and who, beginning to wonder himself whether any trouble was abroad, left his room for a minute round about two o'clock. The Rowes heard no actual words, but Taverley heard a sentence which he believes ran: 'Well, if things get too hot, there's always a way out.' When I asked Taverley whether he could swear to this he said he could not. He was also vague about the time, and was not a very satisfactory witness. Still, his information fits into the story, and helps in some degree to support my theories.

"What caused this quarrel, and what lines did it take? From the events of the next day, and particularly from Mrs. Chater's attitude and actions, I deduce that Chater told her what had happened, either voluntarily or through the pressure of her questions. I am reasonably certain that Mrs. Chater knew that Turner was dead (though Chater may have told her this was due to an accident, and that he had fallen into the quarry), and also that she knew Chater had stolen the poison. The remark overheard by Taverley assists this deduction. She became thoroughly alarmed, and after condemning her husband for his actions—not, I imagine, on moral grounds—there was a division of opinion about immediate policy. Very likely she wanted to fly. In that case, Chater would point out that flight would direct suspicion against themselves. He overrode her arguments at last, and they settled down to their final sleep on this earth.

"Their moods next day must have been unenviable. Chater concealed his, and even when the death of the dog was being discussed he retained his outward composure. If Mrs. Chater's mood was not remarked, this would be because even at the best of times she appeared to be on the verge of a nervous breakdown. But Chater knew that Turner's body would shortly be discovered, and also that Thomas was a danger, despite the hold he had over him. Probably his alert mind interpreted correctly the attitudes of Bultin and Pratt in excusing themselves from the meet. Had he a dog's chance of escaping justice when Turner's body was discovered, and his identity revealed?

"He made an attempt to secure an alibi. I found this out when, having ploughed through Earnshaw's reticence, I made him repeat word for word all the conversation he could remember having had with Chater at the Meet. Reference to my note of my original interview with Earnshaw (before his admission that he was under Chater's thumb) will show that more questions were discussed between them than I was first informed. As a matter of fact, the question of Chater's behaviour to other guests was a subsidiary one. It was the relationship between these two men themselves that loomed above all else.

"The attempt to establish, provisionally, an alibi was made by Chater just before the hunt began. He instructed Earnshaw to remember a perfectly mythical interview on the previous night which, if necessary, would account for Chater's time during the period of the murder. Note here that Chater did not know he had been heard in the hall by John Foss, and imagined that the only other person he had to silence was the butler. The butler might logically have entered into his mind when stealing the poison.

"It was this instruction that set Earnshaw thinking, and that brought to a head his subsequent rebellion, later in that day. Circumstances threw them together during the hunt. They had ample time to converse on private matters. Earnshaw, pressing for information which Chater would not supply, gathered that Chater wished him to perjure himself, if necessary, to cover some exceedingly serious matter, and with praiseworthy though tardy courage refused to play his part.

"The quarrel began in a wood, just after they had become separated from Taverley and Anne Aveling. The nerves of both men were on edge, for, added to their natural animosity, each had a separate cause for worry—Chater because of his crime, and Earnshaw because he knew that Anne had deliberately left him behind, and that his chance of winning her was slipping away from him. Earnshaw tried for a while to lose Chater, in the hope of finding Anne, but Chater hung on to his heels. Chater was not going to let Earnshaw out of his sight till he had come to an understanding with him.

"The quarrel grew. By the time they had reached Holm and had sat down to their lunch it was at bursting point. 'I did not kill Chater,' Earnshaw said to me, 'but perhaps it was as well I did not have the opportunity.' Then he recounted, as nearly as he could remember it, their last conversation while waiting for the lunch to be served.

"'What did you do last night?' demanded Earnshaw, not for the first time.

"'Mind your own business,' replied Chater.

"'I intend to make it my business,' said Earnshaw.

"'Oh, what does that mean?' asked Chater.

"'It means that you can smash me,' said Earnshaw, 'and I am going to find out how I can smash you. We all make slips, Chater. I made one years ago, and have been paying for it ever since. *You* made one two or three hours ago when you asked me to lie to provide you with an alibi.'

"'I didn't ask you,' said Chater. 'I ordered you, and you'd better obey the order.'

"'Use your own terms,' answered Earnshaw, 'but I'm disobeying this order so I won't have to obey any more. When I've found out what you've done—and, by God, I'm going to—we shall be quits, if it's anything less than murder!'

"'What the hell are you talking about?' retorted Chater. 'And keep your voice down!'

"'Did you kill a dog last night, by any chance?'

"'No, I didn't, and killing a dog isn't murder, anyway, any more than killing a stag. But—for the sake of argument—suppose it *was* murder?'

"'In that case, I'd smash myself to hang you!'

"'Bah! Talk!'

"Then Earnshaw said, 'Listen, Chater. We're down to rock-bottom with each other now. I've nothing to boast about, though I have tried to live down my past and stage a come-back. I'm not even suggesting that a political career is always as clean as growing potatoes. But I haven't sunk quite to the bottom, and if you've committed murder I'll see you swing, whatever it costs me. Now you know.'

"Then Earnshaw got up and left him. And, between three and four hours later, was back at Bragley Court with the knowledge that a man had been found dead in the quarry, and that Chater had fallen from his horse.

"He no longer had to fear a living Chater. But what of Chater's ghost? Earnshaw was sharp enough to realise that when the police came along an awkward situation might develop for him. He decided to lie low and to see how events shaped themselves.

"Fortunately for him, the truth about Chater's death was found inside Chater's hat.

"Taverley had mentioned to me that his discovery of Chater at Mile Bottom was due to seeing his hat lying on the stubble. I count it a bad mark against myself that I did not examine the hat more closely when I saw it beside Chater's body where it had been placed in the studio. But journalists sometimes score, and it was Bultin who discovered—or who expedited the discovery of—the little glass tube in the hat's leather lining. This discovery will probably cause his own size in hats to increase.

"Leng identified the glass tube. It was the tube that had contained the poison stolen from his cupboard. This, coupled with Chater's fingerprint, not only proved who stole the poison, but also proved how Chater met his death.

"He took the poison with him, concealing it in his hat. He had two reasons for this. One, he did not want to leave it about. Two, he might want to use it. I have the evidence of the innkeeper of the Rising Sun, at Holm, that Chater was in a very nervy condition. 'Stayed till I thought he was never going to leave,' said the innkeeper. 'I said to my wife, "That man's got something on his mind." Kept biting his nails, and once up he jumps, as if he thought somebody was coming, and twists his head round, and then sits down again. I watched him through the door. But that was only by himself, mind—when I was there, cool as cucumber.' The innkeeper had Chater tabbed.

"When Chater left the inn, he hesitated to return at once. He rode around. Maybe he lost himself. Maybe he didn't care. Maybe he decided to return and face things. But when he got to Mile Bottom, he acted on impulse or design, took the tube from his hat, drained it, replaced it—and so ended his life.

"Why did he replace the tube? I had questioned Leng, and understand the poison would begin to work in about thirty seconds—and then work swiftly. He had time to replace it. His reason may have been just to get rid of it that way, instead of throwing it down, or he may have done so subconsciously. At a moment like this, knowing his end was upon him, a man's trivial actions would not necessarily answer to the normal rules of logic.

"And so we come finally to the last tragedy—Mrs. Chater.

"Her general attitude has been described, but her active participation in events did not begin until she was asked to identify the man who had been found in the quarry—Turner. Like Miss Wilding, she refused to view the body, saying she knew nothing of the man; and it was at this moment that her control gave way. In a full knowledge of the facts, her condition is easy to understand. Her husband had killed Turner. He was absent, and could not advise her. Moreover, she learned almost immediately afterwards that his horse had returned without him, and she was a distracted woman groping in the dark.

"Into that darkness entered the figure of Earnshaw. Earnshaw was a man who would benefit considerably by an accident to Chater. Her mind seized on this, and, after rushing up to her room and locking herself in, she obeyed a second impulse to leave the room and tackle Earnshaw on his way to his own room.

"But her short interview with him gave her no satisfaction. His threats increased her terror and her rage. On her way back to her bedroom, she saw Bultin put the knife in the drawer, and when, a little later, Dr. Pudrow gave her the news of her husband's death, the final threads of sanity snapped.

"We know how, profiting by the temporary absence of Pratt, she stole the knife from the drawer and descended to Earnshaw's room. The button Price found outside that door was the button I myself found, later, to be missing from her dress. (Her interview with Earnshaw had taken place by the stairs, some little way from the door.) We know that she found Earnshaw's door locked. We know that, using the information supplied by her husband on the previous night, she escaped from the house, went to the shed, found the bicycle Turner had left there, and rode away on it. Mad revenge, when thwarted, yielded to mad terror. She fled before the police came.

"It was ironic that, flying from danger, her means of escape should have played the final trick upon her. I have ascertained from the Smiths, to whom the bicycle belonged, that the chain was loose and constantly needed adjusting. Turner had ridden the bicycle hard on the previous day. It may be assumed that Mrs. Chater, on her last ride through the darkening lanes, rode it equally hard. A steep hill was her undoing. The constable who found her, and who notified us at Bragley Court, said she was already dead when he came upon her. The chain was off its wheel, and the knife lay in the road about five yards away.

"Mrs. Chater, from all accounts, must have been a pathetic creature. Probably she had little to look forward to, and the defective bicycle may have proved a blessing in disguise.

"Indeed, Fate has taken matters largely out of our own hands by dealing out justice to the various miscreants in her own way, saving in the case of the butler, Thomas, whose punishment is not our particular concern."

As he closed the book, a thought struck him.

"Odd, I never found that flask!"

Chapter XXXII

The Truth

Man's calendar, saving when its events intrude, has no interest for other creatures. A kennel was empty, and there was one stag less in Flensham Woods, but otherwise life underwent no change in the bracken and the briar and the burrows, the trees and the streams around Bragley Court. The cock-pheasant did not know that a man had fallen down a quarry near his sanctuary of russet foliage, nor would he have cared a feather if he had. Man was an incomprehensible biped causing birds to shift from one place to another when he came too close, and occasionally sending loud bangs through long sticks; but the cock-pheasant had always avoided the bangs, and the idea that man possessed sensations to arouse pity or hatred or love did not exist. (The idea hardly existed in the more intelligent creature, despite his mental advantages, that a pheasant possessed sensations of any significance.) The sly old fox at Mile Bottom was similarly ignorant and callous. Had a man fallen from his horse near the fox's earthy home? Granted temporary speech and understanding, the fox might have stated in a Court of Law, "Yes, I do vaguely remember some disturbance or other. A horse nearly put his beastly hoof in my front door. But he didn't quite, and I was very drowsy, and really and truly I'm not in the least interested. Can I go now, please? You're thoroughly boring. I want to walk out with a badger."

A hind wondered why her companion was not about to-day. These were disturbing times. Another stag had vanished into the void a week previously. But the hind did not cry her eyes out, and felt anxious mainly for her own safety, denied the comforting knowledge that, unlike yesterday, to-day her safety was ensured, and would remain so for many months to come.

In Bragley Court itself, however, life had completed a transformation. Faces that had smiled were grave. Voices normally resonant had dropped to whispers. None of the guests had departed, for an unwritten law was holding them to their engagements, but there was no enjoyment for them on this grim Sunday. They were merely awaiting the release of Monday morning.

And yet in certain breasts there was a sense of unvoiced relief. The tide of tragedy had ceased to flow, and there were no indications that it would flow again to drown survivors. Sir James Earnshaw, sensitive to every little breeze that blew, and subtly testing the situation in so far as it affected himself, began to hope that his past had died with those who had previously kept it alive. Kendall alone knew his secret now—and was Kendall interested officially? "Thank God I have escaped Bultin!" thought Earnshaw. The relief of this consoled him partially for the fact that Anne had also escaped from him.

Zena Wilding was another guest whose heart was beginning to beat more quietly. She tried to feel pity for the man who had duped her, and who now could trouble her no more, but her feelings were numb. She could not say whether official necessity or journalistic lust would force her story into momentary limelight. Perhaps an unpleasant experience lay ahead of her, and one morning she would find her name among the headlines. But she had been conscious of Kendall's sympathy when he had interviewed her; and even Bultin, as though events had stirred him out of his usual cynicism, had once given her a smile that was almost human.

But it was the Avelings themselves who had contributed most definitely to her comfort. In the privacy of their room Aveling had said to his wife, "I think, after all, my dear, I won't back that play."

"Why not?" Lady Aveling had answered. "I heard Mr. Rowe telling you he was willing to back *you* if you did." And then she had added, in a manner that had somehow taken him back many years, "We've always had pluck, you and I—the Avelings face things."

Lady Aveling had then marched straight to Zena's room, and had told her the money would be found.

In the drawing-room, Edyth Fermoy-Jones murmured, "The evidence certainly points to suicide—one must admit that—but, well, there might be other theories."

"What other theories?" asked Mr. Rowe. "I don't see 'em!"

"I wish you'd do something, Ruth," muttered Mrs. Rowe. "We're all just sitting about."

"Didn't it strike any one as significant, Mrs. Chater disappearing so suddenly?" demanded the authoress.

"If you mean she did it, how could she have?" exclaimed Mr. Rowe. Conscious that he had raised his voice, he dropped it and repeated, in a lower tone, "How could she have? Why, she was never out of our sight the whole blessed afternoon! And then what about that glass tube thingummy?" He turned to Bultin, who was watching Pratt play Patience. "What made you think of that hat, Bultin?"

"There's your seven," said Bultin. "On the eight of clubs."

"Damn smart, that was," persisted Mr. Rowe. "How did you get on to it?"

"Don't disturb them, dear," whispered Mrs. Rowe. "Why don't *you* get a pack, Ruth? They can't do Patience while people talk."

"I do mine while you talk!" responded Mr. Rowe. "However, if Bultin doesn't want to talk, that's all right."

"You've blocked your ace," said Bultin. "I came upon Taverley practising fielding by throwing ping-pong balls into a hat. He bet he'd get all twelve in, and he did. When he took the hat up he said, 'Hallo, what's in the lining?' It was a cigarette. Why not take the Jack? De Reszke Minor. Ivory-tipped. Kind Chater smoked. Looked like Chater's hat. 'I wonder if he used his lining as a pocket,' said Taverley, 'and thought this hat was his? I missed it from the rack before dinner on Friday.' There, what did I say—if you'd taken the Jack you'd have done it."

It was the first time Bultin had told this story. He had allowed the inspector to deduce that his brainwave had sprung from inspired virgin soil.

"Well, I'm blowed!" blinked Mr. Rowe, impressed. He watched Pratt sweep up the cards and begin shuffling them for another attempt. "What are you going to do about your picture, Pratt?" he asked.

"Hope for better luck with Miss Rowe's," answered Pratt.

"Yes, by Jove! But you'll be doing Miss Aveling again first, eh?"

Pratt shrugged his shoulders. "Perhaps—if it doesn't preserve unfortunate memories. Of course, there wouldn't be a lunatic butler around this time to interfere."

"Of course not. That chap's going, ain't he?"

"So is the attractive maid, Bessie, who caused the trouble," smiled Pratt.

"What! Sacked, too?" Pratt shook his head and began to lay out the cards. "Oh, I get you," said Mr. Rowe. "She's agreed to be your model?"

"I understand she has agreed to be Thomas Newson's wife," replied Pratt. "When we menfolk get into trouble, our women are illogically adhesive. Even Mrs. Chater outraged sanity by failing to rejoice in her husband's death."

Edyth Fermoy-Jones looked pensively understanding. She had written about such women.

Mrs. Rowe, less appreciative of Pratt's reflections, murmured, "Ruth, get a pack, as I told you."

Bultin said, "You've only laid out six cards."

"Would you like to do the damn thing yourself?" asked Pratt....

In the ante-room, Nadine Leveridge suddenly broke a long silence. John could now hobble with the aid of a stick, but the ante-room had remained his headquarters, and Nadine had drifted there in obedience to a natural impulse. But she also had a definite object, and before she left the room there were certain matters she had determined to clear up. One of them she tackled now.

"What's on your mind, John?" she asked. "Tell me."

"Oh, nothing really, I suppose," he answered. "Anyhow, we won't talk about it."

"But I've come especially to talk about it," she objected. "Conscience worrying you?"

"Can anybody ever hide anything from you?"

"You can't—much! You're not satisfied that you've done your duty. Perjury's a new experience for you, and you don't like it."

"You don't mince your words," he murmured.

"It's never been my habit," she replied, "and I'm not breaking my habit with you. But if you've committed perjury—to the extent of informing the inspector that you'd told him everything when you hadn't—well, you were acting on my advice, so I'm your partner in crime. It's no good shaking your head. It's true. And, that being so, shouldn't I know the degree of the crime I've partnered you in?"

"What does that mean, exactly?"

"It means, John, what information did you withhold from the inspector, exactly?"

"Well—I never said a word about Anne."

"Thank God!"

"But—but—if—"

"John!" she interrupted. "You've not known Anne long, but you've known her long enough to answer this question: Do you think Anne Aveling is capable of committing a cold-blooded murder?"

"Of course not."

"Or any kind of a murder?"

"She'd have to have a damn good reason."

"I see. And then she might?"

"And then she might," answered John unhappily. "You see, Nadine, I'm not mincing my words now, either."

"I'm glad you're not. And I agree with you that if Anne had a damn good reason—I mean, a reason that seemed damn good to her—she *might* commit murder. But it wouldn't be a cold-blooded murder. And she had no reason of any kind—damn good or damn bad—to murder Mr. Chater."

"I suppose you're certain of that?"

"Sufficiently certain not to give it a second thought. You know, don't you, that everything is pointing to suicide?"

"Yes."

"And, of course," she continued, "if any one *not* Anne were arrested, you'd come forward with the rest of your knowledge?"

"I'd have to then."

"Naturally you'd have to. You couldn't risk the wrong person paying the price. So why worry? Why not continue to wait as you're doing, and save the hell of a lot of unnecessary bother? We're not supposed to speak ill of the dead, but Mr. Chater was a rat, and if a rat commits suicide, as this one seems to have done—well, it can be quite convenient."

"Yes—if he commits suicide," answered John slowly. Then he shot an abrupt question at her. "Do you know that Anne came down *twice* last night?"

"You only told me once," replied Nadine.

"I know. It was Anne herself who told me of the second time. She said she came to get the book she'd forgotten."

"Well, that explained that, didn't it?"

"Did it? I didn't hear her come down the second time."

"Is that important?"

"It means she didn't come down for the book for quite a while. Long after one would have thought she needed it. She waited. When I was asleep she came down. Then she remembered—afterwards—that I might have been awake, and in case I had been she volunteered her information, coupling it with an explanation. Yes, and I've not told you this," he went on. "She hinted that she might get into trouble if I passed the information on."

For the first time, Nadine looked definitely alarmed.

"Her reason was that she would be blamed for having disturbed me," added John quickly. "Good enough, do you think?"

"I—don't know," murmured Nadine. "I don't know any more than you do. Excepting that, whatever happens, I stand by Anne.…John, we must get this settled. The difference between you and me is that if I have an instinct I believe in I'm ready to follow it blindly, but you've got to prove yours. Yes, that hateful conscience will have to be appeased, and I know only one way. I won't be a minute!"

She left the room abruptly. She was away five minutes. When she returned, Harold Taverley was with her.

"Now, then, Harold," she said, when they were seated, "I've explained the position to you, and here is the man. It's your move!"

Taverley nodded. He did not show any discomposure, but John had never seen him look so grave.

"Yes, it's my move," he answered, "and I'm going to begin with a general statement. If there's been any wrong-doing in this—matter of Anne—I'm the chief culprit."

"I can't associate you with wrong-doing of any sort," replied John sincerely.

"Thanks. That's nice of you," said Taverley. "Just the same, don't bank on it. One thing I never interfere with is another man's conscience. And I won't interfere with yours—"

"Oh, for God's sake, cut the philosophy!" interrupted Nadine. "This isn't a question of ethics! It's a question of— how much we love Anne!"

"I'd commit murder for her," answered Taverley, "though I don't happen to have done so."

"What have you done—if anything?" demanded Nadine.

"I'll tell you in a minute. But first I'd like to ask Foss a question or two. You've said nothing whatever to the police about Anne's coming down last night?"

"Nothing at all," responded John.

"Have you kept anything else back?"

"No—I don't think so."

"What about the morning—before the meet? Were you questioned about that?"

"No. Should I have been?"

"Well, let us pretend you are being questioned now, and that I am the inspector—and I have just asked you to tell me all you saw through that door—which I remember was open part of the time—between about a quarter-past and half-past."

John took his mind back. He recalled the details with perfect clearness.

"At about a quarter-past ten," he said, "Lady Aveling was talking to me in here. The door was open. I saw Anne pass through the hall and go towards the stairs."

"Correct," replied Taverley.

"Then Lady Aveling left me, and Mr. Rowe looked in. I was still keeping my eye on the bit of the hall I could see— you know, watching people pass by—" Nadine smiled to herself; she knew the particular person for whom John had been watching. "And while Rowe was talking to me, I saw Bessie go towards the staircase."

He paused. Taverley sat on an impulse to ask a question. Nadine, watching Taverley, read both the impulse and the restraint. John felt the atmosphere suddenly tighten.

"Bessie was carrying a tray," he said. "I noticed a blue water-bottle on it....Then Rowe went, and *you* came in, Nadine. Our chat was cut short by Miss Fermoy-Jones. That woman—oh, well, never mind! You left, and she jawed on and on—five minutes, perhaps, but it seemed five hours—and during that time I saw you and Anne come down, Taverley—and then Anne suddenly left you and went upstairs again, I think—she looked a bit queer. A moment after she had gone up, Chater came down. Then you came to my door, Taverley, Miss Fermoy-Jones left, and you waited till Anne returned."

"Did you notice anything particular about Anne's mood?" asked Taverley quietly.

"I should say I did!" answered John. "It was quite different. Almost—hysterically gay. She lugged you off—and that was that."

"But there's something more," suggested Taverley. "I can see you haven't quite finished."

"Yes, I noticed one thing more. Bessie again. Coming down with the tray. The blue water-bottle was on it, broken."

"I wonder why you noticed that?" murmured Taverley.

"A broken water-bottle—wouldn't anybody notice it?" replied John. "I'd noticed it originally because it was rather a pretty one."

"It was Mrs. Morris's water-bottle," said Taverley slowly. "Her special one. Anne broke it because she had poisoned the water."

Nadine's hand went up to her heart. John sat very still. Taverley did not continue for a few moments. His mind seemed suddenly to have stopped. Then he frowned at himself and went on:

"Anne's story is very simply told, but probably no one could ever tell the agony behind the simplicity. Probably no one will ever know Anne's character completely. I know her as well as anybody, but there are depths that beat me. I think she ought to have been a boy. Her parents wanted her to be. But, thank God, she isn't! She's a mixture of hardness and softness. Each hates the other, and tries to cheat it. But—my view is—the softness wins. She has spent hours and hours with her grandmother, being that grand old woman's companion while she suffers—and then coming out of the room blinded with tears. She hides her tears, just as her grandmother hides her suffering.…My God—yes—I understand Anne!"

His voice had become a little unsteady. He continued, almost apologetically:

"I expect I'm a bit soft myself where those two are concerned.…Anne told me what she had done while we were riding together on the afternoon of the meet. I speak as though it were weeks ago, yet it was only yesterday! She knew her grandmother wanted to die—she had told Anne so often, though never complainingly—and Anne found the way of granting the wish on Friday, during dinner. She had left the table during the first course, because she had forgotten to say good-night to her grandmother. On her way down she overheard a conversation between Thomas and the cook. She found that the cook kept some painless poison in a cupboard over his bed. She decided to steal it that night. You interrupted her at her first attempt, Foss. At the second she succeeded."

"I heard that Chater's fingermarks had been found on the cupboard, Harold," interposed Nadine.

"Yes—by a rare bit of good fortune," answered Taverley. "I think he must have intended to steal the poison, and then changed his mind. He may have overheard the conversation, too—he was out of the dining-room at the time—or he may have got on to it in some other way through Thomas. Anyhow—as we know—he didn't steal it. Perhaps he thought better of it, or the cook may have moved at the crucial moment and made him lose his nerve. Anne nearly lost hers.

"The poison was in a little glass tube. Anne kept it on her. All night she was torn with doubts. But next morning, just before the meet, she went in to see her grandmother again, and found her in such pain that she made up her mind to take the first opportunity to bring the old lady peace.

"The opportunity occurred as she left the room. Outside, on that wall-table you may have noticed, Nadine, was Mrs. Morris's water-bottle. Bessie had brought it up, and—as I have since found out—had been called by Chater into his room. Anne seized the chance impulsively, poured the contents of the tube into the bottle—and a second later I came along, found her in a very agitated state, and brought her downstairs.

"Well, as you know, she went up again. Panic had got hold of her. She went up to smash the bottle. And that, she expected, would end the incident.

"But I knew—and so did you, Nadine—that something was wrong with Chater's complexion when we came upon him at Mile Bottom. And, remember, I had just heard Anne's story. While you were both away getting help, I had a search, and I found Chater's flask a little way off. He had obviously drunk from it before falling—otherwise the flask would still have been in his pocket. He had obviously taken the poison in that drink. And he had come down from his room a minute after Anne and I had come down, and before Anne had gone up again—they actually met on the stairs—and he had passed by the water-bottle on the table.

"The bedroom water-bottles had not yet been filled that morning. My own bottle was empty, I remember. Chater always drank his spirits diluted. The deduction was clear. He diluted his whisky from the bottle, and Anne did not notice in her hurry that some of the water had gone."

He paused and shrugged his shoulders.

"Well, what would you have done?"

"Probably what you did," answered Nadine, "only not half so well. What did you do?"

"Actually, very little—but, aided by other circumstances, it proved enough," he answered. "I had made Anne give me the little glass tube, saying I would get rid of it. Instead of getting rid of it, I eventually stuck it in the lining of Chater's hat. If I had thought of this at once I should have stuck it in his pocket, but by the time the idea came—when we had returned to the house—the hat was the only thing available, for by that time I couldn't get near Chater's body alone."

"How did you manage to get near the hat?" inquired John.

"I brought that back myself," Taverley answered. "That was easy. I also brought back the flask, though nobody knew this. At first I put it in a locked drawer in my room, but when the inspector interviewed me before dinner he got too interested in flasks. So, when he'd gone, I took it out of the drawer and kept it on me. Lucky I did. My room was searched while we were dining."

"Where is it now?" asked John.

"Same place," replied Taverley, touching his hip pocket. "It's been thoroughly cleaned, but I'm not using it. *You* know, don't you, Nadine, that I've had this old flask for years?"

"I gave it to you," answered Nadine.

Taverley smiled rather wearily.

"All this seems thoroughly unscrupulous. Perhaps it is. I even told Kendall I'd heard the Chaters quarrelling in their room—as the Rowes actually did—and invented a remark I pretended I'd caught. But I'm not shielding a murderer, you know. Just helping events to take their happiest course, and trying to avoid increasing the tragedy. My greatest difficulty was to direct Kendall's attention to the hat. I mentioned it casually to him, with no result. To have done so deliberately would have been fatal."

"But it was Bultin who looked in the hat," said Nadine.

"Yes—after I'd played a little trick on him to give him the idea."

There was a pause.

"What's Anne's own attitude?" asked John.

"I've had the devil's own time with Anne," Taverley answered. "But I convinced her at last that her confession would just about crush things here, and that if anything happened to *her*, a county cricketer would drown himself. Well, Foss, what about it?"

"Don't ask fool questions," replied John.

Two floors above, the subject of their discussion was sitting by her grandmother's bed.

"Here's that piece, Grandma," she said. "The squiggly blue bit. I'm beating you this time—I'm finding them all!"

She looked up and smiled. Her grandmother smiled back. Peacefully and motionlessly. Suddenly Anne's heart began thumping like a great hammer. The next moment her face was buried in the bed, and she was sobbing with a wild, unbearable joy.

Chapter XXXIII

Death and Life

"And now, John," said Nadine, entering his room late that evening, "*us*!"

"That's what I've been wanting to talk about more than anything else," replied John. "Do you know, Nadine, we haven't talked about us since the evening you brought me here!"

"Two evenings ago," she reminded him, as she sat down.

"It seems more like two years," he answered. "Lord, what a lot has happened since then! Have you reckoned up the tragedies?"

"Yes, and I can only find one." He stared at her. "The death of poor Haig. Tell me, John, is Mr. Chater's death a tragedy? Don't be hypocritical. I want your true answer."

"I don't think the world's poorer by it," John admitted.

"And Mrs. Chater's?"

"One can feel sorry for her—though once you told me it was difficult."

"I was wrong. I can feel sorry for her now. And that makes me all the more convinced that her death isn't a tragedy. She'd have had a stickier end in a lunatic asylum. Yes, and after a heart-to-heart with Zena Wilding, I think the same might be said of Bultin's 'Body No. One.' By the way, Zena told me Lord Aveling was backing her play, and that Lady Aveling is all for it. So that doesn't sound like a tragedy, either."

John smiled grimly.

"One would think, from the way you're talking, that we've all had a merry time!" he said.

"It's been a ghastly time," she responded, "but it's had some mighty good effects. Quite a number of the survivors have had a shake-up they badly needed. Do you know, I believe even Bultin is one per cent. more chastened! And Anne has discovered sanity and escaped from Earnshaw. But let me go on with my list. The ruined picture. Was *that* a tragedy?"

"I never saw the picture," answered John, "so I can only guess."

"Guess that it deserved to be ruined, and you'll be right! Of course, Thomas, the butler, is out of a job; but that attractive maid—do you remember I remarked on her looks the first afternoon?—she's doing the serial-story stuff, and following her erring man to reform him."

"Do you mean she's going, too?"

"Handed in her notice, I hear. I'll give her a big tip....And dear Grandma Aveling, who has done her last jig-saw—ask Anne if *that's* a tragedy, though the blinds will remain down to-morrow?...I've seen her. Anne asked me to. I was rather afraid—I loathe illness, though I can stick it—but Grandma Aveling gave me an entirely new idea about death. I—I don't think I've ever seen anything more lovely. So perhaps this week-end has done me a bit of good, too!...Well, that only leaves the dog. I can't find anything redeeming about that."

"You've missed out a stag," said John.

"Are you going to be trying?" she asked.

"I hope not. But hunting people—when they're nice, as

most are—always baffle me. Hunting is the one thing you and I won't agree on."

"It was one of a thousand things the late Mr. Leveridge and I did not agree on," replied Nadine. "Which almost brings the conversation back to us, doesn't it?"

"Yes," he nodded. "Nadine, will you marry me?"

She looked at him solemnly as she answered. "That was the way to ask me. I knew you would do it. But this is the way to answer you. No, John. Even in this short time, I've learned to love you too much."

To her surprise, he was not depressed.

"That's as good as I could expect in two days," he smiled. "You'll let me have your London address?"

"It won't be any good."

"You never know."

"How old are you?"

"Forty-three."

"Do I take off twenty years?"

"About that."

"And I am—"

"As old as you feel," he interrupted.

But she shook her head.

"A woman may be as old as she feels, to herself," she said, "but to a man she is as old as she looks."

"Very well," he answered. "You don't look bad to me."

"Idiot! Use your vision, and now put twenty years on *me*! When you're forty-three, and pretty girls of twenty-three are flitting all round you, will I look as good to you as I look now?"

"I say, Nadine!" he exclaimed. "You don't think much of men, do you?"

"Men can't help it, any more than women can," she retorted. "It's not a question of ethics, but of simple common sense—of facing things as they are, and not as you want them to be. But even putting aside the question of age, what do we know about each other?"

"Only that we love each other," he replied. "That seems enough."

"May I risk hurting you?"

"Of course."

"You were in love with somebody else two days ago."

"I guessed it was going to be that. I'm not hurt. You were right to remind me—only, as it happens, I didn't need to be reminded. You see, this is quite different."

"It always seems quite different, John, and it's always the same."

"That's another thing we'll disagree about, Nadine," he smiled. "And I win, either way."

"How?"

"Why, if I'm right, it *will* be different, and if I'm not, and all love *is* the same, you and I won't do any better by looking elsewhere. So why try?"

She gave a despairing little laugh.

"Just a small boy!" she murmured.

"Do you dare come six inches closer to the small boy?" he challenged.

"That's our trouble," she answered. "I daren't!" She bent forward, then drew back quickly and jumped up. "It's unfair! I won't do it!" she exclaimed. "Yes, of course I love you, and of course you love me. But—you'll deny this—you were ready to tumble into anybody's arms. Well, that train tumbled you—and my wretched feminine instinct finished the job. If you'd turned out to be clever or cynical or immoral, we'd have been a match, and at this moment might be planning to buy tickets for Monte Carlo. We'd have kissed more than just once. And ahead would have been half a dozen glorious months, which would have ended naturally or stormily, according to our moods." She had turned away from him.

Now she turned back and faced him squarely. "I don't want any stormy memories of you, John. I don't want you to have any unhappy ones of me. Believe me, my dear, I know best. Some queer freak of chance has made us fond of each other—just now—but we haven't been designed for each other. I'd give you the hell of an experience—"

"You're not forgetting, I haven't asked you to go to Monte Carlo with me?" he interrupted. "I've asked you to marry me."

"—and I dare say that presently you'd bore me stiff. No, I'm not forgetting that. I'm remembering it hard—and thinking for both of us.... The tragedies of this week-end are shouting warnings at us!" she exclaimed. "All due to physical passion, or physical misfits!"

"You didn't call them tragedies a little while ago," he reminded her.

"John, that's the small boy arguing again, and you know it! They *ought* to have been tragedies! Instead, they were just releases!"

"All right, Nadine—I'll try and grow up in my arguments," he said. "Are you going to take the warnings yourself? Are *you* going to give up physical passion?"

"I'm going to give up the misfits!"

"Now I'm going to risk hurting you. Did you give your husband the hell of an experience?" She frowned at him. "Was that a misfit?"

"We didn't fit anywhere!" she retorted.

"Did he regret marrying you?" The frown remained, but she was silent. "Did you regret?"

"John—you're impossible!"

"You can't have it both ways. I'm impossible when I'm a small boy idealising you, and I'm impossible when I'm a man realising you. I'll tell you something. In my first conversation with Taverley, he read me like a book, and he warned me against you. In the strict, always-play-cricket Taverley manner. You wouldn't have been offended if you'd heard him. He warned me in much the same way you're warning me yourself. Well, I didn't take his warning, and I'm not taking yours. Life's a risk, however you look at it—isn't it?—and I prefer to take the risk with somebody I've made a solid start with."

"Do you call ours a solid start?" she asked.

"It seems to me astonishingly solid," he replied. "Anyway, there hasn't been any moonlight."

"No, but there have been other things equally devastating. Give me your hand a moment." He held it out, and she took it. "I know we had to have this conversation, John. It couldn't be otherwise. But we're both confused—tired—too close up to events to see them clearly in perspective. We mustn't rush into this madly." His heart rejoiced, but he said nothing. "I'm speaking as your companion now, in a very queer world. You've no idea how queer it is that a man like you should want a woman like me—and that a woman like me—"

She withdrew her hand.

"Yes, mad, John, absolutely mad. I'm nearly ten years older than you are."

"I'll still love your white hairs."

"You say all the hackneyed things so convincingly!"

"I'll repeat the most hackneyed thing of the lot. Will you marry me?"

"Will you ask me again in six months—if you want to? Then we'll both know."

"It's a bargain, Nadine. I'll keep it."

Then silence entered the room and lingered for a while. It was the silence of life, destined to be broken. Not far above them lay the completer silence of death, no less happy.

"Nadine," said John suddenly. "I wonder—would it be possible—understood?—if you helped me upstairs to see Grandma Aveling for just one moment before we go?"

To receive a free catalog of Poisoned Pen Press titles, please provide your name and address through one of the following ways:

Phone: 1-800-421-3976
Facsimile: 1-480-949-1707
Email: info@poisonedpenpress.com
Website: www.poisonedpenpress.com

Poisoned Pen Press
6962 E. First Ave. Ste 103
Scottsdale, AZ 85251

CPSIA information can be obtained at www.ICGtesting.com
Printed in the USA
BVOW08s0401280715

410673BV00001B/1/P

9 781464 204890